DOCTOR WHO

SCREAM OF THE SHALKA

PAUL CORNELL

BBC
BOOKS

1 3 5 7 9 10 8 6 4 2

First published 2004
This edition published in 2013 by BBC Books, an imprint of Ebury Publishing
A Random House Group Company

Doctor Who is a BBC Wales production for BBC One.
Executive producers: Steven Moffat and Caroline Skinner

The Random House Group Limited Reg. No. 954009
Addresses for companies within the Random House Group can be found at:
www.randomhouse.co.uk

A CIP catalogue for this book is available from the British Library.

ISBN 978 1 849 90647 0

Penguin Random House is committed to a sustainable future for our business, our readers and our planet. This book is made from Forest Stewardship Council® certified paper.

Printed and bound in Great Britain by Clays Ltd, Elcograf S.p.A.

Commissioning Editor: Ben Dunn
Editor and Creative Consultant: Justin Richards
Project editor: Vicki Vrint
Cover design: Black Sheep © BBC 2004

To buy books by your favourite authors and register for offers, visit:
www.randomhouse.co.uk

For Gary Russell

Chapter One
Unwelcome Visitors

It was a high, sunny place, where everything was calm.

Dave McGrath had come to the islands to work on attachment with the New Zealand Geophysical Survey. He was due to stay six months, but he was already so in love with the place that he'd made the first tentative enquiries about immigration. He'd flown into Auckland at four o'clock in the morning, and had been stunned just by the clear smell of the air as he'd walked to his taxi. Despite the jet lag, every turn on the empty two-lane roads presented him with some new joyful sight. And every time he'd expected bureaucracy to get in the way of something he'd wanted to do, there was instead a wave of the hand and a promise that all was 'sweet as'.

The kiwis, he'd swiftly decided, were the least frightened people on Earth. Everything was going to be fine. Nothing was going to happen. His new friends at the Survey had, last weekend, cajoled him into throwing himself off a bridge with a bungee chord wrapped round his ankle, and he'd actually done it, freed from his fear. Every morning he woke to clean air, clear skies. Even the rain tasted good. He thought that it was when he'd gone whale-watching off Kaikoura that he'd finally got it: he'd seen the giant, serene bulk of a sperm whale surface and lie there, calm in the sun, breathing. And something inside Dave had relaxed in a way he'd never known before.

His mate Tony was more phlegmatic, had started to remark on the way Dave was grinning all the time. Tony just wondered at the pies that were available in every service station, and why all the chocolate tasted different. But Dave could tell that, underneath it all, he too was having a great time.

Their work took them up onto the slopes of Mount Ruapehu, a volcano that looked so classically like a volcano should – a black cone rising out of the lava plain, with clouds around its summit – that Dave had laughed at his first sight of it. They had taken radiosondes out of the back of the van, at the highest car park, and had started the long tramp up the slope of small, grey stones, the colour broken by patches of white lichen and weird, tiny flowers. Tony muttered something about how stupid they must look, with red, half-inflated balloons in their hands, as if they were on their way to a fancy-dress party.

The radiosondes carried instrument packages, each designed to monitor wind-speed, pressure, and other changing circumstances in the heights of the atmosphere.

They reached the designated site, checked their position with the GPS, and then released the sondes, Dave waiting for a moment, watching Tony's balloon spiralling upwards into the blue before letting go of his own.

He detached the radio from his belt and clicked the button that connected him with the light aircraft that was somewhere up there, where Maggie would be filming the progress of the sondes while keeping up a stream of abuse at her husband, Geoff, who was the Survey's pilot.

'Mount Ruapehu field campaign to tracking aircraft, over. Tracking aircraft? Can you hear me?'

He clicked the button. There was just the hiss of static from the receiver.

'Weird.' He glanced at Tony. 'What's going to be interfering with it up here?'

Tony was shielding his eyes, staring up into the sky, trying to catch the plane. They could both hear the drone of the engine. 'Probably a new radio station. Volcano FM.'

This had become a running joke between them, how as they drove around the North Island, the radio stations gained eccentric little monopolies of their own in the most out-of-the-way areas, where there was no competition. 'Volcano FM, cool. Rock by day, lava by night.'

'Is that the aircraft?' Tony was blinking at something.

Dave followed his gaze. There was something sparkling up there, high against the blue. Sparkling and … burning?! For a moment he felt fear again, but no, a moment later he realised, that wasn't an aircraft. It was a blazing light source, swiftly growing from a point, showing almost no parallax as he moved his head from side to side.

Which meant it was coming straight at them!

'A meteor!' he yelled, full of wonder. He'd never seen one that had amounted to more than the streak of a shooting star. 'Sweet!'

'Sweet as!' laughed Tony back.

'It's going to land just over the ridge!'

'No, they always look like that, from what I've read.'

'Not this one, mate. Look at it, we're seeing it head on!'

They waited for a moment more. And then they both started to run, their boots slipping on the grey rock and dust, trying to get over the ridge into the low valley.

They got there just as the meteor hit, a liquid burst of flame smashing rock into gobbets of fire that fell all around them, the volcanic rock returned to its original state.

The noise hit them a moment later, a concussion that rolled across the valley, nearly knocking them off their feet.

They slid down the slope, coughing in the sudden smoke as darkness rolled across them, cutting off the sun.

'Look at it!' gasped Tony. 'I never thought I'd get to see one of these close up!'

But Dave was blinking, wiping the back of his hand across his eyes. There was something … no, surely there couldn't be? 'Mate…' he said. 'Do you see something moving down there?'

He could see it in snatched moments through the smoke as the wind blew it right and left. The shattered rock. The hiss and glow of new lava. And something twisting on the ground. Moving with the unmistakable motion of life.

'It's just the smoke. No. No… I see it too!'

They made their way awkwardly through the smoke, waving it away from their faces. Their clothes were being blackened by it, the stuff of interplanetary space, which would soon be going into the washing machine and brought down to Earth, thought Dave randomly. His senses were full of the illusion before him, waiting to be proved wrong.

They stopped as they both became aware, at the same moment, that it wasn't an illusion.

Slithering on the dust in front of them, coiling and uncoiling like it was getting its bearings, was a tiny green snake. Its skin shone, like it was chitinous, or somehow ceramic. The green was that of a polished mosaic tile. It had a hood, like that of a cobra, and its eyes were blank, covered with some kind of membrane. The most startling thing about it, though, was its face.

It had features, an intelligence about it. The tiny thing looked almost human.

'What is it?' Dave heard himself murmur.

'Some kind of worm…'

Dave couldn't believe he was awake. He suddenly had a vast new life before him. Papers to write. An endless new area of research. One, above all, that would keep him here, in the land he'd come to love. There would be prizes and speeches, of course, but those were nothing beside what this creature actually was, what it stood for, the sudden freeing idea that mankind wasn't alone in the cosmos. 'You know what this means, eh? Life in an asteroid! If life can flourish there, if it can survive that impact … well, then it's everywhere!'

'Cute little guy…' Tony had picked up the remains of a branch from a scrubby bush that had been blown apart by the impact. He squatted and hesitantly reached out to try and lift the creature from the ground. 'There's a home waiting for you in Turangi. Come here…'

It took a moment for Dave to register what happened next. The sound hit him first. He had a moment's thought of whalesong, of something loud and strong that communicated information. But this didn't have the homely, Earthlike quality of that noise. This was a scream, a tearing, screeching, horrible noise that made him want to run. He found that he'd instinctively covered his ears.

It was the snake. The snake was screaming. A sound that seemed far too loud for such a small creature.

And then, with a twist of its body, it was gone.

'What was that?' he shouted. He was looking round frantically at the ground, that ancient fear of the running rat or spider. 'Where is it?'

'It burrowed into the rock!' Tony was staring at a tiny, bubbling pool of lava that Dave was certain hadn't been there a moment ago. 'I think it *made* it molten!'

The wind changed direction, and suddenly the smoke was on them again. Immediately, Dave found that he couldn't breathe. 'The gasses … from the meteorite … Got to get some air!'

They jogged to a short distance away, out of the range of the smoke. Tony was shaking his head, his face a picture of astonishment. 'Dave, this is huge.'

'You're telling me. We have to find it!'

'We have to get a crew down here. Fence this off.'

'Sure. Just give me a second.' Dave took deep breaths. 'Okay, let's get back to the van.'

They started back the way they had come, heading for the upper car park, trying to run despite the pollution in their lungs and the rocks sliding beneath their feet.

Dave was feeling strange. All the hope that had bloomed inside him when he saw the creature had shrunk away when he'd heard that sound. It hadn't been a good sound. It had spoken of something wrong, to him. Something that didn't belong here. Something that was going to rip all that he'd found here apart, as the sound itself had ripped the air apart.

He was surprised to find that his arms had fallen to his sides, that his legs had stopped running. He was standing still, watching a little slide of volcanic gravel across his boots.

Tony looked back to him. 'You all right? Why have you stopped?'

Dave didn't know. But he could see something of what he felt reflected in the look on Tony's face. 'Why have you?'

Tony looked annoyed, and made to get on. 'Come on.'

But he didn't. He just looked back at Dave again.

And Dave understood now. It was like this was a dream. Or rather a nightmare. That feeling when you can't run. And something huge is coming to get you.

He felt cold from his stomach, the sunlight on his arms making him shiver. 'I can't move,' he said.

He was afraid. Afraid like he'd never been before. Scared like one of the possums they'd run over at night on the road, locked in their headlights, unable to run. As something hurtled at him.

'Me neither.' Tony sounded angry under the fear. As if he was being unreasonable with himself. 'I want to… It's like some kind of nerve paralysis. I keep telling my limbs to move, but…'

'I know. There's something… Can you feel it?' Dave could feel the direction from which the fear was coming, now. Up into his stomach. From below. From deep under the world. 'Something underneath the ground.'

The roar made them both start, ducking their heads reflexively. Dave looked around desperately.

A few metres away to the right, a crack in the ground had split open; new, white-hot lava becoming exposed as he watched. Adrenaline rushed through him. He wanted to run like an animal. Wanted to get away. Had to!

But the rage in his blood moved nothing. He couldn't run. Couldn't move. Mustn't! The thing underneath the world would get him if he did!

And then, sickeningly, his limbs suddenly jerked into life.

He was moving again. So was Tony. Slowly, deliberately.

Towards the lava.

'What's going on?!' screamed Tony. 'Stop! Grab something!' He started to beat his hands on his own legs, as if trying to knock himself off his feet. But then he jerked upright, swinging into a parody of a walking posture.

'I can't…' whispered Dave.

'Dave!' He could hear Tony screaming behind him. His feet were carrying him to the edge of the lava now. 'Stop! Don't go in there!'

And now Dave could hear another scream. Something which scared him nearly as much as that earlier sound had, when it rose up into the clean, clear sky with the smoke and obscured all his hopes and dreams.

His boots slipped on the edge. His hands refused to grab anything as his body gave way and plunged into the chasm.

There was just a moment before the heat shock of the soft, caressing lava burnt Dave's consciousness away.

And in that moment, he realised that the scream was his.

Chapter Two
Enter the Doctor

With a wheezing, groaning sound, a battered blue wooden box materialised on a street corner opposite a pub called *The Volunteer*. This was the TARDIS, an advanced craft from a distant and mysterious world. Originally, it had had the ability to change its appearance to blend in with the background wherever it landed. But on one of its owner's early trips to Earth, many years ago, that mechanism had got stuck, leaving it in the same shape it had assumed when it had landed in the London of 1963. So it still looked like a police box, something which had largely vanished from British streets since that date, a sort of telephone box from which the public could call their nearest police station, and where police officers could store traffic cones and the like. But the craft's appearance belied its nature. This was really a machine capable of travelling anywhere in time and space. Tonight, it had arrived in a small town in northern England.

The battered wooden door was hesitantly opened, and a man stepped out. He had an elegant, curious face, with eyes that darted around his surroundings. And at the moment he was frowning a dangerous frown. He wore the sombre black tailcoat of an Edwardian gentleman under a heavy cape, with a Keble College scarf thrown over one shoulder. He would have merited hardly a glance on the streets of Edwardian London, but he looked somewhat out of place in the twenty-first century. This was the adventurer in time and space known only as the Doctor. Although he looked human enough, he was actually an alien from a far-off world. Among the many strange and wonderful things about his alien nature was his ability to regenerate, to replace a worn out or fatally injured body with a new one, which brought with it a whole new personality and outlook on life. It was something all his people, the Time Lords, could do. This form was his ninth. He had long ago come to admire and respect the people of Earth, and had helped save their world from many alien threats. But he could also be impatient at how primitive and aggressive they could be. He knew Earth well, from many visits, but he was first and foremost a traveller, someone who just ended up somewhere at random and liked to explore what he found there.

At least, that had often been the story in the past.

But now there was a look of worry on the Doctor's face, a tension born of responsibility. As if these days he was at work rather than on holiday.

He paused on the threshold, then glanced back into the interior of the police box.

'No,' he called, his accent indicating the kind of classical education that one only got in the better schools in the southern spiral arm of the Milky Way, which just goes to show that accents tell lies, 'it's *not* where we're supposed to be. I'm going to take a look around.'

He stepped out and locked the door behind him.

There was nobody in sight. The sign of the pub swung in a slight breeze, and the streets were quiet enough for the Doctor to hear it creaking. There was no noise even of distant traffic. No people were visible. There wasn't even a solitary dog to howl at the lonely spectacle. And yet a clock in a jeweller's window indicated that it was only nine o'clock in the evening.

The Doctor turned his eyes skyward, and raised his voice, certain that the mysterious beings he was addressing could hear him. 'I don't want to be here. I won't do it. Whatever it is.'

No answer was forthcoming from whatever powers the Doctor was talking to.

He looked back to the empty streets and sniffed. 'From the smell of the air, England, 2003. But there's something *odd* about it. And where *is* everybody?!' For a moment he wavered, as if his curiousity could allow him to step back into the TARDIS and be on his way.

As if it could.

'Oh for goodness' sake!' he muttered, annoyed at his own nature. He opened a panel on the front of the police box, the sign that indicated how the public could call for help and advice, and plucked out a mobile phone, as blue and stocky as the craft itself.

Then, at a march, he set off for the pub.

Alison Cheney pulled back on the beer pump with exactly the right pressure to deliver one perfect pint of this easy-flow, easy-down-the-gullet nonsense that you'd never catch her drinking. Junior Beer, she'd called it before she'd started working here. She was only in her mid-twenties herself, but that didn't stop her from looking down on those who didn't like to taste what they were drinking.

Or that was how she'd used to feel. And talk. A joke from before the time when everything had gone wrong. Working at the pub hadn't changed her attitude. The way things were now had.

She placed the pint expertly on the bar towel in front of old Tom Crossley, who'd come in like he always had, always did, always would. Unless something terrible happened to him. He was their only customer. Alison wondered if he'd noticed that anything had changed in the last few weeks.

His rheumy eyes fastened on the miraculous pint and she managed a smile. 'There you go. On the house. I've got a sore throat and I'm too ill to use a till.'

He managed the same thin smile back, and she knew. Tom was just as aware of what was going on as she was. He came here to ignore it. The same way she did. 'I love you. Marry me, Alison.'

'You gonna take me away from all this?' Alison realised at the sound of her own voice that she had forgotten how to flirt. The last few weeks had pummelled that out of her. She went to the big plastic container of jelly snakes at the end of the bar, unscrewed the lid, and threw back a mouthful, chewing hard. She'd been eating too many of those lately, as well. 'You want some of these too?' she asked Tom.

Max, the landlord, a man balding before his time, wandered in from out the back, rubbing his throat. 'Alison,' he croaked, 'don't give away beer.'

'Why not?' Alison toyed with the wage slip she'd left on the bar in front of her. 'We're never going to get any more in. We might as well empty the cellar.'

'It might just ... stop.'

'And you're not paying me enough for this. I'm the only barmaid in town.'

'It'll stop.' Max sounded certain. 'It has too.'

Alison felt like screaming at him. 'Everyone's been saying it's going to stop since it started. Everyone's waiting for it to change. But nobody's *doing* anything. Everyone's too scared to leave their houses!'

Tom got to his feet, off his stool, took his pint with him as he retreated from the bar. Max had stepped back the same distance, looking Alison up and down, waiting for something terrible to happen to her. 'I don't agree with her,' he said carefully, addressing his words to the carpet. 'This is all her. I *told* her to shut up!'

She sighed at them. She almost wanted it to come for her. It would be better than the waiting.

They all looked round as the door opened.

Into the pub came the most eccentric individual that Alison could ever recall seeing. He was wearing Edwardian clothing, as if he wore it every day. The costume lacked the stiffness or just-dry-cleaned look of something brought out for fancy dress. And it was perfect in every detail, right down to the watchchain on the breast pocket.

She looked up from it, and found that his eyes were waiting to meet hers. They were the eyes of a troubled prince. They wanted to sparkle, but they could not. Because of some great burden.

The eyes broke contact with her, and took in the awkward distance between the three of them.

Then the man marched to the bar and locked his gaze on her again. He seemed to have concluded something, though surely he should know what was going on here.

Alison didn't know everyone in Lannet, but she was pretty certain that this man was a complete stranger. And that in itself made him interesting. And incredibly dangerous.

'A single glass of Mersault ninety-six, if you please,' he snapped. But then his tone softened into a smile. 'I've heard so much about it.'

Max and Tom shifted, not sure whether or not to relax.

'Sorry,' Alison winced to have to say it. 'We only do dry or sweet.'

'And I don't do sweet.'

Alison took that to be an order for dry, and went to get the bottle and a glass. When she turned back, he'd snatched up her payslip from the bar and was peering at it. 'Miss Cheney. Any relation to Lon? Wonderful chap. Hairy hands.'

'What are you on about?' She found her hands were shaking as she put the glass down in front of him.

Max stepped forward, bringing up the point they were all interested in. 'Haven't seen you around here.'

'No,' murmured the man. 'In a bustling town centre on a Saturday night, I suppose you don't get many strangers.' He threw back the drink in one shot, winced mightily, and slammed down the glass.

Of course, they all jumped.

He raised his eyebrow at the reaction. And then leaned in to stare at Alison, examining her expression. 'You're scared,' he said. 'Less than these two are, though.'

'That's why they're both looking at me like that,' she found herself explaining. 'They're scared of anyone who *isn't*. Scared somebody might talk.'

'Do you want to do this, Alison?' yelled Max. 'Do you really?'

Alison gave him a look, but bit her tongue. She had Joe to think about, she thought. And her Mum and Dad, and everyone else who loved her who wasn't caught up in all this. But she didn't like Max and Tom reminding her of it.

The stranger had wandered over to the jukebox in the corner, and was looking at it like it was some heirloom in a sale that took him back to his childhood. He reached out an elegant digit to hit a button.

They all tensed, of course. Max really should have switched the thing off, but having the lights on it still flashing felt normal, and they had to keep everything normal.

The finger stopped, and the man looked back at them. Those eyes again, working everything out. As if he really didn't know. 'So,' he said. 'None of you are going to tell me *anything*. You haven't even thought to charge me for the drink. And there's no Pachelbel on this jukebox.'

He strode to the door, and turned back for a moment to look accusingly at them. 'I'd have thought he'd get a look in on "Smooth Classics 2". But no.'

And he left, leaving the door flapping behind him.

Alison let out a long breath. She didn't know which had been worse, all the questions the stranger had been asking, or the terrible desire that she had to tell him the answers.

Chapter Three
The Underground Terror

A humanoid figure stood opposite the street corner where the TARDIS was. It had been watching the time-and-space craft for some minutes, standing completely still, its cold eyes examining every detail of the new object.

The figure was green, its features smooth, like a polished marble statue. Its mouth was flexible and muscular, the only part of it that spoke of function over form. It was androgynous, and had no need for clothes. It was a representation of a human-being as seen from a distance, as seen from a superior culture.

It took big, controlled breaths of an air it did not care for.

This was the chosen form, for now, of a being called Prime.

Prime turned at the noise of the pub door opening. It had already watched as a tall, thin man in anachronistic clothing had stalked out and off into the streets. It had arranged for him to be watched.

Was someone going to follow him?

The woman called Alison Cheney had opened the door, and taken a step or two out into the cold night. She was looking left and right. As if she had indeed wondered about pursuing the man.

Prime moved out of the shadows, just enough so that she could see it.

Alison turned at the movement, and registered its presence. She glared at it for a moment, defiant. But that was all right.

Defiance was meaningless without action. Prime had only appeared to this human, because this human was important. But she did not know that as yet.

'It's all right,' she said. 'Whatever you are. We're all being good.'

She went back inside, closing the pub door behind her.

Prime had made its decision. It turned back to the anomalous blue object, and opened its mouth. It emitted a soft, warbling harmonic, playing the currents of air with a sound that was part of its culture. It delighted in the way the noise reached down into the world, finding its way deep into the ground through all the cracks and pipes and conduits the humans had forced into their planet.

It could hear a response from far below.

The Doctor stalked the streets, his nose in the air, his eyes and ears taking in every detail of the empty, echoing town. It was called Lannet, as a sign revealed. In Lancashire, if local newspaper hoardings were to be believed. There were people here: there were lights on in upper windows; very low sounds of music and speech. But the people were inside, behind closed doors, in hiding.

Something was terribly wrong here.

A sound came to him, distant, uncertain, and he followed it to the kerb.

A wisp of steam was rising from a manhole cover. A sight one might see early in the morning in Berlin or New York, if the season was right. But not here.

The Doctor dropped to his palms, his ear to the manhole cover. He had no fear of traffic. He would have heard it coming a mile away.

Deep underground, echoing up from the depths, came a high, warbling scream: the sound of something alien.

'Either something very odd is going on down there,' the

Doctor whispered. 'Or the rats have discovered the delights of the D'Oyly Carte.'

On the street corner beside the pub, the pavement under the TARDIS had started to glow.

It became red, then white hot, then dissolved into crumbling, shifting lava. The police box shifted from one side to the other as the ground collapsed underneath it, then swiftly fell into the morass, its own weight dragging it down as lava sizzled and spat around it.

Finally, all that was left was the light on top, which flashed rapidly, as if the machine was trying to exert all its strength against something that was stopping it from dematerialising and getting away.

But it was no use. The lava closed even over that, and a hissing, steaming scab of cooling lava was all that was left on the pavement to indicate that the TARDIS had ever been there.

Alison came back out of the pub, her coat on and her bag in her hand, ready to head home.

She saw the pool of lava, and of course she had no idea what it signified.

But she thought she did.

Looking over her shoulder, she turned and walked off at speed, reaching quickly in her pocket to find the keys to her car, trying to stop her hand from shaking.

The Doctor turned a corner, and stopped as he saw something extraordinary.

Standing on the pavement, rising out of the ground itself, was a vaguely human shape made of rough rock. It was like some weird, modern, statue. It expressed pain and grief, like something reaching, agonised, upwards, while the rock dragged it down.

If he could have been sure that it was art, the Doctor would have declared it a masterpiece. These days he had a taste for horror in the gallery.

He reached out to touch it, half expecting it to be hot. But it retained only a slight warmth, the warmth of living rock in a cold street. His fingers found the roughness of pumice, the light, air-filled chambers of stone that would float in the sea. 'Solidified lava,' he whispered.

'Never knew what hit him!'

The Doctor turned slowly at the sound of the voice from behind him. He didn't want to give away his surprise. He liked to keep up a veneer of confidence, even now when he had none. Especially now.

An old lady was sitting amongst a cluster of well-filled plastic carrier bags in the metal-gated doorway of a grocery shop on the other side of the street. She muttered something more under her breath, looked away for a moment, and then jerked her head back to stare at the Doctor, as if puzzled he was still there.

'Who?' asked the Doctor. He pointed at the statue. 'That?'

'No!' The old lady scowled at him. 'My Oswald. He was run over in 1987. He was such a lovely kitten. Grew up to be an awkward cat.'

The Doctor walked over to her. 'He must have used up his nine lives. Rather like me. I'm terribly pleased to meet you, what's your name?'

'Miss Mathilda Pierce.' The old lady said it like she was reading it from a card. An ancient memory.

The Doctor took her hand, holding onto it for a moment as a reflex born of years on the street made her pull it away. When she was sure he wasn't going to hurt her, he planted a kiss on her dirty knuckle, for all the world like they were at a dance. 'Charmed.'

She could see he was different, then. 'What are you doing

here?' she asked, taking back her hand.

He sat down beside her, moving a couple of her bags of belongings out of the way. 'I don't know,' he sighed. 'They –' He raised a finger to the sky. 'Keep putting me in places where terrible things are going to happen.'

'Oh, right,' nodded Mathilda. 'Spare change?'

The Doctor started to rummage through his pockets, finding all manner of bright and shiny coinage. 'Let's see, what have I here… Atraxian semble seeds… You'd need to grow those into a tree before they'd be worth anything. Zornic groats? No, you don't want currency that talks back. Do you lot use Euros yet?' He held up a big coin with the symbol of the European Union and the King's head on it.

Mathilda looked down, her face clouding. 'You're being cruel to me.'

The Doctor gently raised her chin and smiled at her. 'Oh, never, Mathilda. I'm a homeless person myself. It's the first thing I am.' He searched in his other pocket for a moment, and found a handful of pound coins. 'Here!' He dropped them into her hands. Then he pointed again to the lava figure. 'What do you know about that lump of rock?'

She shook her head, afraid to say.

'Only you're the first human being I've seen on the streets tonight, and I was hoping for some assistance.'

'Nowhere else to go.' She picked up on the wrong thread of his question. 'I left my house. The floor wasn't solid.'

'Not solid?'

She leaned closer, whispering. 'I used to have twenty-eight cats. But they all ran away. All the cats and dogs and birds have left this town. All the animals.'

'Why?'

'Cats get scared of things they can hear. You know, it's how a tiger marks its territory.'

'By low frequency sound,' the Doctor was nodding along

23

as if talking theory with a fellow academic. 'A booming in the throat. Keeps all the other top predators away. But what about the people? Why aren't they out and about?'

Mathilda looked pained that he had to keep asking these sorts of questions. 'You seem a nice young man. You should stay off the grass!'

'Why?'

She looked around, and then whispered to him again, pointing to the ground. 'It's down there...'

'What?'

She stopped, as if she'd heard something and what she'd heard had scared her.

A moment later, the Doctor heard it too. A slight shifting of the pebbles on the road in front of them. A humming that became a vibration, unsettling his spine, working its way up him with a cold feeling of dread. It was as if something was physically creeping up his backbone.

The sound suddenly erupted into reality, the windows of the shop behind them creaking as in an earthquake and the bags jumping off the steps. The whole shop-front was shaking now.

'Oh no!' Mathilda was looking around desperately. 'No! Oh stop it!' She was shouting to something the Doctor couldn't see. 'Please! No!'

'It's all right!' yelled the Doctor, trying to keep a hand on her shoulder. 'It's just some sort of earth tremor! Hang onto something!' He was trying to find purchase against the steps, to stop them both from falling. But surely the worst that could happen was that those windows would break? He flung up his arm to save Mathilda from the flying glass.

Everything went black. His vision contracted as the full force of the vibration swept over him.

He fell without being able to hold onto anything to break the impact.

Mathilda was screaming. The Doctor's vision cleared to see that she had her hands over her ears.

And then she was falling.

She collapsed into the Doctor's chest.

The vibration suddenly stopped.

The Doctor looked around, waiting for another attack, but none came. He placed his hands gently on Mathilda's neck, feeling for a pulse. 'Are you all right? Mathilda? Mathilda!' No pulse could be found. The old lady was motionless. No breath, or sense, or life remained.

He stood up quickly, and she fell, cold and dead, onto the step.

The Doctor stared down at her, horrified. As he watched, the step grew red hot underneath her, causing her clothing to smoulder and a horrible smell of burning to assault his senses. Then the step grew white hot, liquefied... And Mathilda's body fell into the ground, awkwardly, the rock opening and closing around her, leaving only a mass of bubbling lava.

The Doctor numbly reached up to find a wetness on his own face.

He saw his reflection in the intact shop windows. A trail of blood had fallen from one of his nostrils.

He wiped it away with one swipe on the back of his hand.

'All right,' he whispered, his voice full of cold fury. 'All right.'

Chapter Four
The Enemy Revealed

Joe Latham was a General Practitioner, the young, enthusiastic sort who liked to get to know his patients. His cheeky grin and old-fashioned good manners had made him a hit with the kids and the old ladies, and he had been a candidate for promotion, in line to be the senior doctor at his practice within a couple of years. It had helped that Lannet was his home town, that he had roots here. He'd only been to London once, for a rugby match. It was okay, he'd said to his mates on the coach afterwards, but there'd been nothing there you couldn't get from Lancashire with a satellite dish.

He'd met Alison in Lannet's only club, Bella Bonito's. She'd thought he was a vet, and had pursued him round the dance-floor, drunkenly asking him what was wrong with her cat. It took a quick conversation with her mates to discover that Alison didn't actually own a cat.

He'd realised, after she'd stopped chasing, that she was gorgeous, actually. And could talk about anything, with her London accent, and had only just missed out on getting onto *University Challenge*, because some bloke on her college's team couldn't get the wives of Henry VIII in the right order.

He'd had to stop himself from calling her the next morning. But as it turned out, she called him at teatime, still hungover, and asked if he was really as nice as she remembered him being.

And so they started going out. And kept in touch when her term started. And when her course was over, she'd come back here and it seemed right that they should get a place together. So they had.

She'd been going to go back to college that autumn. But one morning she'd just told him she was going to stay here with him instead, because she loved him and he couldn't move, and she didn't want them to be apart.

That had worried him, for a bit. The pressure it put on him to live up to that. She mentioned it every time they had a row, and said she regretted saying it afterwards. She'd told the university that she'd resume her studies at a later date.

She had to work, because his wages couldn't keep them both, and she wanted to. But Joe had been a bit surprised when she'd got a barkeeping job down the *Volunteer*. He'd expected her to be something a bit more high-faluting than that. To work in the library or something. But he hadn't asked. He was out in the daytimes, she was out in the evenings, so they saw each other just for moments. It worried him, off and on, that she'd taken the job to do that, to put off living with him long enough to realise that she shouldn't be staying. There was a hole at the heart of them, but they kept walking around it. There were things that they didn't talk about, because why talk about them?

And then everything had changed, and they hardly talked about anything at all.

Right now, Joe was slumped on the sofa, watching television with the sound turned down so low he couldn't really hear it. He didn't need to. It was the snooker. From Sheffield. Where life seemed to be going on as normal. Or maybe they were all just acting normal too.

He smiled when he heard the familiar key in the lock. The prospect of Alison getting home not only cheered him up, these days, it flooded him with a terrible, momentary feeling of relief. One more work day, and they were still alive.

She came in, smiled a small smile at him, and put her coat on the peg. 'Hiya.'

'Hey. How was work?' Joe got up from the sofa and went to embrace her.

'This weird guy came in, asking questions.'

Joe smiled. 'You always get the nutters. They can tell you're going to listen to them. He won't last long, though. There aren't many left.'

Ally kissed him, then took the remote from the arm of the sofa.

Joe found he'd taken it off her again before he'd even thought about it.

Which made her look at him like he'd done something wrong. Again. 'I was only going to see what's on,' she said.

'It's just –'

'I know. Don't raise the volume so we can actually *hear* anything.'

'You can hear it well enough. And there's the subtitles. You're able to make sense of *EastEnders*. Next-door hasn't got theirs turned up and the street's quiet. I like it like this.'

She dropped onto the sofa, rubbing her brow. 'Don't say that, Joe. Don't say you like it.'

He sat carefully beside her, wondering how he could make this better. The tension between them had risen and risen since the changes happened. 'Sorry. I went into my surgery today. There were even a few patients.'

'Great.'

'All throat complaints.'

'Yeah. I've been getting hoarse. And it's not like I've had anyone to yell at. Must be a bug going around. Be the death of me.'

He looked at the ground, and then realised he was doing it and looked back to Ally, afraid. 'Don't.'

'I don't care anymore, Joe. This has to change.'

'We have to keep on living, Ally. We have to keep on going in case –'

'In case there's a chance to fight?' She looked hopefully at him for a moment, wanting him to join her where she was.

'That's not what I meant,' he said, looking away, consciously keeping his eyes off the floor. He didn't want to see how Alison was looking at him, either.

They both jumped at the knock on the door.

'Don't worry,' Alison snapped, getting to her feet. 'I'll get it.'

Alison hadn't wanted to fight with Joe when she got home. She hadn't wanted to do anything apart from fall asleep on the sofa with the last cold beer from the fridge in her hand and the last pizza in the oven.

But she wanted to turn the volume up. Even at home, she didn't want to shut up, she wanted to shout.

But she nearly slammed the door when she saw who was standing outside.

The man from the pub. He was looking thunderously at her. As if this was all her fault.

'What are you doing here?' was all she could think to ask.

'Around the corner,' he said, 'a lovely old lady has just died. Does anyone here care?'

Joe was up from the sofa as the man stepped inside. Alison was too numb to stop him.

'Who are you?' Joe was even keeping his voice down now.

'It's the weird guy from the pub.'

Who rounded on her again, intent on her like he'd seen and disregarded Joe in an instant. '*You* care, don't you?'

She started to shake her head.

'You were going to tell me. What's going on? Why is everybody staying off the streets?'

Joe was looking between them like they were talking treason.

'How did you find me?' she asked.

'Your payslip had your address on it.' He marched into the room, hardly looking round, picked up the phone, listened to it for a moment, and then replaced the receiver. 'The phones don't work. There are no current newspapers or magazines in shop windows. Nobody on the streets. So this town has been cut off for, what, three weeks? And somehow nobody in Britain has noticed. What have you allowed to happen here?'

'Allowed?' Alison was almost proud that Joe had found his voice, even raised it a notch.

He finished his walk with an absurd little glance around their living room that seemed to find it wanting. 'As you humans allow so many things.'

'"We" humans?' Alison had a sudden sinking feeling. Maybe this guy really was a nutter. With that weird confidence they sometimes had. Just when she'd started to hope.

Joe was squaring up to him, his arms wide, saying 'come on', in that wouldn't-hurt-a-fly doctor way of his. 'How can you come in here and start –?'

But the sweep of his hand caught a tea mug that Alison had left on top of the folded-up table.

It fell and hit the ground.

Smashed with a sound so loud that Alison could hear every other sound in the close stop too, as everyone tensed.

Joe stood there. Paralysed. So did she.

The strange man slowly looked down to where the mug lay in pieces. 'The floor,' he said. 'You're afraid of something coming up out of the ground. You're all pussyfooting around! Walking on eggshells!'

With one bound he was at the little table they kept in front of the sofa. It was covered in beer bottles, tea mugs, magazines, a glass vase with some old flowers that once Alison would have thrown out.

Joe realised before she did what the man intended to do.

'Don't!' he shouted.

With one sweep of his arm, the man cleared the table, sending the vase crashing to the floor, the mugs flying, bursting against the walls, the bottles shattering everywhere.

Alison put her hands to her ears and closed her eyes. Joe put his arm around her shoulders.

'If you don't tell me what you're afraid of,' he was shouting now. 'I'll keep making noise until I find out for myself!'

Alison couldn't help it. She went for him. 'You –'

He caught her hand before it slapped him across the face. He'd moved so fast she hadn't seen it.

Suddenly he was looking deep into her eyes, those very old eyes of his interrogating hers, with a little hope now, a little humour. 'So,' he murmured. 'One of you is willing to fight.'

'You give me a *way* to fight and I'll fight!'

He kept looking at her.

'She doesn't know what she's saying!' insisted Joe.

He kept looking at her.

'Tell me,' he said.

And Alison found she had the courage to do that. 'Three weeks ago, like you said. Some kind of sound. Deep underground. A vibration. It was there when you listened to the pipes. It was there when you slept. Right at the edge of hearing.'

Joe took a step towards them, sounding desperate now. 'Alison, don't!'

'Joe, I have to do this. Somebody has to!'

The man had let go of her hand now, and was pacing, his thin, elegant hands laced behind his back. 'I've heard this noise myself. It seems you're living above an angry landlord with a long broom-handle, who wants you to stay very, very, quiet!'

He sounded like a doctor, like Joe had in the old days, talking about something very serious with the lovely assurance of someone who knows all about it, who's expert enough to be flippant. That confidence gave her the confidence to come out with something she'd never told anyone, not even Joe. 'I see one of them on the street, sometimes. Keeping an eye on me. I saw it tonight.'

'I don't know what she's talking about!' Joe shouted. 'I've never seen anything! Everything here is normal! Please, leave us alone!'

The mysterious stranger ignored him. 'Tell me about the solidified lava. That was a person, wasn't it?'

Joe looked at her. She had to take a deep breath. Take a moment to let it out. But now she was determined that she was going to. 'That was Kim, my mate from work.'

He didn't react so much. His eyes just noted that, filed it away. She had the reassuring sense that it meant someone, somewhere, was going to get slightly more of a kicking. But there was also something reserved about his expression, something not quite as caring as it should have been, as if he was still making up his mind about her. Or about something bigger than her. 'Go on,' he said, quietly.

'Max didn't like her because she talked too much. More than me, even. She wanted to get a message out. Wanted to do something. Then one night on the way home the ground opened up, and she … she started covering herself with lava. Just kept smearing it onto her body. She was screaming all the time, calling out to us to stop her.'

'But we *couldn't*,' insisted Joe, gently.

'We couldn't move. In the end, she didn't have hands any more, and then she put her face in and just…' She had kept from thinking about this for such a long time, she had to make an effort not to cry. If she started, she'd never stop. 'Just solidified there.'

The man nodded, took it in, made his decision. He put his hand on her shoulder. 'I'm so sorry,' he said. 'I give you my word: this ends tonight.'

Alison stared at him. There was no question in his eyes at all now. He really meant it.

And then Joe was suddenly in his face, angrier than she'd ever seen him. 'Well, thanks for that! Because we might *see* some of those punishments now! The lava is for the ones who really push it. If you're lucky, you'll just get your brain fried by the sound! Do you know what it's like to be a doctor, and stand by and watch these things, and not be able to *do* anything?!'

The stranger almost chuckled, a sound like a catch in the back of his throat. 'Oh, so many answers to that. But no interest in giving them.' He snapped back to Alison. 'No wonder you're so afraid.'

'The sound *makes* you afraid,' she insisted.

There came sounds of movement. Not from any of the houses, or from the road, but from where Alison and Joe had had nightmares about hearing them. From underneath. From the floor.

'Oh no,' whispered Joe. He started to step backwards.

The sound was coming from beneath them. The vibration. The modulated scream that had infested their town. It was rising, coming closer.

It was in their imaginations now. The sudden burst of superheated rock. Or the sound that rose up and shook your brain apart. Alison wanted to run, wanted to pull the door open and sprint down the road, but the sound held her, made her feet too scared to move, trapped her!

'Get behind me,' snapped the stranger.

33

'They say they're down there!' Joe was yelling. 'In the rocks! They say they're monsters!'

'That's why I've been sent here,' said the man.

Alison stared at him, certain he was telling the truth. 'Who *are* you?'

He flashed her a jagged smile. 'I know about monsters. I'm the Doctor.'

The sound hit them.

From out of the ground, through the floorboards and carpet, burst two terrifying figures.

They were green, they shone like wet stone, they had the hoods and muscles of powerful snakes, their arms those of statues.

They advanced on Alison, Joe and the Doctor, slithering across the remains of the floor. The scream was coming from their faces, rippling the air between them and their prey.

Chapter Five
The First Victory

The Doctor was staring with intense interest at the two creatures as they advanced on Alison and Joe.

While he stared, he was backing towards a standard lamp, unconsciously working out spaces and ranges while consciously making deductions about the alien species he was looking at, a species that, in all his travels through time and space, he'd never set eyes on before.

And while doing all that, he was, of course, talking. 'Ah! You must be the aliens. I've heard so much about you. It's been a long time since anyone screamed at me, and then I think they were only waiting for Elvis to come on. But my poetry went down tremendously.'

He got to where he wanted to be just as the creatures got to where he wanted them to be.

He grabbed the lamp and swung it like a club.

It smacked into the head of the first creature, knocking it from its shoulders and sending it bouncing off the far wall.

The creature's body thrashed and writhed, knocking the furniture in all directions.

The second alien spun with snakelike speed, and opened its mouth. From it came that terrible screaming sound, that seemed to melt the air itself with sheer, sickening force.

But the Doctor had grabbed a metal serving dish from under the table.

The scream was reflected back at the creatures, the force of it distorting the metal in the Doctor's hands, rippling the air.

The bodies of the monsters wavered for a moment, their structures warping under the force of their own weapon.

Then they exploded. Their bodies dissolved into bursts of expanding green liquid.

The Doctor grabbed Alison and Joe. 'Run!' he bellowed. He sent them stumbling past the remains of the creatures towards the door.

On the threshold, he stopped for a moment to look back. The green goo was congealing, tendrils forming and snaking back together, all the pieces finding each other with questing, urgent motions.

He slammed the door closed behind him.

They sprinted out of the house, out into the night of the quiet close, their breath visible in the air. The Doctor led them towards the small row of shops that stood beside Alison and Joe's house: a newsagent, a florist, a hardware store right next door.

He chose the hardware store.

'You killed them!' yelled Alison. She sounded half terrified, half elated.

'I do not kill,' snapped the Doctor. He grabbed a pin from her hair, and in one smooth movement slipped it into the lock on the shop door. 'They're obviously bioplasmic creatures, masses of goo. The bodies are just crusts, scabs!'

'"Obviously"?' spluttered Joe.

'They'll knit themselves back together. Their eyes don't look much use, so they probably live underground, navigate by sound, and the hoods focus a sonic weapon to stun their prey. Right now, that's you.' The door clicked open, and he grabbed them both and thrust them inside. 'In!'

* * *

Inside the remains of Alison and Joe's lounge, the two aliens had nearly reconstituted themselves. The gobbets of green ooze had become threads, pools, structures, and two nearly complete creatures were forming, lying across the furniture.

It wouldn't be long before the monsters were mobile once more.

The Doctor ripped the lid off a large metal drum. He'd barged into the hardware shop, pulling items off the shelves, and then yelling at Alison and Joe to find him things when his own hands couldn't work fast enough.

'What are we doing here?!' shouted Alison.

'Fertiliser bags! Come on! Empty them into the container! Quickly!'

The couple heaved another heavy bag of fertiliser between them. The Doctor ripped it open and dumped the foul-smelling chemical into the drum. 'And newspaper! Alison, over there!'

Alison grabbed a pile of old newspapers from behind the till.

'You're insane!' Joe shouted at the Doctor. 'What do you think *you* can do?!'

'Surprise them,' muttered the Doctor, working the fertiliser into a particular shape using black plastic bags. 'Resist them. And possibly perform a few show tunes. So hush.'

He grabbed the newspapers from Alison, and started to knot them in a kind of origami, his fingers moving faster than the eye could follow.

'Don't just stand there!' he cried at Joe and Alison.

But then he realised. He could feel it himself. That terrible vibration, distant now, but soon it would come closer. The monsters were whole again.

* * *

The skin closed over the last inch of the creatures' new bodies, once more formed into their half-human, half-snake appearances, the green mass inside contained within shining ceramics.

The head of the one the Doctor had wounded adjusted itself an inch on its moorings, the creature shaking it left and right until it sunk again into place on its shoulders, pulled there by its constituent plasma.

Before the process was even complete, however, the monsters had started to emit their shrill hunting cries.

'I want to move, Doctor,' whispered Alison, staring at her frozen feet. 'But it's like this terrible … fear. The vibrations –'

The Doctor grabbed her by the shoulders and looked into her eyes once more. 'You fought back before. You can do it again.' His voice took on a note of bitter contempt. 'Or are you just the same as all the other sheep?'

She angrily shrugged off his grasp. 'Shut up and show me!'

Joe watched, helplessly, as she ran to help the Doctor with whatever he was making in the metal drum.

The pavement outside the hardware shop bulged for a moment with the backs of two creatures. For them, the ground was as easy to travel through as the sea was for a dolphin. Or for a shark.

The killers dived again, preparing for the upward thrust that would surprise their prey.

'It's not that I'm a coward,' Joe was yelling. 'You show me an army and I'll join it. But this is just *us*! How can this work?!'

'You do go on, don't you?' the Doctor snapped. He was searching his pockets while Alison finished packing the drum. Lots of small, practical items flashed through his dextrous hands: string; circuits; screwdrivers; a multi-bladed knife of alien design with a strange symbol on the hilt... 'If I can find a little something to add to this then Johnny Alien is going to get a good seeing-to. From just us! Ah!'

He'd found it. A tiny velvet bag. He dived to the drum, inspected what Alison had done, and then poured the contents of the bag into it: a stream of fine purple powder.

'Why aren't you scared of the sound?' asked Joe.

'I believe I may have let that slip before,' murmured the Doctor.

'You're not human.'

'Decent of you to say.'

'What are you?' Alison's eyes were wide.

The Doctor glanced at her. 'Mildly annoyed.' He conjured a match from his pocket and struck it on his nail. 'There!'

And he applied the flame to the trail of newspaper that led into the drum. 'Out!' he bellowed. 'Now!'

The two creatures burst up through the floor of the shop, the tiles and floorboards splintering and melting into flaming shards before them.

They stopped, their eyes trying to pierce the gloom. The sounds fluted inquisitively between them as they communicated, searched, formed a sonar picture of the room.

One was about to dive back into the earth to continue the search elsewhere. But the other stopped it. It could sense movement. It communicated the shape and location to its fellow, and then the other creature could sense it too. The warbling scream they exchanged contained a wealth of detailed information, with shadings, subtleties of meaning, the entire weight of their magnificent culture brought to bear on this tiny landscape.

They made their way slowly across the floor of the shop, spreading out. They moved their heads from side to side, seeking the nature of the sound and motion they could sense. The humanoids had evaded them before. They would not do so again.

One of the creatures stopped by the metal drum. It had a sack thrown across it, a momentary bit of camouflage that the creature tossed aside.

Even its feeble eyes could see the brightness in front of it.

A tiny flame that had reached the end of its trail of newspapers.

The end of its fuse.

The creature's vestigial eyes widened in shock.

The Doctor, Alison and Joe stumbled to a halt across the road from the shop.

'How big is this going to be?' Alison had swiftly worked out what they were making. Now she was looking around at the other houses, realising that theirs was the only one close to the shop. 'Only it's right next to –'

The explosion blew them off their feet.

The hardware shop vanished into fire.

The gravel bounced off the driveways.

The grass in every direction blew flat.

The ball of flaming gasses rose into the air, the shop and the house beside it, and no other buildings, consumed and turned into falling, cascading, scraps of rubble and debris.

Alison sat up and stared at it. 'Our house,' she whispered.

The web of sound that united the alien intelligences shuddered, then disintegrated. For a moment, they thrashed, lashed out, in all their dark places, shocked by the sudden disconnection.

They turned down into the rock, by instinct, and made it liquid, and swam for home with compulsive, erratic strokes, seeking contact, lost and uncertain.

Their screams of information had become screams of distress.

The Doctor leapt to his feet, shaking his fist at the blazing building.

'Got you!' he shouted. 'Got you!' He sounded triumphant, to Alison's ears, but also surprised, as if he'd succeeded against all his own expectations. The thought swam into her head that he was trying too hard, pushing himself against something.

'What have you done?' gasped Joe, staring at what remained of his home.

The Doctor glared at him. 'Everything. The sonic pulse from that will stun those creatures underground. For hours, if I read their looks right. The ones who were in the shop will take days to reform. There's no thumping from downstairs now, so, listen –'

He spread his arms wide and closed his eyes, as if he was luxuriating in a world that had suddenly become comfortable again. From all around them came the sound of people. Individual voices raised, doors opening, cries and shouts and sobbing, and in the further distance, cars and sirens.

All the way down the close, the lights were coming on.

The Doctor opened his eyes again. 'That's the sound of you being free.' He pulled an odd-looking, blue mobile phone from his jacket. 'I told you this would be over tonight, Alison. And I kept my word.' He looked suddenly complicated again, and took one stride towards her. 'So … this is goodbye.'

He looked like he had problems with those.

Alison could only whisper it back at him, though she didn't want to. 'Goodbye.'

He frowned at her. Then turned on his heel and stalked off.

He stopped a few paces later, and turned back to them with a little, awkward, curl of his lip. 'Oh. Sorry about the house.'

And with that he was gone.

Alison didn't know what to do next. She felt like crying or laughing or something. She reached out and hugged Joe to her.

Together they listened to the sounds of Lannet waking up.

Chapter Six
Military Matters

The Doctor strode through the streets, watching people coming out of their front doors, clustering together in groups, getting into their cars and racing off, all suddenly aware that they didn't have to stay put and be silent any more.

He waved and smiled every now and then. He felt relieved. His work here was done. Nobody had got hurt because of him.

It was a fragile sort of feeling, he knew.

And it was all shattered, as it had to be, when he turned the corner by the pub and saw that the TARDIS had gone. There was just a crust of lava where his time-and-space machine had been. 'Rumpty!' he muttered, which was very rude if you were one of the few people in the universe who understood what it meant.

He looked upwards again, addressing the great powers that he knew were watching him with all the disparagement that the fools deserved. 'Haven't I done enough?' he asked. 'They're going to be fine!'

But again, there was no answer. He hadn't expected one. They would play their game. He would be their pawn. Until he could persuade, cajole, escape, destroy... He put the thought out of his mind, took the mobile phone from his jacket pocket, and hit a speed-dial button. The humans were going to need help, it seemed, and so was he.

'Secretary General!' he made sure there was a smile in his voice as the call connected. He knew that just his number showing up on the private call display would have already made the old chap slump in his chair. 'It's me!'

The Secretary General replied in his own language that yes, he knew, and grudgingly asked if this was something to do with the end of the world again?

'Yes, spot of bother in Lancashire…'

The Doctor wandered off into the awakening town, filling his friend in on what was happening to his world.

Prime staggered, trying to control its breathing.

It fell against a wall. The scream had been disrupted. It had depended on the scream for support and communication, and without it it felt isolated, cut off from its troops, alone!

This condition could not be allowed to persist.

Prime folded its arms around itself, cursing that it made a habit of wearing a body akin to that of the native lower creatures. It closed its eyes and instinctively considered for a moment how to focus its own scream to do this.

The scream found its place. The ground beneath Prime liquefied and gave way like the welcome embrace of geneswap. The heat enveloped this awkward crust, and folded over Prime from feet to head.

Then all was welcome darkness, and warmth, and falling towards the forward base. It could feel, around it, the screams of hundreds of its warriors, all doing the same. The feeling comforted it. Whatever had happened to the scream could be made right, with this army of their people at hand.

Prime emerged from the ceiling of the forward base and fell the last few metres, landing on its feet. Around it dropped the others, some of them in planned descents, some of them just falling in panic or injury.

Two warriors arrived in liquid form, droplets pattering down from the roof, splattering into each other, gradually creating mass enough for consciousness. The warriors waited, afraid, as the critical point approached.

Prime, as befitted a commander, turned away a few moments before it could be sure of their continued survival. It indicated its experience of combat, its willingness to deal with life and death for the great race it served.

The forward base had been created in less than the time it took this planet's moon to circle the globe below. The technology had been brought here in small, portable units, and had been fitted together through fine manipulation of the mother rock, waiting for them as always, wherever they went in the universe, the constant that spoke of their superiority and fitness to survive.

Prime went to the control console, where a technician stepped back to let it see for itself. Prime used the controls to focus the scream, to gain as much information on what had happened as possible. It made inquiries, calling its own scream into the device that amplified and replicated it across the entire operation.

After a while, it understood. On a screen on the wall, the image of the house exploding flickered into existence, a violent event that kicked the vibration sensors, made them roar with chaos.

Prime looked at it with contempt. A shaped charge, designed to blind them. A gesture, almost an accident, the only negative in what so far had been a perfect operation.

And yet... There was the unknown factor. The object that had been located in the settlement of the lower creatures. The being that had emerged from it. The scream said he had been in the vicinity of the explosion. As had the lower creature called Alison Cheney.

Prime had to know what this meant. The warriors knew

this. They swarmed around the anomalous blue object where it stood on the security dais, anticipating what Prime would do now.

Prime modulated his scream to let them know that now was the time. They acknowledged it, and moved out of the way.

Prime approached the blue box, and directed his scream to modulate the air between it and itself. It still felt strange, with these lower creature organs, despite having served in such operations many times before, to scream changes into the world.

It took a while for Prime to find the necessary frequencies and points of vulnerability. The blue box was much more than it seemed. It contained some great power that had, in stillness, set itself against the scream. This was worrying. The technology might even match Prime's own!

But eventually the doors of the blue box began to bulge and warp. Prime was at the edge of its endurance. It could not keep the scream at this level for much longer. And yet it would not show weakness before its warriors.

It was about to fall, unconscious, when the doors flew open.

The warriors warbled and hooted in satisfaction, their screams giving Prime support and warmth. It did not falter. It made its way towards the box with pride, and pushed through the doors, screaming in triumph.

The control room of the TARDIS had changed its appearance many times. Its owner had spent hundreds of years balancing the demands of modernity and tradition, function and style. There had always been the technological elements of his own culture, their magic of circuitry. But there had also always been the beloved items encountered on the ship's journeys, the antiques old and absolutely new, the art and craft from races that his own people had disregarded.

Now the room felt lived in, designed for comfort and then tested on that basis for many years. It was dark, the roundels shining with a warm evening light. A light designed to salve the inhabitant from whatever awful burdens the world might have placed on his shoulders. Comfortable chaises longues and chairs stood on well-worn carpet, and bookshelves lined the walls. The screen that displayed the cavern outside was subtly set back on one wall, where a tapestry would slide down to cover its existence. A large grandfather clock stood ticking incongruously in one corner. The console itself was made of fine, polished wood now, with dials and levers of shining metal, a device that complemented, not dominated, this study befitting some ancient Oxford professor. Or rather, one particular ancient Oxford Doctor.

It was a room meant for two. Two chairs stood by the fireplace, which was marked with the roundels of many teacups and wine glasses. There were dashings of liquid and glass, the marks of old disputes and moments of violence. Every piece of furniture was somehow scarred, if one cared to look close enough.

A figure still stood in this room, though the Doctor was absent, its mind considering the history they had shared here, and regretting the invasion that was about to occur.

The doors burst open, and in marched the alien that the figure by the console had already identified as their leader. It had completely ignored the doormat.

'Yes?' asked the Master.

The alien stared at him.

Prime's gaze and scream had taken in the advanced but at the same time primitive nature of the control room in an instant. Then all its senses had focused on the creature that had asked it that impertinent question, as if it and its forces following were a minor inconvenience.

The creature was clothed in black, a simple suit that buttoned at the collar and black gloves. It had a white beard, flecked with black streaks. Its face was wise, whimsical, with hard eyes that expressed a deal of pain. Prime knew that the lower creatures emulated such emotions in their simple lives, so that was not itself a sign of the creature actually having sentience. But the technology that it commanded might be.

'My dear sir and/or madam!' the being sighed. 'Say something! Do I take it you wish to board the TARDIS by force?'

'Stand aside, lower creature.' Prime would not give a sentient being the respect due to it without first being certain of its status.

The being straightened itself up to its full height, looking affronted. 'I pride myself that I am the dearest companion to the owner of this craft. So I am very much afraid I shall not. As to the nature of our respective intelligences, might I suggest that, as the common saying goes, empty vessels make the most noise?'

The Master had understood much of the nature of the alien's political and social outlook from the four words it had uttered, and had chosen his own carefully in response. And, as he'd predicted, the being responded by reaching directly for its most obvious cultural weapon.

It opened its mouth and screamed.

Which was why the Master had kept his finger close to a particular pre-set that he had programmed into the TARDIS controls. The old craft had been unable to resist such a complex sonic attack, but the Master knew of old that often the wisest strategy when dealing with a new enemy was to surrender, learn, and then counter attack with the dagger one had kept behind one's back.

Living with the Doctor had constantly reminded him of the wisdom of that approach.

The Master was a long-time acquaintance of the Doctor. They had been at school together, on the Doctor's home planet, where the Doctor had known the Master first as a childhood friend, later, as they grew older, as a nuisance and a bully. Then, for a long time, they had been enemies, with the Doctor stumbling over some scheme of the Master's – usually a plan to gain vast cosmic power – and annoyingly foiling it. But during this time there had often been an underlying fondness between them, a sense that they were somehow just playing a game, that they were fellow adventurers, just with different approaches. The Master had grown more desperate and ruthless as time had gone on, using up his natural ability to replace a dying body with a new, healthy, one, and having to move his consciousness into increasingly more complicated host forms. The Doctor had still beaten him every time they had met.

But now they travelled together, thanks to the events of the last time they had encountered each other. It was fitting that they had ended up, however awkwardly, on the same side. Fitting, but still somehow frustrating.

Now the Master flicked that switch.

The walls of the control room warped in a moment, subtly changing their shape in accordance with the mathematical design the Master had been working on since the ship was sucked down through the Earth by some sort of vibrational force field; a field, incidentally, that was strong enough to prevent the craft from fleeing into the space-time vortex.

The scream echoed around the room and bounced right back at the doorway.

The alien went flying out of the doors.

The Master grabbed the door control, but the warriors

behind their leader rushed into the gap, their screams reaching inside the ship with new notes, new attacks. 'As you just found out for yourself,' he murmured, never one to avoid gloating over a downed enemy.

But he knew this battle was only just beginning. And he wished for a moment that he could retreat to the safety of his grandfather clock. 'I can continue to reflect all your screams,' he told the advancing mass of aliens, his hands darting over the controls, his mind busy with the mathematics. 'But dear me, how tiresome.'

The British military command structure had been taken by surprise by the message it had received from New York. It wasn't often that one was advised by a third party of an invasion of one's territory. Still, the Cabinet Office had contacted the Prime Minister, who had been at home with his family, and had briefed him on the nature and severity of the threat. The Prime Minister had reacted with horror. Everyone who had taken up the office had asked the older civil servants involved with the intelligence services whether the records contained in the Grey Book archives could possibly be true. The whole nightmare was back, complete with United Nations involvement on sovereign territory. The Prime Minister had put the Grey Book back on limited circulation status, called in the Chairman of the Joint Intelligence Committee, and asked who had been earmarked to respond to such situations, should they arise.

There were still UN structures in place, of course, but these had devolved to the point of being supposed offices deep in the UN command apparatus, the reactivation of which would take days, and a lot of goodwill. The very fact that the UN had contacted them seemed to be an indication that the first response should be a British one. Which suited the Prime Minister. It was hard to say which would upset the body politic more, the appearance of alien monsters or blue helmets on British soil.

The JIC Chair got, within twenty minutes, the Grey Book 'Woodland Surprise' list sent to his laptop, and picked out a number of names and units. There would have to be a larger evacuation group, with the mission of getting all the civilians out from, say, a twenty-mile radius of Lannet, under some pretext. Those units could have lower security clearance. The news editors would have to be brought in and briefed. Some of the older heads in Docklands knew the form about aliens, anyway, and they'd lead the others. But the main aim now had to be designating a regiment from near Lannet to go in and take on an initial engagement with the hostile force, on a search-and-destroy basis. They needed to be combat ready, and within a couple of hours of the combat zone. They'd make the first encounter, and sort out targets for Two Para and the SAS's incursion groups.

The Royal Green Jackets were live-ammo training on the Yorkshire moors, and one man within their ranks was highlighted on the JIC Chair's list.

Major Thomas Kennet. In the photo he had a certain look on his face, that the Prime Minister liked: a competent belligerence.

He looked like a man willing to grab the unknown by the throat.

And that was how the military came to Lannet. Twin-engined Chinook helicopters descended into the market square, and while a token force took on law-enforcement duties and prevented looting – not that there was any threat of it – the majority of the troops started to organise the setting up of a perimeter and the movement of every single human being to areas outside of it.

And then there was the combat platoon. That landed

separately, and brought in the heavy ordinance. Their leader had been given a brevet rank of colonel, to be de facto in charge of the whole operation.

Major Thomas Kennet was in his late forties, with white hair cut back to his scalp, a hard chin and a gleam in his eye. He'd served in the Gulf, and he didn't like the look on the faces of the people he was rescuing here, in comparison. They hadn't welcomed his men. They'd just been scared, and wanted to get out of here as soon as possible. That fear hadn't made him afraid in turn. It had made him angry. Top of his daily list of things to do was a duty of care, get the civilians out first. He'd heard the stories, like everyone did when they got to the higher ranks: that sometimes there came strangers to England's green and pleasant land. And like all professional soldiers, he was pleased to be in actual combat circumstances again. However, he couldn't help but wonder how good his boys would have to be to deal with something this far outside their experience.

There was, of course, one person who could help: a legend in the British military, whom many people in fact regarded as a myth. But the UN liaison had insisted that he'd been the source of the call. Kennet had sent his first jeep speeding through the streets of people – they seemed to want nothing more than to get *out* of their houses now – to find and secure him. They'd managed that, with some difficulty, but had reported all sorts of demands, all sorts of calls he was making outside of the chain of command.

He was also not going to budge from the spot he'd decided on as *his* headquarters: a primary school. Kennet had read the Doctor's file in the helicopter, and realised as he did that to do so was surely one of the privileges of being let in on the ground floor of an operation like this. He knew, therefore, that here was not a man to be ordered around. And Kennet had no ego, could turn his decisions on a coin, depending on what the situation needed, something he prided himself on. Ego got men killed.

So Kennet told his people that the primary school in question was where they'd be setting up front-line communications and office space also.

He marched in pleased to see satellite comms being wheeled through the door, and acknowledged the salutes of his lads with the kind of offhand twinkle that said everything was under control, and soon they would get some action.

He had in his head exactly what he was going to say when he first set eyes on the Doctor. He walked into the classroom labelled '3C', and saw the thin figure turn from the blackboard where he'd been working on some obscure calculation. His eyes flickered up and down Kennet, taking him in with distaste.

'Ah!' said Kennet, taking care to sound pleased, to indicate gratitude for the number of times this man, or extraterrestrial, or whatever he was, had saved the human race. 'You must be the famous Doctor!' He took a step forward and held out his hand.

The Doctor ignored it. Alien manners, and all that. Must remember that.

'Major Thomas Kennet,' he continued, snapping his hands behind his back. 'First Royal Green Jackets, commander of this operation.'

Finally, the Doctor spoke. 'I specifically asked for a team of speleologists, so I can retrieve my TARDIS. Then I'm away from here.'

Which wasn't what Kennet had been expecting at all. He'd read about a certain arrogance, an occasional impatience with human affairs, and he'd been ready for that. He hadn't expected coldness and distance. 'The evacuation phase should be complete by twenty hundred,' he said, keeping his tone level. 'After that, I need your help.'

'I've put everything I know about these creatures on record. And listed a dozen academics and linguists who'll help you communicate with them.'

Now this Kennet had anticipated. The admirable desire to debate rather than fight. He'd prepared his answers for that. 'We can talk to them when they're no longer a threat.'

'You do that,' the Doctor snapped. 'I won't be here.'

Kennet threw the Doctor's file onto a desk. 'I've read that. Exciting stuff. Help us, and we'll help you get your TARDIS back.'

He watched as the Doctor picked up the file and examined it. He seemed to gaze at the descriptions and pictures with the tired expression of someone who regretted their adolescent excesses. With a flick of the wrist he tossed the file aside. 'How ridiculous,' he sighed. His eyes flicked back to accuse Kennet. 'I seem to attract the military. They're either arresting me, making strong, sweet tea, or killing my friends. Go and find someone else to play your filthy games with.'

Kennet wasn't the sort of man to fly off the handle. His temper was reserved for those who deserved it. He went to where the file had landed on the floor and picked it up, quietly tidying the crisp pieces of white paper back into order. As he did so, he thought about what he might say to cover the anger he suddenly felt towards this man, his thoughts drifting to some of the things he had seen in the town, to that obscene lump of rock on the street corner, to the fear that had been put into those good people. 'Doctor,' he said. 'We estimate the civilian death toll at six hundred and thirty-seven. Now, our job is to put ourselves in the way of that.' He allowed the fire inside him to express itself, just a little. 'While you get to be superior and eccentric.'

The Doctor met his look, and Kennet could see that his words hadn't entirely fallen on barren ground. The man was looking at him with a measure of respect now, and maybe, for a tiny moment, something approaching shame.

He strode quickly back to his blackboard, before Kennet could see anything more. He cleaned off his equations with one sweep of a board eraser, and started replacing them, at high speed, with some sort of design that required many colours of chalk, all grabbed with astonishing dexterity from the runner beneath the board. 'Were the controlled people doing anything in particular?'

'Sitting at home.' Kennet was a little wrong-footed. Were they talking tactics now? 'They were allowed to go to their jobs, but most were so scared they didn't leave their houses.'

'And nobody entered the town?'

'It seems not to have occurred to them. Delivery lorries would dump their loads on the edge of town, and then report back as normal.'

'Such amazing control,' the Doctor sounded almost appreciative of the power of their enemies.

'Only one person reports seeing a creature before you brought them out of hiding...'

The reply came almost before Kennet had finished his sentence. 'Alison Cheney, yes, I've met her.'

Kennet had decided that this man was just determined to keep on surprising him. Hopefully, he had the same effect on his enemies. Fine, so perhaps he could have that tactical conversation after all. 'The big question is, why here? Why just this town?'

The Doctor spun round from the design he'd just finished, blowing multicoloured chalk dust from his hands. 'Because,' he said, 'it's on top of a plug of ancient volcanic rock.'

The design was a geological map, a cross-section of the rocks underneath the town. The plug was visible as a red mass, rising up diagonally to meet the surface, Lannet floating like a small boat atop it.

'I think these creatures evolved on their home planet,' the Doctor continued, 'to take advantage of rock like that, to manipulate it with their sonic cries. The volcanic rock meets metamorphic rock at the hills, here.' He jammed a finger at a blue body of rock that formed the hills above the town. A crinkly chaos that Kennet took to be an intricately rendered cave system ran down through them. 'These caves offer access to very near that point. My team of speleologists –'

'My men and I,' Kennet corrected him, 'will be going down there. With you. And then I'll get to see what a TARDIS looks like. Won't I?'

The Doctor glared at him for a moment. And for just that moment, Kennet thought he might have to fight all day and all night with this man to guarantee a tactical approach that wouldn't put the lives of innocent scientists and cavers at risk.

But the Doctor had one more surprise for him. 'Hoorah,' he said.

Chapter Seven
No Escape

Prime watched as the massed ranks of its warriors advanced by a tiny degree into the open doors of the blue box. It would take time. But they had time. The creature at the controls would eventually come to regret besting Prime in sonic combat. It was a mark of Prime's suitability for command that it had not thought for a moment about how its defeat would look to those it led. It had simply ordered them to attack in its place, that they might understand the forces that had momentarily overcome their commander.

Now Prime was examining the viewing screen that displayed a visual representation of the image information that the scream collected from the surface. It showed the lower creature called Alison Cheney being led into the back of a vehicle, her pair-bonded mate beside her.

Prime was aware of the military intervention of the lower creatures, the evacuation that was already under way on the surface. It had been a minor setback that could be corrected. Now, however, it was threatening to become a slightly more urgent problem, one that demanded a response.

Prime added its own scream to the continuous music of its fellows, making its orders clear.

Joe didn't know what to say.

He and Alison had put what they could salvage from their house into a couple of suitcases that a corporal had provided.

There wasn't much. They had the clothes they stood up in, and fortunately their cards, mobiles and driving licences had been in their pockets. Some of the things from the top floor had been thrown clear. The shattered remains of a wardrobe, which had landed on someone else's drive, yielded a few pullovers, and Alison had folded a favourite party dress into her suitcase.

They couldn't yet believe it enough to talk about it. Everything they'd had was gone. Surely there would be some kind of compensation? But, and the thought made Joe very scared, they had actually aided in the destruction of their own property. What sort of insurance company would understand that? Well, he hadn't. Alison had. But when was he going to get the chance to make that distinction? And whyever would he want to? They were together… He made himself stop thinking stupid thoughts, to get back to the practical things he could help with.

After about an hour, during which they'd just stared at the blazing ruin, he'd used his mobile to call the fire brigade, not that it would do any good. To his surprise, 999 had worked, and he'd got through to an operator who confirmed that he was in Lannet before *he* could tell *her*, and then put him through directly to a military operator. The operator had read him a prepared statement, and told him to stay exactly where he was. The incoming forces had seen the fire, and a military fire engine had been dispatched in their direction.

As it turned out, the local fire brigade, who'd made an issue of going into work every day and responding as normal to any local emergency calls they could (everyone had been sure were going to be the next for the chop) got there before the Green Goddess did. Joe had watched as their neighbours had come out of their houses and cheered them, hugging and laughing as the remains of his house were prevented from igniting those nearby. The arrival of the soldiers elicited more cheers. The military firefighters saw that the professionals had the blaze under control, and ended up being hugged by people, and telling them that evacuation forces would be with them that day.

The soldiers had taken an interest in Joe and Alison, and had provided them with silver blankets and tea. They ascertained where they could go – Alison's parents in Sheffield – and put them at the head of a computer list of residents.

And so when a military truck had arrived in the close, to more cheering, they had been the first into the back of it. The soldiers had got people with cars, those who hadn't driven out of town as fast as they could, as soon as they could, to make their way immediately to a point outside their newly erected perimeter. The truck he and Alison had been put in followed straight away. They were alone in the back, sitting facing each other on two benches, the first evacuees.

Through all of this, Alison had just said 'it's over'.

Joe hadn't been able to find words to reply. Until they were passing along a familiar road out of town, the cars having all overtaken them. He managed a smile. 'So you're finally getting out of Smalltown, eh? Back to the big city!'

The expression on her face told him he'd said the wrong thing. '*We* are.'

'Except I don't *want* to go.' He could feel himself getting angry and defensive. 'That's my town back there.'

She was silent for a long time. Then she very deliberately held her head up, made herself look him in the eye, made a decision. Or at least for now. 'But maybe this is a chance for both of us to start again.'

Relieved, he took her hand and she took his. There was so much unsaid that he wanted to say. He'd been thinking about getting down on one knee soon. But no. This would be such a stupid place to do that...

He realised that she was looking afraid.

A familiar vibration was rising, making the metal fixtures over their heads clatter against each other. Out of the back of the truck, the world was shaking up and down, pronouncedly more so than it had been.

'Tell me that's the truck shaking,' whispered Alison.

The truck was shaking because the wheels were dropping further and further into the crust of a road that had become soft and yielding. The tarmac had returned to its original state, and beneath it the layers of sand and gravel and concrete had liquefied.

Which left the lorry sinking further and further, its wheels starting to splatter the cab with flying asphalt.

The driver realised that something was happening, downshifting and downshifting, trying to get the wheels to find some grip. His mate beside him scrabbled to unlock the weapons box under the seat, where a pistol had been fixed.

But then they both jerked their limbs upwards as the vibration rose into the cabin. Their arms and faces battered against the windscreen from the inside for a moment as they spasmed out of control.

And then they fell back into their seats, blood pouring from their noses, dead.

The lorry skidded to a long, smooth, halt. Sinking further into a growing pool of lava.

Joe and Alison could hear something happening in the cabin. Joe found the catch that opened the connecting window, and wrenched it open.

He took one look at what had happened, and realised that the horror hadn't left them. 'Alison!' he shouted. 'We have to get out! Get out now!'

Which was when the creature burst through the floor of the lorry.

Its scream had preceded it by only a moment as it blasted towards the surface. It sent molten metal and stone flying into the rear of the lorry, lumps of it ripping the canvas and setting it alight.

Alison cried out, jumping back and scrabbling for something behind her. The creature spun and found her, its hands reaching for her.

Joe threw himself at it, kicking it across the head as hard as he could. 'Get away from her!'

The thing grabbed him and threw him back. He hit the wooden seating awkwardly, but staggered to his feet again, determined to get himself between Alison and the creature. 'Run!' he shouted. 'Get away!'

But Alison had found what she'd been after, a fire extinguisher that had been fastened somewhere behind them. 'Leave us alone!' she was screaming at the creature. 'Leave us *alone*!'

She activated the extinguisher and some sort of chemical foam covered the creature. Joe was absurdly hopeful, just for a second. It would have worked in the movies. The creature was linked with heat, and the extinguisher with cold.

The monster, its scream turning into an angry screech, just thrashed its way through the foam, its fingers finding Alison's arm and dragging her towards it.

With a sudden jerk of motion, it had grabbed her in its arms.

Joe was trying to see through the foam. She was fighting it, kicking as hard as she could, screaming things at it.

The creature lifted her high above itself. Then suddenly engulfed her, wrapped everything it was around her.

And dropped through the floor of the lorry again.

A new low splattering of lava made Joe leap out of the way. The foam from the extinguisher cleared. All that remained was a hissing circle of metal and road and molten rock. Bubbles drifted to the surface and burst, bubbles which might have been Alison's dying breath.

Joe found something inside himself give way. He fell to his knees. 'Alison?' he whispered. And then the whisper became a scream. 'Alison!'

Chapter Eight
Into the Depths

Kennet listened to the news on his RT with quiet anticipation. The enemy had broken cover. That was good news.
'Copy that,' he said, flicking the call button. 'If you have
contact, engage with high explosive. Kennet out.'

Kennet had selected one of his assault squads and
equipped them with caving gear appropriated from a local
potholing club. He judged they didn't have long enough to
wait for military-issue gear to arrive. Best to strike before the
enemy had time to prepare. They had driven up to Bowfell
Point, where potholers had created a rough car park, and
had leapt out of the lorries in good order, the men alive with
that sense of nervy anticipation that preceded combat. The
sergeant drilled them with a weapons check while Kennet
had checked in with his security points, and discovered the
first contact incident.

A significant distance away from them all, the Doctor was
putting on his own caving helmet, glaring at the soldiers all
around as if they cluttered up the countryside.

Kennet went over to him now. 'Just heard from the helicopter
units. An evacuation truck is under attack. A detachment is
moving in to assist.'

The Doctor frowned. 'Blast. I thought the explosion would
hold them off. They're surprising me. Which is worrying.
And it's odd. Why continue the punishments after the town's
been evacuated?'

A sergeant in Kennet's employ, of long and weary standing, had come over to hand the major a map and a location tracking device. His name was Greaves, and Kennet had enjoyed his company in several major military actions. 'I don't know,' he answered the Doctor now, significantly allowing himself permission to speak to the civilian. 'Maybe they're alien monsters who don't give a flying one?'

'Greaves.' Kennet realised that he had a special timbre for the word now, which suggested their rank relationship, Greaves' lackadaisical attitude towards it, and his grudging acceptance of that, all in one.

'Sorry sir.'

But they shared a smile as the Doctor turned away.

Kennet marched over to his men, who snapped to attention at their captain's command. 'At ease,' he told them. They relaxed into the stance. 'This is a recon mission. We find the enemy, fix their position, then either retreat for, or call in, reinforcements.'

'How nice for you,' murmured the Doctor, theatrically waving a hand to cool himself. 'I'm just after my TARDIS.'

Kennet didn't acknowledge him. He saw some of the men's eyes glance in the Doctor's direction, looking angry. 'What are we?' he asked.

'Royal Green Jackets, sir!' they yelled back at him, together.

'Good lads,' he growled back. He strode over to the Doctor, unstrapping a handgun from his pack, and slotting in a new rack of live ammo. 'Here you are, Doctor.'

The man actually slapped his hand away. He moved in to within an inch of Kennet's nose, his patience obviously at an end.

Kennet cursed himself. He'd read this detail in the Doctor's file, of course, that the scientist didn't carry a gun, but he'd had no idea that he would carry that principle this far, even into an actual combat mission. The file also said the Doctor was an expert shot.

But that slap was not good news. He could feel his men looking at him. Their pride was tied up with his. He should bellow at the Doctor. Even cuff him back. He considered those options briefly and discarded them. 'Very well,' he said.

'I'm here under duress. Remember that, Major. Don't you *ever* offer me a gun again.'

Kennet just sucked in his cheeks, nodded, backed off. Then, when he was looking back to the men, he allowed himself a moment with them, a raised eyebrow, a meeting of gazes, a shared humour.

They relaxed again. This idiot was nothing the boss couldn't deal with. Just an irritating civvy in the wrong place at the wrong time. A shared burden.

Kennet just hoped that, when they got underground, that burden didn't get them all killed.

Alison had yelled for twenty minutes as the creature that had wrapped itself around her had plunged through the earth. It had kept on screaming, and its scream seemed to be liquefying the rock beneath and around them. It also kept that rock back, had turned it into a blaze of white heat and light that sped centimetres away from her face, but didn't harm her.

It had all stopped suddenly as they had fallen into some sort of huge cavern. And Alison had had another moment of terror, the vertigo of realising they were too high, that animal instinct of knowing that you were going to be injured when you hit the ground.

But the creature around her had enveloped her, pulling her even closer to its ceramic, cold skin, which reminded her of the earthenware pots in her mum's kitchen. It had landed under her, tail first, and rolled around her, and Alison had stumbled into a half-run, free of it, on the ground, without understanding how she hadn't been injured at all.

Now she was staring at a circle of the creatures as they moved in on her, hissing.

She tried to work out as much information as she could, angry at her own fear. Everything was made of rock. All the switches and controls, and the architecture of the ceiling as well, great swirls and columns. There was something round and spinning on one wall, a great glowing vortex. No: no idea what that was. There was a control panel, with a creature – a different variation on the others – operating it. This model had two sets of arms, ending in dextrous, spindly fingers. Its eyes seemed bigger. And was that a row of … brains down its back? There was a big screen, showing some distant figures making their way through caves. They were being watched by some kind of surveillance that didn't suit human sight, so she couldn't see the details. She hoped they were coming down here to give this lot a going-over. And there was a blue box, which looked completely human in origin, something to do with the police, and huge numbers of these monsters were surrounding it, screaming at it, trying to get in.

Whatever.

Her attention snapped back to what was in front of her as the ranks of the creatures parted, and through them stepped her old mate from town, the figure with the arms and legs, who looked almost human. What Joe had said about it had scared Alison, without her showing it back then. She didn't like being the only one who'd seen this thing.

It didn't try to talk to her. It opened its mouth and began to scream, the volume and intensity building and building.

'I'm not going to let you control me!' Alison yelled at it. 'Whatever you are. I'm not your zombie! Get away from me!'

She tried to put her hands over her ears, but the scream

went straight through her fingers, and hit something inside her head.

Unconscious, she fell.

Prime went to the controls, and took the unit from its container. It was the last one. A proud moment. This stage of the plan was complete.

One of the technicians moved in to make the incision, its bladed fingers sharpening themselves against each other with a swish of rock on rock.

The Doctor, Kennet and his team of soldiers were making their way down through the pothole, so far following routes established by cavers. They wore helmet lights, but hadn't taken up gloves or overalls, the soldiers electing to stay in uniform and have ease of access to their weapons, the Doctor not wanting to get creases in his suit.

The Doctor had some experience of caving, on many worlds, and recognised the area they were passing through as one where what cavers called 'poached eggs' were growing. They were stalagmites formed by the lime workings above, a mixture of lime and humus sifting its way down through the rock above over decades, and creating gorgeous mineral flowers down here. They were a sign of human activity that stretched back thousands of years, to when the first settlers here had started the process. Without gloves, where the soldiers touched them, they would become black over time, the pollution on the men's hands rendering them dull and dark. Another sign of human presence.

The Doctor had mentioned that, but the soldiers didn't seem to have paid any attention. Indeed, one or two of them seemed to reach out and touch the formations deliberately.

He was getting this all wrong. He could so easily have charmed them. After hundreds of years of life, of knowing people, he surely knew ways. Instead, he was doing this to himself again, deliberately creating a barrier between himself and these people, because…

Because.

He kept up an informative and educational commentary as they passed through the various strata of rock, touching on many subjects, but centring around the core values of a classical education. Now they were on the level where the caves intersected with the volcanic rock, so he had changed the subject of his improvised lecture from geology to macro-economics. 'Ground floor: caves, aliens, weapons of mass destruction. You lot be careful you don't miss those.'

They ignored him as they had for hours. They came to a branch in the caverns ahead of them, and Kennet stopped to consult with Sergeant Greaves, who was carrying a map.

The Doctor stopped them and pointed down the left branch. 'This way.'

'Oh,' muttered Greaves. 'Now he's driving.'

The Doctor flashed him his best annoying grin. 'I can sense where the TARDIS is.' He widened his address to include the whole patrol. 'If we encounter the creatures, you're not to open fire, understand?'

Kennet stepped between him and them. 'You don't give my men orders, Doctor. Understand?'

The Doctor was about to make him aware of his many qualifications from the best colleges of strategy and tactics, and a certain bowls wager still outstanding with Sir Francis Drake, when a noise from further down the cavern made the soldiers all unshoulder their weapons at once.

It was the cry of something vast. It reminded the Doctor of whalesong, an enormous outpouring of information that also suggested primal force. With it came a shift of air in the tunnels, the feeling of something enormous moving down there, disturbing the natural breathing of the caves.

'What is it?' whispered Kennet. He looked alarmed, but also interested, his gaze seeking to pierce the darkness ahead.

The Doctor put a hand on his shoulder, holding him back.

Slowly, the creature moved into view. It was huge. A giant green bulk of shining flesh. A worm that filled the cavern ahead of them. It was obviously the same kind of being as the creatures the Doctor had encountered previously, but here there was no sign of eyes, or arms, or a hood. Just the brute vastness of a monstrous beast. They had been walking, the Doctor realised with a start, through spaces big enough for it for at least the last few kilometres.

The worm opened its mouth, throwing a shadow over them, revealing a maw of gigantic teeth. Far too big to feed on any earthly thing. Not that, the Doctor suspected, these creatures fed at all. The teeth were there for effect, to scare small mammals like the soldiers.

But the soldiers stood firm, bringing their weapons to bear. 'Dirty great alien monster, sir,' said Greaves, answering Kennet's question. 'Just a guess.'

'Or rather, dozens of them,' muttered the Doctor. 'Joined together as a colony creature.'

From the huge mouth there came the sound again. It nearly blew them off their feet. It was recognisably the scream, amplified to tremendous volume.

The Doctor flung his hands over his ears. He could see the soldiers swaying, their eyes fixed on the creature. The sound was controlling them somehow, holding them fixed in the course of the oncoming predator.

And indeed, the worm lurched towards them, as if intending to crush them.

'On my mark, you men!' The Doctor roared with a parade ground bellow. 'Snap out of it and scatter!' He held it for a moment. 'Mark!'

They scattered. One kind of conditioning had over-ridden the other.

The Doctor risked a cheeky grin at Kennet, but he'd turned to call to the men backing up.

'Grenades!'

The soldiers grabbed them from their webbing.

The Doctor glanced up, then at the swiftly advancing creature, working out the stresses of the different sorts of rock. A push there, a pull here…

He grabbed Kennet by the arm again. 'Throw them into the corner there!' He pointed urgently. 'The sound will hurt it!'

'You heard him!' Kennet added quickly.

'I'm afraid I just *did* give them orders.' The Doctor couldn't help but whisper it in Kennet's ear. He allowed himself a gleeful chuckle. 'And it felt *so* good!'

Kennet gave him a look.

The soldiers pulled the pins, estimated, counted, and threw.

At the same moment, the Doctor threw himself forward. He rolled into exactly the right corner of the cave.

The worm reared up, blasting them all with the heat and violence of its ear-splitting bellow.

And then the grenades went off. The explosions in the confined space produced a burst of rock and fire.

The ceiling came down. Tons of rock that roared down over everything, bringing with it a vast crushing noise of its own, and a torrent of dust.

When the dust cleared, the Doctor looked up to find … that the soldiers had vanished on one side of the rock and he was on the other. He allowed himself a grin for a moment at his own cleverness.

Then he looked up at the bulk of the worm rising over him. And the grin faded.

* * *

Kennet glared at the solid wall of fallen rock that had cut his patrol off from their first engagement with the alien enemy.

His men looked at him, as angry as he was.

'He did that deliberately,' he muttered. 'Well then, move out! Let's find another way!'

And, with the furious major at their head, the soldiers turned and ran to do so.

Chapter Nine
The Shalka

Prime watched on the viewing screen as the Collective Warrior advanced on the stranger who owned the blue box. The Collective Warrior was obeying its orders, intercepting and destroying any lower creatures who came near the forward base. It would be glorious to see it destroy this small creature.

But there were questions Prime needed the answers to. Reluctantly, it emitted a scream that was taken up by the engineer at the control panel, and rebroadcast down the tunnels.

The Collective Warrior stopped, hesitated, understood.

It stayed there, its mouth open, waiting for the tiny creature beneath it to use what passed for thinking processes in these lower creatures.

Prime urged it on, delighting at the trap.

The Doctor gazed up into the vicious jaws of the worm, marvelling at the vast teeth he could see there. An entire system of them, set out for form rather than function, a visual representation of a human nightmare. Old Goya would have been proud. Well, actually, he would probably have just sighed, because Francisco could be a touch dreary, especially towards the end of the evening.

'The teeth are deliberate, aren't they?' he asked the worm. 'What a wonderful species, to have such control over what you're like.' He stood up, flapped some of the dust from his suit, and grabbed hold of one of the smaller teeth in the front of the thing's mouth. It felt cold and wet. He hauled himself up, tooth by enormous tooth, climbing over the creature's rocky palate. The mouth gave beneath his feet unevenly, the crust there breaking into tiny patterns of faultlines. 'Excuse me, I hope I don't taste of boot polish.'

He found refuge in a row of smaller teeth, far back, which, dentistry not being his speciality, he didn't know how to describe.

It was only then, with his feet planted and his handholds set, that the creature suddenly roared again – and from here it wasn't so bad, actually, the scream must be designed to resonate *outside* the form of the creature – and thrashed into the air, making a very obviously false attempt to dislodge him.

The Doctor hung on.

Finally, the worm threw itself flat again, let out another long, communicative cry, and slithered off down the tunnels, swiftly accelerating to an enormous speed as its scream melted the rock beneath it into a smooth runway.

The Doctor relaxed, letting his muscles react to the occasional buckings of a bigger rock underneath them. 'That's it!' he cried. 'You take me home, big boy! Yeeee-hahhhhhhhhhhhhhhhhh!'

Finally, now he was alone, he was enjoying himself.

He pulled the mobile phone from his pocket and hit a key.

The Master hung on to the console with grim determination.

The creatures had been varying their screams, trying everything they could think of to get within the doors of the TARDIS. The Master was rather hoping they would try and just slither in and thump him, because then he would hit the fast-close key, and the doors would crush them, but they retained an annoying hesitancy about the ship's defences.

With a clatter, his face fell off and bounced on the floor.

He sighed. All the vibrations must have worked the catches loose. It was always embarrassing when that happened. He remembered a particular dinner party where he had had to fish for his face in the soup tureen with a pair of silver tongs. The other guests in the TARDIS control room had politely looked aside and commented on other things, but the Master had been able to tell that the Doctor was quietly seething underneath his patrician chuckles.

That had been months ago, and yet he could still taste onions.

At least, given all the screaming, it was lucky that he could no longer get a headache.

He reached down, one hand still poised at the controls, and retrieved his face.

He didn't look at it before he clipped it back in place. He didn't like to be reminded of his current nature: a mind contained inside a program, a program contained within a machine. He had chosen the look of the machine, the way its voice sounded. The Doctor had given him all the dignity he could find for his former foe.

But it was not enough. It never would be.

'Every day,' he whispered, 'presents a new challenge to one's dignity.'

It was at that moment that the telephone started to ring. The old-fashioned bell from the black lacquered chinoiserie instrument sounded odd over the harmonised screaming of the creatures outside.

He tried to make his way towards it, inching around the console, but it was going to prove impossible, the instruments needed his whole attention if he was going to continue defending the ship from the aliens.

The answerphone clicked on. The first time it had seen service in years. The Master was suddenly glad that the Doctor wasn't here to hear it.

In the background was the gentle sound of *her* laughter. The Doctor, in turn, sounded like he hadn't a care in the universe. And indeed, back then he had not. There was the sound behind them of champagne being poured.

'Hello! You've reached the good ship TARDIS! We're rather busy at the moment. Leave a message after the beep and we'll try and get back to you before you call.' The laughter grew closer for a moment. 'Stop that!'

The Master looked skywards. 'We really should change that message.'

'Are you there?'

He realised with some horror that it was the Doctor on the other end of the phone, that he must indeed have listened to that. Why hadn't he thought to change it?! 'I'm trying to get there, you fool!' he yelled across the room, exasperated.

'Well,' the voice of the Doctor continued. 'If you can hear me, have you considered setting up the secondary configuration suite? Nothing can generally get in, I know, but I haven't encountered this lot before, and there's something worryingly confident about them. Cheerio.'

If hearing the sound of her voice had affected him, he had managed not to show it.

And that had been an excellent idea.

The Master waited until he was certain that the aliens were engrossed in their latest attempts to outwit the programs he'd set up in the defence circuitry, and then altered a couple of settings on the control panel. Then he dived under the console. He found a particular lever, and pulled it.

The doors, ignoring the sound blasting them open, simply swung shut. They had been phased, for a moment, into an entirely different mathematical plane.

The dimensional seal whacked closed. Once more, nothing could get in.

The Master fell back against the trunk of the console, his batteries exhausted. 'Why,' he sighed, 'did I choose continuing existence, listening to him being *right* all the time, when I had the option of a slow, painful, death?'

The Collective Warrior slid into the forward base through an entrance it opened up for itself, melting away an entire rock wall of the cavern.

It opened its mouth slowly, as Prime ordered its warriors to surround it.

Inside stood the owner of the blue box.

Prime watched its expression, glorying in its fear and dread.

The Doctor watched as the mouth of the worm slowly opened. In front of him was a vast cavern, full of technological wonders, all rather charmingly made from rock. Inside it stood hundreds of the creatures he'd seen before. They were waiting for him, their eyes fixed on him.

At their head stood a tall, green, humanoid figure, which looked like their leader.

The Doctor could scarcely contain his glee.

He waited until the jaw of the worm had hit the cavern floor, then, with a deep breath, he strode proudly forward, looking around him, waving and grinning. 'Hello! Hello! This is so unexpected!' He stopped for a moment and glanced back behind him. 'Is there someone more famous further back in the monster?'

No reaction. Tough audience.

He saw the familiar shape of the TARDIS, and, still ignoring the leader, put a hop in his step towards it. 'Ah, there the old girl is! It's been lovely, but I must be going…'

He got one step further than he thought he would. So they were either rather sloppy or very confident. The latter, from supporting evidence.

Their leader had stepped into his path. The Doctor smiled brightly at it.

'What are you?' it asked.

The Doctor grabbed its hand and pumped it enthusiastically, aware of the rest of the creatures closing in round him, cutting off his retreat, not that such a thing existed. 'No,' he laughed. 'It's *how* are you. And how are *you*?'

'I am Prime, War Chief of the Shalka Confederacy.'

'And that's *who* are you!' Shalka, Shalka, Shalka. No, it didn't ring a bell. War Chief, which indicated an otherwise civil society. As did 'Confederacy'. A union of many different groups. Promising. The top monster? No, probably just the chief here and now. And there had been pride in the title. That confidence again. So... 'I'm the Doctor. I'm from a highly advanced alien species. Entirely different league to you. I only come to this planet for the wine and the total eclipses. And I do love a nice old-fashioned invasion.' He nodded upwards. 'I think this lot could certainly do with a spot of regime change.' He spun on his heel, doing a rough head count while apparently gazing admiringly at the Shalka army. 'What a turn out! There must be, oh...'

'A bridgehead force of two thousand Shalka,' Prime interrupted. 'That's the information you wanted, isn't it?'

Oops. Move on. '*Shalka*, eh? Never heard of you. So, forgive me,' he lowered his tone to a confidential whisper, 'but you can't be *all that*.'

He didn't pause to see the reaction, just used the moment to leap through a handful of the creatures and get to a shining circle that spun on the far wall of the cavern.

The power that shone inside the ring was unmistakable. It was like looking into a crushing whirlpool, somehow controlled and focused and hung on the wall. The butterfly tunnel inside was a visual representation of the chaos of the space-time vortex, the other-dimensional void through which the TARDIS and other such vehicles passed in their travels.

It was a bit of raw universe displayed like a hunter's trophy.

'Ah-ha!' The Doctor pointed at it like he'd only just realised what he was looking at. 'I like your wormhole.' Then he slapped a hand to his mouth. 'Oh dear. Do *you* call it that?'

He continued his reconnaissance of the cavern, noticing exits towards small, bolelike caves where Shalka were curled up, at rest. The mass of the army followed him, obviously under orders not to harm him. So Prime was sizing him up at the same time. It didn't quite know who he was. Best keep it that way.

Prime strode after him, intercepting him once more near a boiling pit of open lava. 'Instead of pretending to be a fool, just ask your questions!'

'Well,' the Doctor grasped his lapels and twiddled his thumbs. 'I am slightly curious. Why did you only invade a tiny bit of Lancashire?'

'Our ambition is greater than that!'

The Doctor's eyes boggled. 'You mean... Nottinghamshire?!'

Prime was silent. Didn't react. Just stood there, breathing.

'*Like* the humanoid form, by the way! Differentiates you from your henchworms.' He bent to sniff the vapours that were steaming off the lava pool, doing his best to analyse them. 'You speak and breathe air. They don't.'

'I value understanding my enemy.'

'Do you?'

'I've experienced so-called human "culture". The random noise of individual minds. Lower creatures such as humans aren't united like the Shalka.'

The Doctor took that in, folding his hands behind his back, walking over to where one of those unusual Shalka with too many brains and arms was working at a console, directing the low murmur of its screams into what looked like a big, silver, rather gorgeously retro microphone. Lower creatures. Classic monster attitude. And they had a hive culture, made up of individuals, but united by the scream.

'Your technology's based on sound, built around your natural attack mechanism. Advanced enough to control a black hole,' he nodded at the wormhole gate. 'And hollow out spaces like this, all within a few weeks. I'm impressed!'

He reached out a finger to touch a control, but the Brainy Shalka knocked his hand away.

The Doctor straightened up, turning to gesture to Prime once more. 'You know, not that I care either way, and I hate to say it, but… If it's a dying homeworld job, you don't *need* an invasion. The humans don't use the inside of their world. Rather than be their conquerors you could be their lodgers. Much more fun.' He let his hopeful expression fade. 'Though you'd probably have to take a turn cleaning out Wookey Hole.'

'Our homeworld is not dying. It is the centre of our empire of a billion worlds!'

The circle of the Shalka army had become a spiral, the watching warriors having followed the Doctor in a half circuit around the cavern. Prime had followed that motion too. Perhaps that was something that came with the snake-like form, a fondness for spirals, a spatial weakness, like the human love of symmetry and threes.

It had allowed the Doctor to end up standing outside the TARDIS. He flipped the key out of his pocket. 'Well, as the actress said to the bishop: I'm not human and I don't care. I'll just get out of your way.'

He expected them to rush him, then. He was horribly surprised when they didn't.

'I think not, Doctor,' whispered Prime, moving slowly forward. 'I think *you* are a lower creature too.'

It opened its mouth and added an urgent note to the scream of its fellows.

The crowd of Shalka parted. Through them slithered two of the warriors.

Between them hung the struggling form of Alison Cheney.

They were standing over one of the lava pools that lay all over the cavern floor. Her feet hung centimetres from the steaming, red-hot rock.

All the Doctor's confidence in his own abilities fled. Dread hit him in the stomach.

She had been hurt already, there was a scar across her forehead.

His eyes met hers.

'Doctor!' she called. She was kicking, thrashing, trying to get her feet up from the heat below. She was desperately glad to see him.

She thought he was going to save her.

He tried to find something clever to say. He could not.

'I think you have a lower creature's weaknesses, Doctor,' continued Prime.

The Doctor found something. Something that caught in the back of his throat as he said it. A last gesture in the pretence that he didn't care. 'Does this mean… you're offering to cook?'

Prime started to laugh. It was a horrible sound, the cold mirth of a statue.

The Shalka started lowering Alison towards the lava.

She started screaming as the heat hit her. She tried to helplessly kick her legs up, to thrash out of the way.

The Doctor could see it. Every detail. What was about to happen. Alison would be seeing it too, would be replaying what had happened to her friend.

He tried to hold out. He tried to close his eyes and think of the greater good.

Then he opened them, and saw the terror in her eyes, and he bellowed, 'Stop it! I'll do whatever you want, just *don't hurt her*!'

Prime held it for a moment, then made a little noise.

The Shalka raised Alison away from the lava.

Prime advanced on the Doctor, completely triumphant, laying a hand on the Doctor's shaking shoulder. 'And being a lower creature,' it whispered, quite gently, 'you will do as we say.'

Chapter Ten
In the Hands of the Enemy

The Master had been trying to use the scanner to establish what was going on outside. He had been about to try and take off once more, but as he was beginning the sequence, he'd been astonished to see the Doctor step out of the mouth of a giant wormlike creature and start wandering around the cavern like he owned the place.

At one point during his state visit, as he'd been inspecting the space-time vortex that these creatures had hanging rather daintily on the wall, the scanner had been overcome by interference. The creatures were using their all-pervading sonic force field to interfere with the ship's systems again. Since then, the Master had been unable to ascertain what was happening outside.

He was relieved, therefore, to hear the familiar sound of the key in the TARDIS lock. A moment later, the Doctor strode in.

'Ah, my dear Doctor!' The Master moved from the console to welcome his old enemy. 'Where have you been?'

But behind the Doctor came a group of the creatures, led by Prime.

The Master turned sighingly back to the Doctor, and saw for the first time the expression of desperation and defeat on his face. 'Tell me that you haven't done something foolish? Again?'

The Doctor looked aside.

'Well, I'm afraid that I won't let –'

He leapt for the console.

But the Doctor had pulled that infernal device of his from his pocket. And pressed the control.

And the Master knew no more.

The Doctor replaced the remote control in his pocket.

He felt numb. Despair had overcome him. Had brought his memories thundering back to consume him.

The Master stood fixed, his hand reaching for a control.

The Doctor felt exactly the same. Would that he could lose consciousness in that impotence, also.

Prime was looking around the control room, unimpressed. 'Is this all?' it asked. 'A simple toy?' It moved back to the Doctor and angled its green face at his, mocking. 'It was hardly worth your humiliation.'

Kennet had taken his patrol back to a fork in the caves, at which he'd set up some heavy weapons, ready to hold the line as Greaves led another group of men on a quick recce down the other way. The map had indicated several possible ways down, and Kennet was determined to explore them all.

But ten minutes ago, creatures had appeared in this tunnel, and had started battering his patrol with their sonic weapons. Grenades had destroyed a couple of them, but heavy machine-gun fire just ricocheted off their ceramic hides. Kennet remembered an article he'd read in Jane's concerning ceramic coatings on suborbital nuclear warheads. His men weren't sustaining injuries as such, but they were wavering, attempting to disobey orders and stop firing, even yelling that they were going to turn their weapons on their fellows. There was obviously some kind of controlling effect going on, similar to what had beset the town, and Kennet was aware that his sudden commands and drills wouldn't keep them together forever. He could even feel the effect himself, getting under his guard like post-battle syndrome, like the fear of a sniper.

Greaves ran back from the tunnel, the two men with him turning to fire behind them. 'More alien monsters, sir!' he yelled. 'I make it three at least!'

Kennet held his decision for a moment, making sure it was his. Then he swung his arm and called the order. 'We're not going to make it that way, either! Retreat! Retreat! In good order now!'

They fell back into lines, each group firing to cover the last, jogging back towards the entrance, following their map.

Behind them, rock fell to obscure the creatures, blocking the tunnel.

Kennet turned, coughing at the sudden blast of rock and dust. He cursed under his breath. The reconnaissance expedition had succeeded only in shutting off a way to the aliens' base.

Alison didn't know what was worse: that she'd injured her head; that she'd been put in a cell; or that a few minutes later they'd opened the door and locked the Doctor in here with her.

He'd hardly said a word to her. He'd just glared at her, then started pacing back and forth, looking too furious to speak. It felt like he was angry with her. She would have felt angry back at him for that, apart from the fact that he'd just saved her life.

That felt like it was the problem. Horribly.

Finally, he stopped, turned, glared at her again. 'What are you *doing* down here?'

'They grabbed me. That sound they make protected me from the lava.'

He slapped his palm on the wall, with a force that made Alison jump. 'I should have let you die.'

'Oh cheers!'

The Doctor continued, staring away from her, muttering as if she was an object, or like she wasn't even there. 'They might have thought that was who I was, then: the detached alien observer. But no, as always, only the monsters *know* me!' He turned and faced her again, his glare replaced by a look of self-disgust. 'Only they know how *weak* I really am.'

'You gave in because they threatened me! Anyone would have done that!'

'Well, I did *try* to do something else, last time this happened.' He walked away, turning his back to her again. 'Which is why I told myself that I would never get into a situation like this again.'

'What happened?' She stared at his back, watching how tense he was, how much he was letting out, almost against his will. He had held this inside so long, she realised.

'It doesn't matter.'

She couldn't handle this any longer. She got up, pulled him round by the shoulder, looked him in the face. 'Talk to *me*. This is *not* my fault. How do we get out of this?'

He didn't turn away again. 'If it was just me, I'd improvise something. These days, when I have someone else to worry about…' He threw up his hands. 'Why couldn't you have offered to sacrifice yourself or something?! It was all down to me!'

She almost laughed. 'I'm not going to sacrifice myself for Lannet! It's the dullest place in the universe!'

'Oh I think not! You should see *my* home planet.' He turned away again. His whole tone implied that that was never going to happen, that she was still the stupid human who had spoiled his fun, made him vulnerable.

'I was thinking about leaving,' she said, 'when all this happened.'

He stopped and turned back, to her surprise, suddenly interested. 'You were about to leave Joe?'

It wrongfooted her. 'I don't know. Maybe I was hoping he'd come with me.'

'Did he know how you felt?' What was he thinking, behind those careful eyes?

'I'd just started telling him how unhappy I was. Only then the place got invaded by aliens, and hey – priorities. And now I'm just hoping he doesn't get … you know … killed. Because that would be so bad now. With things up in the air between us and everything.' She sighed. 'Really selfish of me, right?'

The Doctor had taken a step towards her, his eyes searching her face, as if he'd found understanding in an unexpected place. He hesitantly reached out, and put a hand on her shoulder. 'No. I understand exactly. And completely. Believe me.'

Alison wanted to tell him how great that was, that he'd moved from thinking he should have let her fry in lava.

But suddenly it felt like something had hit her across the eyes. Pain rushed into her skull, making her grab her head and cry out.

She was aware, vaguely, of him jumping away, the hand leaving her shoulder. She folded down onto the ground, trying to stop the awful feeling.

Which faded … and vanished.

She rubbed a hand across her face.

He squatted beside her, moving her hair aside to examine her forehead. 'Where did you get that wound?'

'I don't know. Maybe when the house exploded. I've been getting headaches ever since they brought me down here. But nothing like that.'

'Perhaps it's the atmosphere. Prime keeps air circulating down here rather than slipping in and out of its lungs. But there's a lot of volcanic gas around.' He fumbled in his pocket and produced an asthma inhaler. 'Do you fancy a puff of my huffer?'

Alison stared at it. 'Euw.'

The cell door slid open, rock rollers on rock, lubricated with a hiss of lava, and in came Prime.

'We now understand the principles of your craft,' it said.

The Doctor boggled at it. '*Do* you?! Could you explain it to me?'

'A simple cause-and-effect device. The usual lower creature conceits. Its operation will prove well within our abilities.' Prime stepped aside, and into the cell slithered two Shalka warriors. 'So... Now you die.'

The Shalka grabbed them and hauled them out of the cell.

Alison was alarmed to find that, as they were dragged across the cavern floor, through the watching, hissing, Shalka army, the Doctor not only failed to struggle as she was, but actually resumed his bitching at her. 'Your plaintive cries didn't help,' he muttered as their captors stopped in front of the spinning vortex of the warp gate. 'Oh, help me, Doctor, help me!'

'I never said that.'

'Well it felt like you did,' the Doctor retorted. 'If you'd been less convincing with your appeals, we wouldn't be here now.'

'Right. You'd be free and I'd be dead.'

He opened his mouth and then closed it again. 'No need to go on. Point taken. Slipped my mind.'

Prime had moved to a panel of controls set on a rocky outcrop some distance in front of the gate. It turned to address them. 'The space-time tunnel to our homeworld is created by the sonic control of a singularity. Set like this, it can transport our armies instantly across thousands of light years. But set like this –'

Prime thumped a switch. The intricate swirls of colour inside the wormhole became pure blackness. Alison could feel all the dust and vapour of the rocks around her suddenly start falling in its direction. Her jewellery lifted off her skin. A couple of small rocks rolled and then fell into the black pit set in the wall, and then whirled away.

Gravity had suddenly turned in that direction. It sat alongside the normal gravity of the rest of the cavern, obvious only within a short distance from the gate. You could sense the great power it took to keep things in place, the feeling of chains of rock holding physics in check.

It felt like the start of a very horrible theme-park ride.

She took a look at the Doctor. He had shut up, and was concentrating fiercely. He didn't look like he had a way out of this.

'It's a black hole again!' whispered Prime. 'It crushes whatever is thrown into it down to a mathematical point. We use it to dispose of our waste.'

'What about her?' the Doctor suddenly shouted. 'You can't –!'

The Shalka had eased their grip slightly as their prisoner had addressed their commander.

And in that moment – Alison didn't see how – the Doctor was free. He tried to leap for the controls ...

But one of the Shalka threw its weight around its centre of gravity, and caught him a blow with its tail. The Doctor staggered and fell, sprawling short of his target.

He leapt to his feet again, but the other guard was on him now.

Alison tried to run, but the first Shalka caught her hands and held on, dragging her across the floor with one sweep of muscle.

The other Shalka was battering the Doctor, knocking him from side to side with its tail, a predator smashing the consciousness of some tiny helpless bit of prey. It leapt back, and continued the battering with a warbled blast of its scream, throwing the Doctor limply from side to side.

'Leave him alone!' Alison shouted.

Prime turned to look at her. 'Lower creatures always assume *their* cries will have some effect on *us*,' it said. 'It's very strange.'

It opened its mouth as Alison was about to scream something else at it.

And screamed back.

The pain hit her right between the eyes.

The Doctor staggered to his feet, holding up his hands to fend off the latest rush of blows.

And saw Alison fall, her face pale, blood pouring from her nose. 'Alison!' he bellowed.

All his nightmares had come true. Again.

Prime's scream continued. It moved its head to indicate him.

He tried to leap for Alison, to help her, though he knew, sickeningly, that help was too late.

But the two Shalka warriors grabbed him. They held him high above their heads.

The assembled might of the Shalka army warbled with victorious joy.

And then the warriors threw him into the warp gate.

The cavern spun off to become a distant point of brightness in a world of infinite, in-rushing darkness. A darkness that engulfed the Doctor.

He screamed only her name as he fell.

Chapter Eleven
Into the Vortex

Prime stood over Alison's form, using its own knowledge of lower-creature anatomy to make certain that she was still respiring. Around it, the warrior Shalka were vanishing into the walls of the forward base, returning to their individual assignments once more.

When Prime was certain Alison was still alive, it emitted its modulated scream. One of the guard warriors picked the lower creature up, and wrapped its arms around her again. It activated its own scream, and without hesitation, vanished with its burden into the rock of the cavern floor.

The bulge formed by its bulletlike passage sped under the floor and then up the side of the cavern wall, vanishing into the roof.

Prime threw its head back, and laughed once again like it had heard the lower creatures laugh. The lower creature called the Doctor had actually thought they would harm Alison Cheney! He had had no idea of how much they valued her.

Of how much use she was going to be.

And now he had taken that ignorance to his death.

Prime returned to the controls, and started to reset the warp gate to its travel configuration.

The technician Shalka were proud of their position in the Confederacy hierarchy. They had been specially developed from protein strings, genetically enhanced to gather memes until, at the age of birthing, they came forth from the great rock egg chambers with extra appendages jutting from their protoplasmic forms.

When they formed their first shells, those appendages formed nodules that curved and increased the areas of the protoplasm that had been set aside for information processing and memory. The nodules became brains.

They used their first screams, as they were now entitled to do, to carve themselves extra limbs, and filled them with their protoplasm, each technician deciding for themselves how they should appear, how they would be best suited to perform their function for the Confederacy.

They largely chose the same basic shapes, but, uniquely, unlike the warriors or the herders or the breeders or the Primes, the choice was theirs.

That was the source of their pride.

The lead technician and several others were examining the interior of the space-time craft. While the others examined the function of the console, it was the lead technician's job to reactivate the artificial intelligence that stood, one hand poised, where the technicians had placed him on entering the craft. Artificial intelligence! As if the lower creatures had an intelligence that they could pass on to their own creations!

The lead technician ran its scream up and down the harmonic range, adjusting its senses until it received the correct sort of feedback from the electronics inside. A sonic remote control had already been installed, which made the lead technician's task easier.

The being jerked into life, its finger thrusting into the air, reaching for the place where the control had been.

'– you hurt yourself again!' it finished. It looked around, brushed its jacket down, folded its hands behind his back … and smiled. 'Ah,' it said. 'Thank you. My plan worked perfectly.'

The lead technician and the other technicians looked at each other.

The being stepped boldly towards them, waving a hand in the air, as if they were simpletons who required instruction. 'Well of course it was a plan! I knew he would deactivate me, because otherwise I would prevent him from hiding all the secrets of this craft.'

The lead technician moved in on the being, wondering at the extreme confidence it was displaying. Lower creatures typically cried out and ran. This one seemed, worryingly, to know exactly what it was talking about. And there were certain anomalies in the control systems that were definitely much more complex than they appeared to be at first glance.

The being had moved to the console, and was shaking his head, sighing and tutting. 'And I see he's done just that!' He turned to them and slapped his hands together. 'So, now you need me to tell you how to work the *real* systems. In return for safe passage off this suburban nightmare of a planet, obviously.' He waved away this trifle of a detail. 'Now, where shall we begin?'

And he dived under the console and set to work.

The lead technician and the other Shalka exchanged an uneasy sonic communication. Had they just agreed to something?

Joe was sitting beside the road in which the military lorry was still stuck. Its wheels had set in hardening lava. The surface of the road was a mass of different textures, a pattern of solid spiral waves which waylaid the white line in the middle. It was sickeningly beautiful under the sunshine. It was dawn now. There was dew on the grass.

He'd sat inside the truck, after Alison had vanished, waiting for them to come back for him. He'd wanted that. Wanted to fight something. But they hadn't come. After a few minutes he'd felt able to climb out, and jump over the lava onto what remained of the road. He'd found that was hot and sticky too, and had had to leap, asphalt on his boots, over to the verge.

As he got there, he'd heard a roaring, and felt the rush of air above him as a military helicopter had come in to land. The troops had leapt out, thrown down some sort of sacking on the road surface, and had run across to him, carefully hustling him away from the lorry. They formed a perimeter around the vehicle before dashing inside it to investigate. He explained, as fast as he could, what had happened, to a grim-looking captain. The soldiers reacted with anger to the bodies they found in the front seats.

They'd wanted to send him off on an evacuation lorry, but Joe had made a case for staying, firstly as a doctor, and then, when they put further pressure on him, just by insisting that he wasn't going to leave the spot where Alison had vanished. So they had let him sit there, for now.

He didn't know why he'd done that.

He had always known, he thought now, that he she was going to vanish one day. Maybe that was why grief was taking so long to come. Or maybe it always did. He had just never thought, at any moment, that she might die.

He was a doctor, he was there to stop death.

The soldiers were now digging out the truck, freeing its wheels from the road with a drill. And a new group had arrived, these more obviously prepared for combat, bringing with them heavy weapons. One of them, when he'd asked, said that this was one of only two recent contacts with the enemy, so they were preparing in case they came back, but none of them seemed to actually expect that. They were mostly taking photos of the inside of the truck, gathering data, Joe supposed, on their opponents.

One of the new arrivals, a sergeant, marched over to him,

finally. 'It's still not safe here, sir. Possibility of lava, becoming dry later.'

'I can't believe she's gone,' Joe told him.

The look on the soldier's face said he didn't have time for this. 'Sir, the next evacuation truck comes through here in ten minutes. The sappers here were waiting until the road hardened up, we're here to defend the trucks if there's action. It's going to stop here, you're going to get on it.'

'Or?'

'Or you may force me to stop calling you "sir".'

Joe felt an anger that he didn't know he had welling up inside him. 'I'm not going anywhere without –'

The vibration made them all react. The soldiers by the truck looked up and unslung their weapons, looking around for the source, one of them pulling out some kind of sensing device and pointing with a shout towards –

The verge where Joe was sitting.

The sergeant had unslung his rifle and shucked the safety catch. He was looking round to the left and right, keeping it against his body. 'Anybody got contact?!' he yelled.

The shape burst out of the ground in a moment. It was a shape beneath the grass, then there was a moment of green over green, like a dolphin surfacing in the blink of an eye. Then it had gone and there was just –

'Alison!' Joe yelled, leaping up and getting between the sergeant and his girlfriend, who was now lying there, on the grass, beside a swiftly cooling pool of steaming new lava.

They all rushed over to her, the soldiers looking around for further contact. The guy with the sensor was shaking his head.

'Alison!' Joe got to her, knocked the soldiers' hands off him, started to examine her.

'Stretcher party!' the sergeant was yelling.

She opened her eyes and blinked at Joe, like she was astonished to see him, like he was a dream.

'Are you okay?' he asked. Her vital signs were fine for someone under stress, and she didn't look like she'd been injured, apart from that nasty scar across her forehead.

'What are you doing here? Where am I?'

'You're back in Lannet! Where have you been?!'

'They let me go,' she whispered, remembering. 'Why would they do that?' She suddenly sat bolt upright, struggling against the medics who'd arrived with the stretcher. 'The Doctor! They killed the Doctor!'

'Shhh!' Joe squeezed her hand, easing her back onto the spinal board. 'It's okay now. You're with me. And we're getting you out of here!'

The Doctor had been inside black holes before, of course.

But previously they'd been black holes with parentheses. One had been inside a black hole, *but…* Largely due to the benefits of advanced technology.

This time it was just him, plunging into the psychedelic void beyond the event horizon. Small bits of rock from the cavern were falling with him. Ahead he could see the dark point of the singularity, the total nothingness of absolute pressure that would crush him in an instant when he hit it.

And the thing about being inside a black hole was that he *was* going to hit it. All roads led there, no way out.

He'd taken a breath before he'd been thrown in, and had held it, switching off his need to breathe, telling his body to recycle everything, though he didn't know why he'd bothered.

He was, in all practical respects, already dead.

He grabbed his mobile phone and hit a number he'd taken earlier that day. He waited, listening to it ring. The Doctor's mobile was dimensionally transcendental, part of the TARDIS. It could contact any communications network in time and space, and was currently sending its signal via another dimension, allowing it to avoid the trap of energy falling into the black hole.

He got the answerphone message. 'This is Major Thomas Kennet, First Royal Green Jackets. I'm not available at the moment. Please leave your communication, over.'

On another occasion, the Doctor might have smiled at that. 'This is the Doctor,' he said, talking swiftly as he watched the black point rushing closer. 'I'm terribly sorry, but I'm afraid that I'm about to die. The aliens are called the Shalka. I'll text you the co-ordinates of their base. They have a warp gate to their homeworld. Knock that out and they may do a deal.' His fingers fluttered across the keypad, sending the co-ordinates in a message alongside his current vocal communication. He took a breath, wondering at what he should, or could, say next. 'I know you don't know much about me, Kennet, and this is hardly the time to start a friendship, but just know this: I was finished anyway. Hopeless. I can't do this any more. I got her killed. Again. It's not the first time, so it's apt I don't continue and I'm happy with that. I do however have some last words for the universe. They are –'

The phone beeped.

The Doctor glared at the message that had appeared on the screen. 'Battery low?!'

For a moment, he felt as though this was really the end. In the most ignominious possible manner.

But he was the Doctor. There was something inside him that wouldn't stop. And now, especially now, he valued his dignity too much to die without it.

'I will have my last words, blast you!' He fumbled for a screwdriver, and took it to the back of the phone, knowing he could coax a few more seconds out of the battery by cross-wiring the power coupling to the receptors. 'This is not,' he muttered, 'how I want to spend my last few remaining –'

It unfolded in his head. The whole thing. Every detail, down to what he was going to say at the end. In that moment, his speech caught up with his thoughts. 'Seconds. Time. Time machine. TARDIS!' He yelled at the phone in joy. 'You're part of the TARDIS! If I can get you to remember that…'

He changed what he was doing, found the chameleon-circuit link, used the last of the battery power to activate it, aware, over his shoulder, of the singularity rushing up at him like a killing blow.

The phone *unfolded*.

Once, twice, and then quickly, faster and faster.

Until it was the size and shape of a blue police-box door.

There was still a tiny control panel on the door for the Doctor to work with, as per his instructions to the circuitry that controlled how every bit of his space and time craft looked. The mobile phone wasn't just stored behind the sign, it was a functioning part of the craft, and every part of the craft connected, across dimensions, with every other.

That was how the blasted thing worked! He'd been so foolish not to realise it earlier!

One panel on the door began to metamorphose into the familiar sign from the front of the police box. 'I just need a door handle!' yelled the Doctor, frantically manipulating the tiny controls. 'Don't worry about the sign!'

And as always, somehow, the TARDIS grudgingly listened to him.

There was a door handle in the Doctor's hand.

As the singularity howled up at him like a bullet, he wrenched the door open and leaped into his TARDIS.

The leap ended in a bound into the TARDIS control room, from a door that had appeared on the wall only a second before.

The room was full of technician Shalka, all of whom had turned, a stunned expression on their faces, to stare at the Doctor.

'Ah!' The Doctor said. 'You look busy! Many hands and all that.' He flexed his fingers in the air for a moment to emphasise the punchline, but he was seriously coming to believe that this lot were never going to be rolling in the aisles.

He waited a moment to be able to deliver the line he'd thought of inside the black hole, but, worryingly, the opportunity did not arise.

So he let go the bracket of the heavy wardrobe that he'd jauntily grasped and made his way to the console, leaving the door open behind him, aware that any moment the Shalka might attack with their screams again, intending to kill him, since they knew now that was exactly what their leader wanted.

The Master looked up from beneath the console, and the Doctor was gratified to see that, just for a moment, a huge, generous smile lit up his face. 'Doctor! You're alive!'

The three technician Shalka who had been down there with him popped up beside him, hissing.

'I mean,' he changed his tune, 'how dare you profane a craft of the glorious Shalka Confederacy with your presence?!'

The Doctor ignored him. His fingers closed around the rail at the edge of the console. 'I'm the Doctor,' he grinned at the Shalka who had begun to slither round to encircle him in the same spiral attack form they had battered him with before throwing him into the black hole. The look on their faces said that this time they would finish the job. He made eye contact with as many of them as possible, greeting them personally. 'Hello! Hello, hello, hello...' He glanced at the Master again. 'And that's the Master, who I see isn't holding onto anything –'

The Master pursed his lips in a silent 'oh' and discretely gripped the console.

The Shalka all opened their mouths to kill the Doctor.

'And this –' he finished, calling aloud to the flapping door behind him as if emphasising to an off-stage actor that he'd missed his cue –

The door that was falling through the black hole hit the singularity.

The door inside the TARDIS that led to that space slammed open to the roaring, all-consuming vortex.

The Shalka were wrenched off their tails and flew screaming out of the door. With them went everything in the room that wasn't nailed down. A vast plume of books emptied the bookshelves, filling the air with flying volumes.

The Doctor hit the door control. The door that led to the singularity slammed closed again. Everything fell to the floor.

'– is a black hole,' he said, much later than he thought he would have been able to. 'Bye.'

The Master let go of the console, looking round at the chaos of books and paintings that formed a fanlike pattern on the floor. A lot of the china had been smashed. He brushed his suit down for a moment. 'I can explain,' he said.

But the Doctor was already working the console again, frantically flicking switches. 'You don't have to.'

'Oh good. Have you saved the day?'

'No!' the Doctor snapped. 'Help me! There's just a chance she may still be alive! If we can do a biological search of the cavern –'

The Master joined him at the controls. 'Who are we searching for?'

'Alison!'

'A young woman. Again?'

'Yes! Again!'

The Master, a troubled but certain look on his face, reached out a finger and hit a control. The TARDIS began to dematerialise, the familiar sounds of the wrenching of time and space drowning out the Doctor's yells of protest. 'No! Stop! We can't take off anyway! The Shalka force fields!'

'Have now been set to hold the TARDIS in the secondary configuration mode. Once we change it –' He reached for another lever.

'No! I have to be sure!' The Doctor tried to stop the take-off.

But the Master grabbed his hand and held it away from the console. 'On this, your programming of my electronic brain was quite specific.' His voice was hard. 'We leave the girl behind, Doctor.'

The Doctor met his gaze for a moment, fury building inside him once again. How dare this tin man, this automaton that contained the soul of a man whose life he'd saved… But he saw the look in the Master's eyes, that beneath the ice there was something desperately caring.

He had made this device to contain him, to stop him. It was his own desires he was fighting.

He sagged, stepped back from the console, let the column rise and fall as the Master freed them from the bonds of the Shalka.

Left her behind, almost certainly dead, to be dead for certain.

'I can't do this any more,' he said.

The Master slowly turned, as the ship finally broke free and sailed into the space-time vortex, and looked at him once more. He indicated the shattered room around them, and the lack of enemies within it with an all-encompassing sweep of his arms. 'And yet … you just did. As always, Doctor, you are doing at least two things at once.' He turned back to the console with a little tut of feigned annoyance. 'Perhaps your most infuriatingly human trait.'

The Doctor stared at him for a while, but no more was

forthcoming. Then he found a chair, took some books from it, and sat down.

The brilliant escape, the funny line to cap it, despite the lack of timing. And the girl was still dead. The last act had not materialised. The world, and himself, remained so far from what they should be, so imperfect.

He found that in his hand he was holding a manuscript copy of *Hamlet*, signed by the author in an unsteady hand.

The Doctor threw it aside and closed his eyes.

Chapter Twelve
A Captive and a Mystery

Major Kennet had taken over one of the classrooms for his office, having ruled out the headmaster's own office as being too small for his purposes.

He'd entered from the playing fields, having just jumped out of one of the helicopters that he'd sent on a constant surveillance mission. He'd wanted to get a look at the ground for himself. The evacuation convoys were flowing again, the evacuation itself now nearly complete. The military lorry that had become embedded in the road following the enemy attack had been freed, and now all such vehicles carried a heavily armed guard and a seismic sensor. He'd arranged for more of those to be flown in from a tiny company in Switzerland, who were now, presumably, working around the clock and taking on new staff, in ignorance of their product's new military function.

He had a terrible feeling that none of this was going to be enough. Not when their only alien assistance, the source of all their knowledge against the enemy, had fallen to them. It was deeply disturbing that, having saved the world from alien invasion so many times, according to what Kennet had read in his file, the Doctor was not going to save them now. It was a vital difference, a lack of pieces on the board, one of those inequalities that might mean defeat.

Not that Kennet had allowed the news to disturb him for a minute. He'd got this Cheney woman to sign something that said she wouldn't repeat her news, got all he could from her in half an hour, most of which was genuinely frightening detail about the high technological capability of these Shalka, and then sent her off to be evacuated, and contacted later by a specialised debriefing team from the Security Service.

He'd managed to get a couple of hours' sleep, in the rough billet he'd made for himself in a room beside the assembly hall, in the early hours.

As he'd been coming along the corridor, he'd heard a strange noise emanating from his office. For a moment, he'd suspected enemy action, and had taken his sidearm from its holster. But this rending, tearing noise didn't sound like it should be associated with vibrations coming up from the ground. It was somehow more basic than that, as if the universe itself was being worked like clay.

He'd opened the door on guard, ready to retreat and call for reinforcements.

Instead, he simply stopped and stared at what had now appeared in the corner of his office, neatly lodged against the desk.

He knew what it was immediately from the file he'd read. There'd been a photo. But the absurd shape of it, in the flesh, made him smile.

The prospect of victory pulled from defeat made him smile too.

The door opened, and the Doctor stepped out slowly, gently locking the door behind him.

'Well,' Kellet muttered, trying not to sound as pleased as he felt, 'I'm surprised to see *you* back here!'

The Doctor looked ashamed for a moment. He seemed to be choosing his words carefully. Kennet was amazed at the change that had come over the man. Now he seemed sombre, tired … defeated. And nowhere near as annoying.

'Major Kennet,' he said, 'you must forgive me. I've insulted your profession, taken command of your men, been inexcusably rude and hopeless in the face of –'

Kennet realised very quickly that, no matter how annoying he'd been before, what he didn't want from this man was apologies. 'I meant,' he said brusquely, 'that Miss Cheney said you'd been thrown into a black hole!'

The Doctor stared at him. 'Alison's alive?!'

Kennet suddenly understood, and realised how his first words to the Doctor had been misinterpreted as criticism. 'That's correct.' And he told the Doctor how she'd been found.

For a moment after he'd done so the two men smiled warmly at each other.

Until the Doctor seemed to realise that and shut his smile off. 'Why did the Shalka let her go?'

'She doesn't know. We can get her in for the whole story.'

'Yes,' the Doctor paced, his fingers knotted behind his back, 'shortly. But for the moment, I'd prefer it if she wasn't too close at hand.' He glanced away for a moment, as if puzzled by the complexities of humans. 'And she and her boyfriend *really* need to talk.'

Kennet, meanwhile, had wandered up to the blue box that had caught his attention when he first entered the room. 'So this is the TARDIS? Fascinating. I haven't seen one of these since I was a young man.'

'One of these what?' the Doctor frowned at him.

'A police box.'

'Oh, just for a moment I thought you meant, but no, of course not, silly of me, do go on.' The Doctor seemed to have been taken off guard for a moment.

Kennet put a hand up to touch the craft's surface, and felt it vibrating slightly against his palm. It was vaguely warm. It felt exactly like painted wood. But the … presence of the thing left one in no doubt that here was something immensely powerful. It felt like touching magic.

But while he was letting the little boy inside him get madly excited about the vehicle in front of him, Kennet's military mind had been working away too. He'd seen the Doctor at a disadvantage, just for a moment. That chink in his armour had allowed him to see inside. For the first time, he felt he was starting to understand what made the man tick.

He looked at the Doctor questioningly. 'So, now you have this, why are you still here?'

'Indeed.' The Doctor was nodding. 'Indeed! I rather came back because of a message I left for you...' He looked quickly for the answerphone on Kennet's desk, where a figure one had appeared on the New Messages display since Kennet had last checked in this morning. Kennet was quite surprised. The number was for civilian use: his aged father, his son down in Cornwall, a convenience in case ... Well, in case he had to warn them of anything. He'd never liked mobile phones, couldn't handle them after being used to army radios. The military command structure went through the RT and services e-mail. He had no idea how the Doctor had got the number.

Kennet reached for the Play button, but the Doctor gently intercepted his hand, and pressed Erase instead.

Kennet just heard the first part of the message. 'This is the Doctor. I'm terribly sorry, but I'm afraid that I'm –'

And that was where the Doctor cut it off. 'Nothing you needed to hear,' he whispered.

Kennet inclined his head, allowing him that.

The Doctor went to the TARDIS, took out his key once more, and toyed with it.

'So you can manage on your own?' he glanced at Kennet.

'Absolutely.'

'Only … I seem to have found some form. I might not be quite so useless now.'

Kennet knew he had his man now. So much so he pushed it just a little further than he should. 'Well, it's a pity we won't get a chance to find out.'

Greaves entered, at a run, typically without having bothered to knock. 'Excuse me, sir, but we've got one!'

'Greaves,' sighed Kennet.

The sergeant had by now skidded to a halt and was looking affronted to find the Doctor there. 'Oh no. I was hoping you'd got crushed under an avalanche.'

'Greaves,' sighed Kennet.

'Sorry sir, should have knocked sir, permission to speak freely retroactively, sir?'

'Granted,' sighed Kennet.

The Doctor had paid no attention at all to Greaves' complex attitude towards military discipline, and every attention to his first words. He gestured vaguely in the direction the soldier had come from. 'You've captured a Shalka? Could I just…?'

Kennet made himself look puzzled and unconcerned, as if the Doctor's help would be a meaningless little cherry on the top of a wonderful, multi-layered cake he had baked entirely himself. He shrugged like his old Irish Dad. 'As you wish.'

But as he led them out, and heard the Doctor humming a tune under his breath, and was sure that they couldn't see his expression, he allowed himself a secret smile. Got him!

Jack Marker had worked in a butcher's shop in Lannet, the youngest guy in the shop, working for Ken and Josie. His mates had ribbed him all the time about going out smelling like pork scratchings, but they liked the way he could get them half-price steaks at the end of the week.

His nearest family out of town had been an aunt in Leeds. He didn't know what she was going to say when he

showed up on her doorstep with his suitcase. He hadn't
called her in six months. The army had tried to call her,
but she hadn't been in. And did she have anywhere to put
him? They ought to have thought this through better,
put them all up in a hotel or something. One of the soldiers
had started to say something to him about a chemical leak,
but everyone in the refugee truck had started to abuse the
poor guy at once, saying they knew what had been going
on, and nobody had better try to tell them different, and
the soldier had backed off. That was the story that was going
to be in the papers, then. They'd all been asked to sign
something that said they weren't going to let the story out,
but several of the people in his lorry had just not bothered,
or even torn the thing up. The soldiers didn't know what
to do about that, had just finally made a note of those who'd
done it and said they'd be contacted later. It had been
good of them not to get on their high horse about it. They
probably thought that those who did start talking wouldn't
be believed.

Looking at his aunt's doorstep, Jack wasn't sure if he
believed it himself.

He wasn't going to do this. He felt ridiculous, with his two
little suitcases and his stupid story.

It would be wrong of him to go and knock on the door and
ask to stay. It was the wrong thing to do. Terrible. He realised
that his hands were shaking. Something awful was going to
happen if he did that.

There was somewhere he'd rather be. The thought of going
there made him feel better. He didn't know exactly where it
was, but he knew vaguely the direction.

Jack turned away from the door, and started to wander
down the road, feeling his way towards being okay again.

* * *

It was the same everywhere. Evacuees were dropped at railway stations, or on street corners, but didn't stay there. They turned and walked off, sometimes leaving the soldiers who'd delivered them staring, shouting after them, asking if this had been the right place.

None of them knew why they had to go, but all of them went, like water running down a hill.

Alison had been wrapped in one of those blankets they gave to runners at the end of marathons, and had drunk a mug of strong, sweet tea (which even in her state of mild shock she found hard to force down), while the medics checked her over. They'd found only minor cuts and bruises, including that graze on her forehead, a diagnosis Joe had sat alongside them confirming. And so, after she'd answered a lot of questions for a grim-looking military woman who must have been something in intelligence – yes, dead, she'd said, over and over, yes, here's where they threw him, and here's what the rest of the cave looked like – she'd been sent to get straight into an evacuation truck, which had taken them up the motorway to Sheffield.

They hadn't talked much on the way. Joe had asked her what had happened. Alison had lied that she couldn't remember much. The difference between the normal world whizzing by and that scary one underneath had been too much to take in, too much to let out.

The Doctor was dead. That was another reason why she wasn't talking. From the expression on Joe's face she didn't think he'd understand. It felt like the hope of the whole world had gone with the Doctor. Here was a guy who'd wished her dead, and still she felt like she knew him, that she'd lost someone from her own family.

The difference between that frightening world underground and the grey expanse of the motorway, between volcanic fumes and vehicle fumes… It was like one was overlaid on the other in her head. And now the fear was over, she missed the … difference of it all. How weird it had been. How exciting. Though she hadn't thought that at the time.

Her mobile had rung, and she hadn't recognised the number. She hadn't been going to answer, but then she remembered that she'd given her number to the military intelligence woman.

It was her. Stiffly telling her the Doctor was alive. That he was back with the military in Lannet. Major Kennet, whoever he was, had thought she might want to know.

She'd thanked the woman, numb. So, alive then. Not that she was ever going to see him again.

Joe took the news evenly too. What sense this would all make to them would be settled in their memories, thought Alison, long after the fact.

In their dull old memories of the most frightening and exciting times in their lives. Told to their children. Who wouldn't believe them. Because their own lives would be grey.

The clouds lifted slightly, and they were in Sheffield.

Alison's mum lived in a leafy suburb. She worked at the university, and her dad ran his computer business from home. They'd come up from London, the house in Brockley that Alison could just about remember, and made a good life up here.

Alison was staring up at the house, feeling awkward that Joe was getting out of the lorry beside her, and that a few bags of their belongings were being placed on the pavement. Mum and Joe had never gotten on. What she'd make of this… It'd be good to see them again, though. They could live out of the back room.

An army driver had finished putting their bags down on the kerb.

Joe was looking up at the windows, apprehensively. 'I don't think your mum's home,' he said.

'No.' Alison looked around. She couldn't get the glimpse of space and time she'd had out of her head. But there was the wall she'd bounced a ball against a hundred times, knocking it back and forth with her battered tennis racket. 'This is my old stomping ground. I used to play knock down ginger on this street. And now here I am thinking about outer space.' She turned it into a laugh. 'Blimey!'

'I don't want to be here.' He said it so matter-of-factly, one of those huge things that they both needed to think about before they could discuss it.

'Can we talk about this later?'

'No, I mean...' He took a couple of awkward paces towards her, watching his own walk, like he wasn't sure of himself any more. 'I don't want to be here, Alison.' He looked afraid, the old fear, back on his shoulders. It was sickening to see. 'I can feel it.'

And to her horror, now he'd said it, she could feel it too. The vibration that made her shudder from her calves, up her spine. It was distant now. But it was there. It was holding both of them like a fist.

They looked at each other, terrified again.

The army driver, oblivious, placed the last suitcase on the kerb. 'That's the lot,' he said, straightening up. 'I'll be off now.'

Joe leapt at him, his limbs flailing out though his head and body weren't quite at the right angle, and punched him hard up under the jaw. His body flew back, fell off the door of the lorry onto the ground.

'What are you doing?!' she screamed, though she knew.

Joe was swaying on his feet. She could see him straining, trying to get closer to inspect the man. 'I don't know. I didn't mean to do that!'

'Is he okay?'

'He's still breathing!' Joe turned away from the soldier and headed for the truck.

'Oh no,' whispered Alison, as she felt her own limbs jerking into life like a dream, against her will. 'Not now. Not here!'

She tried to fight it with every bit of willpower she had. But she didn't know how. There was a gap where the old familiar links between her mind and her body used to be.

She moved around to the other side of the lorry and climbed into the cab beside Joe.

He started the engine, and drove off. She could crane her head back now, because it didn't matter to them, those things underground, where she was looking. She watched her old life receding again. Watched her suitcases standing on the kerb to puzzle and scare her parents.

She was fooled into thinking she could move freely. She took her mobile from her pocket. 'I have to call the Doctor!' Or at least that woman who'd called her. She could tell her how to get through to him.

She tried to tap a number.

Her hand wouldn't bring the keypad close enough for her fingers to reach it.

She swayed her body back and forth, trying to throw herself against the door to make her limbs connect. But it didn't work.

The only action she could freely make was putting the mobile back again.

'But I can't do it,' she whispered in disgust, trying not to burst into tears. She looked across at Joe. He was driving, his eyes set on the road, only glancing briefly at her. Because that, of course, was how they'd want him to be.

It wasn't that he was relieved to be getting away from here at all.

* * *

An army medical lorry had overturned in the middle of a backstreet, probably because of what had appeared in the road in front of it.

A Shalka lay unconscious in the middle of the street, caught as if going about its business. And indeed, thought the Doctor as he looked down at it, it probably had been on its way elsewhere, surfacing just for a moment to get its bearings, perhaps, on its way ... out of town? He aligned himself for a moment with the direction the beast lay, but couldn't see anything particular on the horizon, in the opposite direction from the caves near which the Shalka base lay.

What had happened was that the lorry had skidded, and its cargo had broken free. A stack of oxygen cylinders had rolled into the road. The valve on one of them had cracked open on the kerb. Even now, a jet of oxygen was hissing across the Shalka's body, into its face. The driver of the lorry had staggered to her RT and called base immediately. The Doctor checked the dial on the cylinder. Not much of it was left now.

A ring of soldiers surrounded the Shalka as the Doctor inspected it, their weapons raised. The Doctor could see the creature breathing, steadily and slowly, peacefully asleep.

'It's the oxygen,' he told Kennet, who had strode over to get a close look at his enemy. 'It got a jolt of the pure stuff and it knocked it out.'

'We can hardly advance on them with pure oxygen.'

The Doctor nodded. It had been hard enough, the driver had said, keeping this area clear of other military vehicles, or anything else that might ignite the highly flammable gas. Its use as a direct weapon would be incredibly dangerous to the soldier wielding it. 'No, but if you can set up something like an oxygen tent...'

'We can get one from the hospital.'

The Doctor turned and called to Greaves and the other

men. 'Get this Shalka wrapped up in one, keep feeding it oxygen, and get it over to the chemistry lab at the school.'

He glanced back to see that Kennet had quickly nodded along, allowing him to give direct instructions to his troops without sacrificing his authority.

He gave the man a smile. Perhaps this was going to work after all.

They headed back to the jeep.

Greaves bent to watch the alien breathing. 'Whatever he's planning to do to you, fella, I wouldn't be in your … whatever you do for shoes.'

'Don't bully it!' the Doctor called as he got into the jeep.

Greaves looked to his commanding officer, but found only a hard stare. 'You heard the man, Greaves. Don't bully the monster!'

And the jeep sped off.

Greaves sighed and glanced to his mates. It had been bad enough when the Doctor and the major had been having a go at each other. But now they were on the same side!

Chapter Thirteen
The Doctor's Experiment

Alison woke as her head jolted to one side, saved from terrible dreams.

They were driving through the country, along a 'B' road, and the rougher surface had woken her up. It was afternoon, and low sun shone through gaps in the trees.

'Ow, my head…' It took her a moment to realise that it hadn't just been the jolt. She had a pounding headache. 'How long have I been asleep?'

'A couple of hours.' Joe was still staring straight ahead. 'No idea where I'm driving. My throat's not feeling so good now, Ally. And I haven't been able to stop for water or anything. I hope the petrol runs out.' She could hear his voice cracking. 'Ally, that poor guy.'

'You couldn't help yourself, Joe. Neither of us could.' She put a hand to her head. She'd never had a headache like this before. It felt like every vein had come alive, and was forcing itself against the skin of her scalp. 'Listen,' she said, 'wherever we end up, I really need to get my head looked at.'

'It's okay, we will.'

'Because it feels like there's…' She'd been feeling along the ridge of her eyebrows, aware that something weird was going on underneath. Now she'd taken her hand away, and her eyes strayed to the rear-view mirror, and her words trailed off as she stared.

A lump was visible inside the skin of her forehead. She was sure it hadn't been there a moment before.

'Something inside,' she whispered.

The captured Shalka opened its eyes. It looked around.

It was lying in a rejigged version of a hospital oxygen tent, on the floor in the chemistry lab of the school where the Doctor had set up his equipment.

The Doctor had been waiting for this moment. He stood beside the tent, his hand on the valve of the oxygen supply.

The alien emitted a quiet moan, a low version of its familiar scream.

The Doctor allowed a little more oxygen into the tent, and the power of the moan reduced a little. The creature seemed subdued, all its energies spent on breathing, low and hard.

'Sorry,' he said. 'Can't have you communicating with your fellows. You're going to get just enough volcanic gas to stay alive and talk to me.' He made sure that he'd judged the creature's level of consciousness correctly, waiting for it to act, and then moved over to another machine he'd set up in a corner. This one – he hadn't decided on a name for it, perhaps later over tea – had a sine-wave indicator on its front. The Doctor turned a dial, and the box produced, through a couple of Greaves' purloined laptop speakers, a mild electronic version of the scream of the Shalka.

The Doctor was good at languages, so good that he could understand instantly most alien forms of communication, but the Shalka had been *too* alien even for him to understand. Still, he had been able to create a message that, he was fairly sure, indicated peace and friendship. 'Hear that?' he asked the creature. 'We humanoids could be part of your sonic network. We're not the primitives you think we are.' He was glad Kennet wasn't here to hear him lumping himself in with humanity in general. That was something he could only do in front of a monster, where the comparison became really obvious.

Greaves entered, without knocking, carrying a steaming mug of tea. 'Here you are, Doctor, strong and sweet.'

The Doctor considered for a moment how many times he had mentioned his preference for taking nothing sweet in his tea, and how it should preferably be precisely blended from three particularly lovely fields he knew of in Ceylon, keeping the whole of the leaf intact while doing so, instead of being made from a damp teabag of unknown provenance found at the back of a cupboard. He thought about mentioning this to Greaves, again.

But no. He was liaising on good terms with the British army once again. Questioning their tea might mean war. 'Put it some distance from me, Greaves,' he finally muttered. 'I'll get to it eventually.'

Greaves did so, obviously having no concept of how long *eventually* was to a Time Lord. He glanced at the Shalka. 'I look at that ugly thing lying there, and I think: I'm glad I took the ring back to the jewellers.'

The Doctor blinked at him.

But he quickly became aware that the Shalka was reacting to Greaves too. It had been watching him, the Doctor realised, as he put the tea down. And now it was screaming softly at him, right on the edge of hearing.

Greaves stopped on his way out, turned back to look at the creature. He continued his thought in a contemplative tone the Doctor hadn't heard him use before. 'I mean, it's… so much more powerful than we are. If the rest of them knew we had it here… It'd be terrible. They'd come for us.'

The Doctor moved to a point where he was just between Greaves and the Shalka. 'You fought them in the caves,' he murmured. 'Are you telling me you were afraid?'

Greaves jumped, took a step back, shook his head. 'As if! Of course not!'

'How's your throat?'

The sergeant rubbed it, puzzled. 'Could be better. I think I'm getting laryngitis.'

The Doctor thought for a moment, glancing between the soldier and the alien. Then he decided. 'Keep an eye on it for a moment, eh? I'm just popping out to do…' And then he realised he had no excuse at all. Might this chap think he might wish to use the bathroom? No, he thought, let us not, as they say, go there. Besides, he had already used the word 'do' and he had no intention of finishing his sentence on that basis. '… Something eccentric!' he finally said.

He marched out of the room.

Greaves turned after the Doctor as the door closed behind him, wondering what his odd behaviour had been about.

But then he turned back as the sound changed. The most urgent sound he'd ever heard. The sound that moved the ground under him, just a little. Unconsciously, he reached out and held onto a work unit. The ground hadn't really moved. He'd just felt, for a moment, unsure about where to stand. About whether to stay or go, about the cold touch on the back of his neck of something ancient.

The image came into his head, just for a moment, of a rabbit held by the headlights of a car, wanting to run for the verge, its blood pounding, but unable to.

His discipline and courage had found that image for him.

He let go of the table, made himself look at the Shalka again. It was nothing to be afraid of. Like some sort of green statue, really. It had increased the volume of its low, warbling cry, and was looking at Greaves as it worked the sound all around the room, making it echo and wind round corners.

Greaves shivered suddenly. He was in charge here, wasn't

he? This alien was a prisoner! He took a step back, but found that he'd taken a step forwards, towards the thing.

Something from inside him grabbed at his chest and throat, a sudden biological urge, like he was about to vomit.

His mouth flew open, locking there, hurting his jaw.

He staggered, trying to raise his arms to gag himself, but he was possessed now, his whole body just a vessel for this one impulse. He couldn't stop it. He couldn't –

From out of his mouth burst the same noise the Shalka had made.

He hadn't thought he could do that. It was like his body was being compromised to do it. He felt the muscles in his throat and diaphragm protesting, reaching their limits, but he was going to be taken beyond them.

He coughed, spluttered, managed to use it to yell 'Doct –'

But that became another convulsive scream.

He coughed again. His eyes were watering. The air in the room was churning, shimmering like heat haze, becoming thick with something. It was getting hard to see. His lungs were trying to take breaths to support the scream, but it was getting harder and harder.

Greaves tried to move, tried to get to the door, but his legs were locked, his head tilted back. He thought about death, right now, being eaten from inside like this! Being used up! It couldn't happen like this!

But it was right that it did, this was for the best, this is what he should be doing. This was what he was for. He managed to slap his hand onto the table, hurting himself, trying to break out of that. If he had to die, he'd do it thinking it was wrong, and that the enemy couldn't win, and that he'd done all he could.

The Shalka, he saw through watering eyes, had started to thrash, to rip at the oxygen tent, to get stronger and stronger as he watched, its scream getting louder and louder.

It burst free.

Greaves felt himself giving way, knew that he was about to die.

He heard a distant crash.

And then the Doctor was back in the room, between them, spraying something right in the face of the Shalka.

More oxygen. The beast fell.

And so did Greaves.

He hit the ground, coughing and spluttering, managing to hold himself up on his palms. He rolled onto his back for a moment, and felt the bruises inside him. It felt like … nothing was permanently damaged. That the Doctor had got there just in time. He managed to look up, and saw that the Doctor was pacing, glancing concerned at the sleeping monster, his hands knitted once more behind his back.

'What … what happened?' Greaves asked. 'Hey!' He saw a deliberate look on the Doctor's face. 'You *wanted* that thing to do that to me!'

'The Shalka's scream doesn't just scare people into obeying…' Greaves wasn't sure if the Doctor was talking to him or to himself. 'It softens them up for long-term control.'

'What are you going on about?'

The Doctor spun and faced him, waving one finger imperiously. 'If you live over a nasty landlord for a long time, you get to the point where he doesn't *have* to keep bashing on the ceiling!'

'So what about this … gas?' Greaves croaked, waving the still thick air away from his face. 'Where did that come from?'

The Doctor gave a nasty smile. 'Out of your mouth. In a manner of speaking. The sonic vibrations you broadcast changed the chemical composition of the air into what the Shalka wanted to breathe.'

Greaves swallowed, feeling the moistness return to his throat. 'So…'

But if the Doctor had been listening to him before, he wasn't now. 'Get it back in the tent,' he snapped. 'I need to talk to your boss.'

And he was off again, the door slamming closed behind him.

Greaves took a moment to get to his feet, feeling his legs tremble as he looked again at the comatose Shalka.

He took another moment to go and find that cup of tea. It was still reasonably hot, and blissfully sweet, and it slipped down his throat in a soothing manner. He leaned on a desk and literally got his breath back, glancing angrily again in the direction of the Shalka. 'I could sue him for that,' he muttered. 'If I could get a lawyer to believe it.'

Chapter Fourteen
The People in the Forest

The Doctor rushed into Kennet's office just as the major was getting out of his seat.

'Major –' he gasped.

'Doctor, I was just coming to see you –'

'Because something's happened to the evacuees –'

'Exactly. We've had calls from relatives who'd been asked to provide places for them.' Kennet went to the door and closed it, so his voice wouldn't carry down the corridor. 'As far as we can tell, *none* of them have arrived.'

Joe stopped the truck at the edge of some woods.

Alison looked around. The lump had remained in her forehead. Every now and then her headache focused on it, seemed to pull at it. She'd tried to ignore it. She was hoping that as soon as they stopped, Joe could grab a knife from somewhere and just hack it out. It was so close to the surface that it would have just been like lancing a boil.

She'd worked out from road signs that they were somewhere in the Pennines. But this seemed to be the middle of nowhere. 'They want us to stop here?' she asked. 'Why? What's here?'

Joe looked pale. He let go of the wheel, and started to rub some life back into his hands. He'd withdrawn into himself, hardly speaking for the last hour.

He fell back into his seat, looking around now himself. So

it was him that saw them first. Amongst the trees. Loads of them. People. Stumbling forward, staring at them, putting their hands onto the truck.

Their expressions were as dazed as the ones she and Joe must be wearing. But they weren't angry or empty. From the woods, a vast crowd of people had emerged … and they were just as frightened as they were.

There was that kid from the butcher's shop. The ladies from the library. That git who liked to skateboard down their close yelling on a Friday night.

Alison had to be with them. She opened her door, and climbed down to the road. Joe followed her a moment later, rubbing his arms. He stared at the mass of people, who were now starting to say hi, to ask them questions, to grab Alison by the hand.

'Everyone we know,' he said.

They followed the crowd back into the woods. The smell of campfires came to Alison on the late afternoon stillness. Nobody knew anything. They all had similar stories of being evacuated, and then feeling they had to come to this place. Many of them seemed to be in shock, a lot of them had been, or were still, crying. They had no possessions apart from what they stood up in. They had come to the roadside to meet her because they'd felt they should.

'The sound is still telling everyone what to do,' Alison muttered, as they headed towards one of the nearest fires. The crowd was dispersing now, to the rough hearths they'd formed – family groups, pub regulars, cricket clubs. They no longer seemed to have a definite purpose. There was a horrible sense of waiting, as if they all realised they'd be given another purpose soon. 'Even when we can't hear it.'

Joe pointed to the fire ahead, over which somebody was turning a sandwich on a twig. 'Isn't that your boss?'

It was indeed Max. And there beside him was old Tom Crossley, the guy who'd been propping up the bar that night the Doctor had arrived. That seemed so long ago now. They both got to their feet.

Max had never hugged her before, but now he did, muttering her name like she was the most brilliant thing he'd ever seen. Then he coughed and held his throat, withdrawing from her, apologetic.

'Alison!' yelled old Tom, folding back beside the fire again, laughing. 'Pint and a short!' He'd brought some cans with him.

They sat down with them, and heard their stories. Max hadn't been evacuated, he'd leapt into his sports car himself at the first sensation that he was free to do it. He'd driven out of town at speed, intending to go all the way to London. He'd stopped at a service station just off the M25 when he'd gone as far as he could on what he'd had in his tank, and there he'd heard the story about the chemical leak. It was only when he'd got back in his car that he'd felt a terrible compulsion to return. So he'd driven back, as fast as he could go, racking up speed-camera violations and somehow avoiding any police cars.

Joe looked seriously at Alison as Max finished his story. She realised what he meant. While Max had been doing that, the Shalka hadn't been doing a thing. And Max said he hadn't felt any kind of vibration. He'd just done as he'd somehow been programmed to do.

A horrible thought struck Alison. 'Has … everyone got something in their head?'

Max and Tom looked at each other, puzzled. 'Head?' said Tom.

Alison hushed him. She grabbed Max and started to look at his brow, to put her palm flat against it. But there was nothing there. 'No,' he said. 'No, I'd know. What's up with you, what have you got in there?'

It was just her. She was horribly special here. When she'd arrived, they'd all come to see. 'Oh no,' she got to her feet and backed away. 'Oh no.'

Joe scrambled up, put his hands on her shoulders, and started massaging them, calming her. 'We can find some sort of blade amongst this lot, and I can sterilise it on the fire. Let's just have a look. See what it is, eh?'

Alison, terrified, could only nod.

Kennet had left the Doctor waiting in his office, pacing and thinking, while he went off to his RT crew. He returned, a few moments later, with a wad of satellite photos, which he slapped onto his desk.

The Doctor grabbed them. They showed huge crowds of people swarming through a forest. 'So where are they?'

'In the Pennines. Middle of nowhere. A place called Edale Wood. Thousands of them. The local police thought it was an illegal rave, and have called for reinforcements.'

The Doctor threw down the photos, thinking furiously. 'That's not on volcanic rock! Their long term control won't work for specifics, just as a kind of group herding instinct. If they want these people to do something specific – and they must, or they'd have kept them on their kind of rock – they must be using some form of direct control!' He slammed his fist onto the table. 'Blast!'

Joe had started to explore the cut on Alison's forehead. He'd found a little girl who'd kept a pen knife in her pocket, and had heated the blade, then let it cool, to disinfect it as best he could.

Alex and Tom watched him. He was aware of a number of the others closing in too. He wondered, distantly, if that was what they wanted to do, or what their masters, these 'Shalka' that Alison had talked vaguely about, wanted them to do?

He so didn't want to hurt her. There was such a distance between them now, and this was the one thing he could do for her. He just mustn't mess it up. 'It must be something from the explosion in the shop,' he murmured, making a tiny incision. It felt weird, to be touching her like this, to be causing her pain. If only he had some anaesthetic. 'Let me see. Tell me if I'm hurting you.'

She winced. 'I don't care! Just get it out!'

Joe wasn't sure what he'd seen for a moment, just as she said that. 'What? Something's just…'

Moved. He must just be tired. It was as if something had squirmed out of the way of the blade.

'What is this?' he whispered.

He worked quickly for a moment, aware that it would make her feel uncomfortable, but now seized by a horrible desire to discover what was going on here. 'Just wait. I think I've nearly got it.' He had a terrible suspicion, that feeling that everything in the world was wrong now, that everything was polluted …

The lump squirmed right into his incision.

He could see it now.

A green stone, gleaming there in the red.

Joe realised a moment before it happened. 'Oh no,' he whispered. 'No!'

The stone opened its eyes.

And screamed.

Chapter Fifteen
The Army of the Shalka

The scream coming from the tiny Shalka made everyone stagger backwards, holding their hands to their ears, doing anything to try and block it out.

But it was no use. Quickly the sound took hold of them, made them stand straight, made them obey.

Alison felt the power of the sound from just over her eyeline, staggering beneath the impact of it like she was suddenly carrying a heavy weight.

Shalka near the forest, just under the surface, at the distance of the nearest outcrop of volcanic rock, echoed and reinforced the scream, leading it back to the forward base deep underground.

The refugees from Lannet all turned to look at Alison. They appeared from between the trees, coming forward from all parts of the forest. In a few minutes, they'd surrounded her, a crowd hundreds deep, stretching back to fill every visible clearing, people broken only by trees. It was a whole town, standing there.

The most frightening thing about them was that they weren't mindless, weren't some kind of zombie, but were talking to each other, and crying and whispering and yelling at her and even pleading with her to make this stop. Not that she could.

Joe was looking desperately around them as they looked desperately back. 'Whatever happens, Ally,' he said, 'remember I –'

'I know.'

Tom let out a cry as his legs lurched forward.

And all at once they were all walking forward together. For just a moment it felt almost comforting, like being part of an army. Alison could feel the body heat from all these hundreds of people clustered together. They made the air hazy. They tramped the forest floor with a single, unified noise.

'Looks like we're moving,' muttered Max.

'Alison!' Tom was yelling, incoherently, looking back to her.

A lot of them were looking to her as they moved. She tried to grab for the Shalka in her head, but her arms were forced back to her sides. She hated the feel of it in there, hated the way she was now directly a puppet.

But she had to do something. She raised her voice, let those who could hear her listen. 'I can't do anything to stop it!' she shouted. 'But we can still shout, right? Everyone! Everyone shout for help!'

They did. The cries started from near her, and worked their way further and further out, until Alison found herself at the centre of a yelling mass of people, the sound coming from further than she could see in all directions.

The crowd came to the edge of the forest, a single track road giving way to a rough, hummocky valley, at the bottom of which stood a warehouse site, at the edge of a small town, surrounded by a high mesh fence.

The crowd surged across the road, making Alison wonder what they'd have done if a car had been approaching, and flowed down into the valley below. They had accelerated to a fast walk now, still yelling at the tops of their voices, their feet stumbling over each other, individuals falling and being hauled up again by the precise, sudden grabs of the others.

Alison could see figures running out of the buildings behind the fence. She hoped they could call for help. Or just get out of the way.

She hoped that this crowd wouldn't be made to become a mob.

Mitch Stannard and his mate Nat worked as caretakers at Barlon Warehouse and Storage. They'd just locked up for the end of the day, doing their first round to make sure every user had locked up behind them, while cars and lorries departed through the main gates. Several small businesses used these facilities to keep stock in, and some of the freight companies used this as a halfway house for long-haul non-perishables. The rest of the units were used by people who needed to store their property, having gone abroad or moved into smaller accommodation.

It was a nice, quiet job. Mitch and Nat had made friends with a lot of the lorry drivers, so they preferred the day shifts, when they'd be about. But the nights were pleasant, when it wasn't raining, with the forest rustling on the hills above. And nothing ever happened. The security barrier was enough to deter petty theft. Mitch worried that one day they'd be hit by a big firm, knowing exactly what they were looking for, with fences already arranged for, say, a whole consignment of pine furniture or microwaves. But Nat kind of thought that Mitch was almost looking forward to that, the way he spoke of it.

They'd returned to the security office after the round, and set to playing whist for the contents of Mitch's vast tin of boiled sweets.

They'd only been a couple of hands in when Nat had noticed something on one of the CCTV monitors. A person so normal that the sight of them there caught him by surprise for a moment, walking straight up to the fence. And then another.

He put down his cards and went to the monitor. 'Mitch, look at this.'

His mate was there a second later. 'What?' he muttered. 'What are they up to?'

That was when they heard it. A low chorus, getting louder, a frightening sound, coming more and more into the range of hearing.

Hundreds of voices, all crying for help.

Nat and Mitch looked at each other, suddenly feeling haunted.

Then they ran out of the cabin.

They stood on the step and watched the vast mass of people stumbling towards the fence, all crying out. It was like the hillside had gained a new layer, and it was rolling down towards them, like human lava.

It took Mitch a few moments to find any words at all. 'Is it one of those rave things? What do they want to get in here for?'

Alison found that members of the crowd around her, Joe included, were suddenly holding her back from the fence. She exchanged horrified looks with him.

It became clear why they were doing this a moment later. Those at the front of the crowd were curling up against the fence, and the ones immediately behind them were clambering on top of them, with the first few of the next row again clambering on top of those. Already she could hear the ones on the lowest level starting to cry out in pain. The Shalka were building a human wall, and the weight of the bodies was going to kill those at the bottom of the pile.

On the other side of the compound, Alison could see a gate. It was locked for the night, but surely they could have hammered it open between them with less slaughter? But it seemed the Shalka just didn't want to move the extra few hundred feet.

She saw the kid from the butcher's shop go under, crushed by feet that pressed down onto his head and throat.

The monsters cared nothing for anything but getting the survivors over the fence.

Alison felt sick to know that she was definitely going to be one of those. That she was marked to survive as her friends and acquaintances died.

Mitch and Nat watched helplessly as the first people got to the top of the wall and threw themselves over it. They fell with shouts of fear and landed with cries. The height of it must have broken bones and dislocated limbs. More landed on top of them, and they stayed there, allowing them to do it. The policy was going to be the same on this side, a human ramp.

Was this some sort of mad cult, who didn't care about their own lives? It was terrible to see, a massacre, but the two caretakers couldn't turn away. They could hear the muffled screams of those underneath.

'We're locked up for the weekend!' shouted Mitch, help-lessly. 'Go away! There's nothing here!'

The fence was giving way, was caving in under the sheer weight of bodies. Nat was reminded of something out of World War One. One of the leading invaders, a balding man, scrambled to his feet, unharmed but for cuts and bruises, and ran towards them.

'Please, just run!' he yelled. 'They're making us do this!'

Nat grabbed his mate and pulled at his sleeve. He didn't like the way the man's arms were spiralling, like wild punches, against his expression and his words. 'Mitch! Get back! Get back and call the police!'

But Mitch hadn't taken it in. 'Get off the fence!' he was

shouting. He kept on shouting it, even taking a couple of steps forward, only now looking to the man who was running straight at him.

He started to move aside just as the man hit.

Nat just had time to see Mitch go down underneath a flurry of blows, before he became aware that they were running at him too.

Men, women, even children. Sprinting towards him. Their faces were scared, they were calling to him for help, but their bodies were jerking and smashing the air.

Nat turned to run, managed a few steps.

They caught him.

He smelt perfume and aftershave and old clothes. The first fist caught him across the side of the face.

Then the heat and the crowd closed on him, and he went under, trying to fend off hundreds of blows, kicks, scratches, pleading with people who were pleading with him.

Darkness took him.

Alison was appalled to find herself walking regally over the fence, her feet crushing the bodies of the dead and the still living. They formed a bridge of flesh for her.

She loathed herself for every unwilling step.

It was a relief to walk on the ground again.

But then she saw Max ahead, beating and beating someone who was already on the ground, at the centre of dozens of people, a target that was motionless and being reduced still further.

'Stop me!' he was screaming at the top of his voice, his eyes wide with not believing what he was doing. 'Somebody stop me!'

Lala Ambedkar was seven. He lived in the village of Ranjintsi, on the coast, in the Pordbander district of Gujarat, in western

India. He knew that because his mum had got him to remember it, in case he got lost.

Most of the people in the village worked at the fish processing plant, or on the sea itself, bringing in the catch. Lala wanted to do that when he grew up. But in the last few weeks, everything seemed to have changed. Hardly any of the grown-ups went to work, and the boats stayed at their moorings. The big red diesel tanker hadn't come this week or the last, which had made Lala angry. He loved watching it connect its pipes to the diesel container at the docks.

He didn't remember much about what had happened, but he'd been playing cricket with his friends in the lane at the back of the Christian school, and he'd fallen during a run. There'd been a movement all around him … something like one of the big fish rising from the sea … and the next thing that wasn't a bad dream was him crying as his mum gathered him up, and ran to the house.

That seemed to have been a long time later, because the light had been different.

Mum had kept saying they should get a doctor, but when they did, he didn't seem to want to get near to Lala. It was like he kept trying, but kept giving up. His dad had said the man was very tired, which Lala would have thought was funny if everything didn't feel so weird.

He'd been cut across his head, but he was being a brave boy. Sachin wouldn't have cried, and neither did he. But everybody treated him like he was really badly hurt, or had suddenly become a Brahman or something. His mum had told him to stay away from the beach where the speckly rocks were. At least everyone had to do that.

Tonight was the weirdest. He should have been asleep, but he'd stayed awake after his Mum had put him to bed, listening to his parents talking quietly, with the radio turned right down. They sounded scared.

He stayed awake because he wanted to … but he really wanted to sleep too. It was like there were two parts of him. And there was this weird noise under everything, like a siren from the plant, but sounding all the time. Like his ears were ringing. And now he thought about it, he had a really bad headache.

As soon as he thought that, he was on his feet, though he hadn't wanted to get up, and walking out of the bedroom he shared with Aj. Aj woke up and leapt up after him, not calling out or asking where he was going, but just following him.

They walked into the kitchen, and Mum and Dad were walking away from the radio, towards them, asking them what was going on, but somehow knowing too.

For some reason, they all went out onto the street, where everyone was waiting. Then they all went down towards the beach, everybody in the village. They started walking along the shore. There was a big full moon, shining down at them, making everything white. Lala thought he saw those big fish surfacing in the water, and again on the beach. He hadn't known they could do that.

Mum and Dad kept pace with him, looking down at him and smiling. But Lala knew it wasn't okay. They were smiling like he was going for an inoculation.

He decided he didn't like this, and stopped. But then he realised that his body had kept on walking. Like he was a cartoon. Like he was being played on a movie screen. He wasn't the boss of himself any more!

Despite Sachin, he started to cry, and asked his mum what was going on. Was this a nightmare too?

Yes, Mum told him, trying to reach out and managing to smooth his hair, though she was walking at a little distance, and didn't seem to want to hug him. Yes. This is all just a nightmare.

* * *

Along the bright daytime main street of Tinton Falls, New Jersey, there marched a sombre, angry parade. They were heading in the general direction of Eatontown, though they doubted that that was where they were going.

They walked through the silent wide streets of low houses, the trees on the corners casting strong shadows on the sidewalks. A smart, middle-aged lady led them, a bandage still wrapped around her head. This was Elise Gower, who sat on the Zoning Committee of the municipal council and had last month been surprised to find that she was going to become a grandma.

She had tried to get the thing out of her head, tried until her husband, under control but also for himself, had wrestled the knife out of her hand.

They marched with a furious look in their eyes. Everyone in town was walking, marching. Some of them had taken up a chant: 'Oh no, we won't go!' Elise led them in that also. She had becoming used to working out how people should lead their lives, to making decisions from a basis of consensus. She was already a leader. But this she hated.

But still, they went.

In the early hours, in the courtyard of what had been the Korchov Collective Farm twenty years ago, and was still thought of that way by all the old timers, a vast group of people had gathered. They'd covered branches with pitch and lit them to serve as torches beside their electrical ones.

They all knew, in their warm clothing and gloves, that they had to follow Anton, who had a plaster on his forehead, and scratches across his face. He was one of the oldest farmers. He'd taken an axe to one of the creatures that the farm boys had started seeing at the edges of the pasture. He'd hacked it through the head, shouting that it was an alien, that they'd come to invade the world! Anton read a lot about aliens. His wife and some of the farmhands had seen it happen, then seen other aliens arrive out of the ground. They'd grabbed Anton and pulled him under, causing Val to faint at the sight.

He'd returned a week later, pointing at his head, complaining that now he'd got an *implant*! But by then everyone knew what the situation was. By then, the aliens had taken over, quietly, from whatever nest they had down there.

Anton had told them all about the aliens in the bar, as much as he could. When he was prevented from speaking, his face would twist into awkward shapes as he forced himself to get the words out. He told them what they needed to know in a kind of backtalk, something he'd got used to under Kruschev, and the aliens didn't seem to notice that. He said they were made of a kind of jelly, that axes wouldn't do any good, that they'd need explosives.

The next day, Alex had gone into the shed by the tin mine, and blown himself and it up, getting rid of all the explosives. Anton said less after that.

Now he was heading, torch in hand, out onto the steppe. They were all following him. The small plants scratched at the legs of the women. At least they had been allowed time to fully dress.

They hated what they were doing, but they were glad that Anton was with them. He would fight at any chance he got. They sang as they went, also: sad, comforting songs about their community.

Their community was all there, about them.

They were sure that their community was on its way to die.

Kennet had rounded up a combat patrol as fast as he could, had them arm themselves with heavy weapons, and got them into the right frame of mind for an engagement, in the changing rooms of the school. He'd explained the mission parameters, and told the men about the various weaknesses and strengths of the Shalka, underlying the briefing notes that were being updated every hour on the comms. Then he'd run with them back to his office, where the Doctor was waiting impatiently, looking at his fob watch.

'In! In!' he yelled at them, shepherding them through the doors of the police box with slaps to their shoulders.

Kennet wondered for a moment why speed was so of the essence if this was a time machine, but a moment later all such concerns were banished from his mind by the interior of the ship.

They had all gazed around in wonder. It had been like a magician's trick. The Doctor had run to some sort of control dais and had started hitting buttons and pulling levers. A moment later, a rather worrying noise had started to grind from somewhere below – and how could there be a 'below'? – and the central column had started to rise and fall. Kennet took that to mean that they were now in flight.

A bearded man stepped out of the shadows. Kennet was surprised that this ship had a crew, the Doctor had never mentioned him. 'Ah,' he said, carefully, 'the military. Would you care for some tea?'

Kennet answered for them all. 'No thank you, sir. No tea for the Green Jackets.' He didn't want them sitting about, wanted them to stay on their feet and focused. The Doctor had told him that the journey would only take two minutes. 'Because, what are we?'

'Royal Green Jackets, sir!' They all snapped to attention and said it loudly at once. Not quite a shout. The room had done that to them.

Kennet looked over to the Doctor and saw him rolling his eyes skywards for a moment. Then he saw him looking, and changed his expression into a very false grin.

Kennet looked back to the bearded man. 'And who are you?'

The man considered the question for a moment, and then

bowed his head. 'My dear Major, I am a mere functionary. What are names, after all, but ideas that can imprison us?'

A smile curled Kennet's lip. 'Or get us imprisoned, you mean.'

The man looked hard at him. 'Excuse me,' he said. 'My presence is required on the other side of the console.' He went to join the Doctor, who looked surprised to see him but nevertheless moved over and let him push some buttons.

Every time he thought he'd worked the Doctor out, Kennet thought, another surprise. He took a moment to look around, marvelling at the chandelier that illuminated the vaulted ceiling from the centre of a compass rose in what looked like marble. This would be something to tell his grandchildren about, when the Official Secrets Act let him. It opened up a vast, new world that made the old one seem narrow and foolish. There were aliens out there, but friendly as well as antagonistic, advanced but also somehow English. What a wonderful world it would be if everyone knew that they weren't so far from the cosmos, that the people from the stars would offer them tea.

He was one of very few people who'd been privileged enough to travel in a TARDIS. The report he'd read named some of the others. In the past, the Doctor hadn't seemed to have used it as a proper vehicle, for ferrying about squads of men like this.

That thought made Kennet worried. Either the Doctor had changed, or the situation was very grave indeed.

He visualised what the situation outside was going to be like once more, draining the nerves out of it with quiet exploration, as his men should also be doing now. They had that expression on their faces, besides the smiles and the continued gazing at the architecture.

Greaves appeared at his shoulder. 'Bigger on the inside!' he whispered. 'Did you see?'

Kennet raised an eyebrow at him. He considered asking the sergeant how even an officer could have missed that, but contented himself with 'I did indeed, Greaves'.

The column stopped moving. The Doctor hit a lever and ran to join the soldiers. 'We're here.'

Kennet looked back to the shadows, where the bearded man was once more standing, regarding them, his arms folded. 'Good,' he said. He turned to address his men. 'Keep the civilians away from the warehouses. Whatever they want must be in there. Fire over the heads of the civilians unless you are directly attacked.'

The doors began to hum open. Low sunlight broke in. A great noise could be heard outside. People. Thousands of them. Screaming in fear.

The noise made Kennet proud inside. They were here to help these people, to put an end to that. 'Make me proud, lads,' he called. 'Uphold the tradition.'

The doors were fully opened. Captain Parker, with a heavy machine gun stood at the front of the patrol. He ran out, as had been planned, firing short bursts into the air to shock the civilians and hopefully halt them.

The patrol ran out behind him, the Doctor beside Kennet.

Pandemonium. They had landed right in the middle of the crowd, who were running for the warehouses in a great mass. A number of caretakers, who had seemingly got out of a small car, were being grabbed and thrown. Police blues and twos were flashing from a nearby road, arriving at speed.

'Don't fire unless you have to!' yelled Kennet as he ran. 'If you have to, fire to wound!' The soldiers were already being grabbed by the civilians, and were firing into the air, fighting back hand to hand, trying to drive a wedge towards the warehouses.

The blue box had vanished into the screaming crowd behind them.

Kennet glanced to the Doctor, who was staring through the mass of people, suddenly shocked. 'Alison!' he bellowed.

And he was off, breaking formation, running into the deadly clutching hands of the crowd.

Chapter Sixteen
The Doctor Takes a Chance

The Doctor ran through the crowd, ducking the ones that grabbed for him, throwing others so that they collided with each other, weaving with the grace of a dancer, never taking his eyes off the point ahead of him where Alison marched, flanked by a sort of honour guard of burly men, including Joe.

He hadn't thought about her being here. Had kept it out of his mind. It was obvious, of course. All these people were from Lannet. But it was still a shock to see her.

The sound was coming from her, he realised. Underneath all of this noise. She was the control point, the source of the vibration. He felt suddenly tense again, haunted once more by the fear of what had happened so long ago. But he would not let it stop him this time. He would not let her be hurt. He ducked a punch meant for his head and sent the assailant tumbling backwards over him. Not for nothing had the Doctor been a Rugby Blue at Keble in the 1930s.

'Alison!' he cried as he ran. 'Alison!'

He'd just got to her when Joe turned, saw him, and with unwilling limbs grabbed him and attempted to wrestle him to the ground. 'Doctor, I'm sorry!' he shouted. 'I can't help myself!'

'I know, Joe, I know!' yelled the Doctor back.

He broke free of his grasp and felled him with a perfect uppercut.

He didn't see where Joe collapsed, he was already through to Alison. He grabbed her by the shoulders and forced her to turn around and look at him.

Then he saw the Shalka in her head, the bloody lump broadcasting the shrill cry. 'What have they done to you?' he whispered.

The battle was going badly. The soldiers were having trouble dealing with an enemy that was shouting to them for help, that was crying and screaming while grabbing for their eyes. The Green Jackets had successfully formed a barrier between the civilians and the warehouses, but the barrier was retreating, step by step. The soldiers were having to wrestle clear of, or club back, numerous assailants that kept stalking towards them, pleading not to be hurt.

Greaves fired into the air once more. 'We'll shoot if we have to!' he yelled at a balding man with blood on his hands. He was hoping to get through to some basic survival mechanism inside the man.

'It's not us doing this!' the man cried back. 'Please!'

Bursts were going into the air all around. It was only a matter of moments, Greaves realised, before his mates would start firing into the crowd. They had held back this long only through vast discipline, but once their backs were against the warehouse walls, then the will to survive would take over.

'Hold your fire!' Kennet was yelling. 'Hold your fire!' He was looking to the Doctor, who was standing beside that girl that had popped up at the side of the road. 'Doctor?' he called.

It sounded like a desperate cry for help.

The Doctor had only seconds. He could feel the soldiers tensing, could see in his head the carnage as gunfire ripped through row after row of the citizens of Lannet.

He looked between Kennet and the Shalka in Alison's head. She couldn't speak, it wouldn't let her, could only stare pleadingly at him.

How dare they? How dare they put innocent people through this?

He was too angry to think twice about what he was about to do.

He grabbed the Shalka with both hands.

Alison screamed as his fingers found the tiny green creature. Blood made it slip through his grasp, but he held on. It erupted in a scream at amplified volume, beyond what its own body could muster, obviously channelling the full weight of its race's power.

The Doctor held on. The vibration began to shake him, through his fingers, into his throat, ripping at his lungs. 'This is the conduit!' he yelled. 'They're using it to control these people! It's living off Alison's body!'

His vision grew dark as the thing blasted its scream into his face. He could feel the power of it taking possession of every organ in his body, crushing them, trying to force him down into its fist.

But he was the Doctor. He hung on.

He made himself look directly into the eyes of the vicious creature and knew he was speaking to Prime and all its kind. Let them know he was back. Let them see who they were dealing with!

'But this...' he bellowed through clenched teeth. 'I ... will ... not ... allow!'

With a mighty heave he ripped the Shalka from Alison's forehead.

She dropped back with a cry of shock.

He slammed the creature between his palms with a blow like thunder.

And then darkness filled his eyes, and he fell.

Everybody stopped moving.

The civilians stopped attacking the soldiers. They just backed away, or collapsed, or sat down. They held each other up for support. Their actions suddenly matched their words, except in the cases of a very few, who'd been angrily attacking the soldiers, and needed a moment to stop their momentum.

The area around the warehouses became quiet, only sobs and screams and cries in the air, cut off from each other, isolated by a tremendous, relieved, silence.

'Cease fire!' yelled Kennet.

He started to run through the people, who stared at him, as if unable to believe that they were still here now they'd woken up.

They cleared a path for him.

He reached where the Doctor lay, sprawled on the ground, motionless. One fist was curled. The other hand lay open.

Alison was kneeling over him, a nasty-looking wound on her head. Others of the refugees from Lannet were tending to Joe. But a crowd had gathered a respectful distance from the Doctor, as if aware that he'd done whatever he'd done to save them.

'Doctor?' asked Kennet, squatting down beside him.

Alison looked to him, shaking, her eyes filled with tears. 'I can't find a pulse!' she whispered.

The Doctor opened his eyes and grinned. 'And with so many to choose from!'

He sat up, rolled the remains of the Shalka between his palms, and popped it into a tiny jar he'd produced from the pocket of his cape.

He looked to Alison suddenly and smiled. She was wiping away her tears on the back of her hand. 'That's two-one to me in the game of "die, Doctor, die"!' He turned back to Kennet. 'Didn't shoot anyone, then? Jolly good. Well done.'

'About time we had some luck.' Kennet watched his men as Captain Parker started to organise them into sorting the wounded into categories. A man was running to the police cars at the gate. Ambulances would soon be on their way.

'About time we made our own.' The Doctor hopped to his feet. 'Why are the Shalka still controlling these people? What's so special about some dull old warehouses?'

Kennet was about to say they'd get the owners to allow a search when Greaves ran up, clutching a radio headset. 'Sir, it's just come over the RT! It's not just this place.' The sergeant looked like he'd come through one great battle only to immediately face a bigger one. 'It's everywhere!'

Chapter Seventeen
A World to Save

As more soldiers arrived by helicopter, and ambulance after ambulance arrived at the gates of the warehouse compound, they returned by TARDIS to Kennet's school headquarters.

Kennet set aside a classroom, and spent half an hour on the military net, compiling all the data he could.

Alison and Joe waited, not sure why they'd been brought here. A military surgeon had checked out Alison's head wound, cleaned it up a little, and applied a dressing, all of which made her feel a lot better. Every now and then the Doctor stalked past, flashing Alison a smile as he went. He seemed, she thought, to want to talk but not to at the same time.

She was just insanely grateful to him for having taken the thing out of her head. She could still feel the lack of it. She kept holding onto Joe's hand as they sat in a corridor. Outside the window, the light was fading. Against all Alison's expectations, she was still in Lannet.

'Why can't we just go?' he said.

'Because they've asked us to stay.'

'Told us, more like.'

'He saved my life,' she said, more abruptly than she meant to. 'If he wants me to stay, I'm staying.'

He looked like he was about to say something at greater length then, but a private strode up and told them that they were wanted in room 2B, or rather, as he corrected himself, the briefing room.

The desks had been pulled back to the walls, and a rough theatre made of the chairs, while images were to be projected onto a screen on one wall from a tiny projector connected to a laptop. Alison and Joe sat at the back, while the Doctor sat one row in front of them. Again, he'd looked back at her when he came in, but hadn't said anything.

Kennet entered, looking grim, and went to the front of the room, while Greaves took up a place operating the laptop. It was night outside now, black against the windows.

The first few images projected on the wall all showed the same thing: huge crowds of people, standing in groups, in varying kinds of terrain. Alison assumed they must be satellite or spy-plane images.

'Twenty-six communities worldwide,' said Kennet. 'There may be others we're not even aware of.'

The Doctor looked up from a sheaf of reports he was studying. 'That's why the warehouses seemed so unimportant. They were. They're arranging themselves precisely around the planet. Do you have a map of them all, a global projection?'

'Give us a second,' replied Greaves, his fingers tapping away.

A moment later, the images on the screen warped into a flat map of the world. On it, evenly spaced in a vast spiral, were dots representing the twenty-six crowds of people that Kennet had mentioned. Straight away, Alison could see there were some gaps. There should be a dot in Britain, for instance, right in the middle. That, she presumed, stood for her community, originally intended to work for the Shalka here in Lannet, but moved to the woods because a few miles didn't make much difference on that scale, and now, hopefully, disbanded permanently.

The Doctor stood up and pointed to another place where a dot should be, if the pattern was to be complete. 'If you get a satellite photo of that part of Siberia, you'll find controlled people there, too.'

'Something coming in, sir.' Greaves looked up from the laptop. Kennet nodded, and the image on the wall changed to a murky vision from on high. A crowd was assembling in what looked like a desert, more and more of them gradually appearing at the edges. The people in the middle were standing rigid, staring up into the sky. 'China,' said Greaves. 'Live from an American satellite.'

Kennet stared at it, then looked to the Doctor. 'They're just standing still in big groups.'

The Doctor had remained standing. Now he paced, his hands laced behind his back. 'We have to stop the populations reaching their destinations. We have to try and coordinate the armed forces in these places!'

They all suddenly turned to look at the screen as something on it lit up. A bright white blur that cut through the centre of the image. A shadow shot across the space within it. That must have been an aircraft, thought Alison. She suddenly realised what had happened. Smoke now obscured the centre of the crowd, but still more people were pushing in from the edges, even now filling the gap. She shuddered reflexively.

'The Chinese have started shooting,' muttered Greaves.

Kennet turned from the wall with an expression of disgust, but he was also shaking his head. 'Doctor, eventually this will be the story everywhere!'

'The Shalka can afford to lose a lot of slaves. I doubt the loss of Alison's whole community will make any difference to their plan.'

'Which is?' Alison was surprised to hear her own voice pipe up and ask the question. She was still staring at the carnage on the wall, imagining what it must be like to be at the centre of that.

The Doctor came over to them, uneasy, making fleeting eye contact. 'You've both still got sore throats, haven't you?'

'And so have I,' called Greaves, 'in case you'd forgotten.'

'So did a lot of people,' said Joe. 'Loads of patients have had it, for weeks now.'

The Doctor looked back to the image on the wall, which had zoomed right in, to the upturned faces of people at the edges of the crowd. Smoke rolled over them, but they kept on looking straight up. Their mouths were open. As if they were ready to all shout at some divine revelation. 'They're using humans to transmit the scream,' said the Doctor. 'They've been subsonically training you up while you've been under the influence.'

'But what for?' asked Alison. 'They can scream pretty well themselves, right?'

'Your vocal chords have evolved in this atmosphere, theirs haven't.' He grabbed a small gas cylinder from a table and twisted the valve open. Suddenly, everyone in the room was coughing and spluttering. He jerked the supply closed. 'The Shalka's preferred atmosphere. Kind of thing you get deep inside a planet, rather than on the surface. That's what our captured Shalka got Greaves to make.'

'What?' Greaves looked stunned. 'How?'

'A chemical reaction caused by severe agitation at the molecular level. The scream forms the nitrogen and oxygen in the atmosphere into the more complex compounds the Shalka like.'

Alison was shaking her head, hating where this was going. 'Why can't the Shalka do that themselves?'

The Doctor went to switch off the image at the laptop. 'This is the fast-track invasion plan. To get you to do it for them. They've been waiting these three weeks until they could activate all their slaves at once, each one led by someone like Alison, with a Shalka in their head.'

Kennet went to join him. 'This new atmosphere –'

'You won't be able to breathe it, and I doubt it'll absorb solar radiation, either. The weather's about to become our biggest enemy. The Shalka will move freely on the surface in the chaos, finishing off the survivors.'

Kennet seemed to take a deep breath, letting that sink in. 'How long have we got?'

'The atmosphere's a sensitive system. Given this many release sites… Once the slaves start screaming…' The Doctor stood against the darkness outside, looking out into the night for a moment. Then he turned back to them, his expression grave. 'Perhaps an hour.'

Lala didn't know why he and his family and everyone he knew had come to stand on the beach, their heads locked back, staring at the sky. It was weird and frightening, not the kind of thing the Lord Vishnu ever wanted anybody to do. But some god must be doing it, since everyone was just doing what he said. But there was so much sobbing, there were so many complaints. He understood now that the god was somewhere inside his head, but he couldn't think how it might have got there.

The sun was rising. Lala and his friends waited on the beach as the tide went out, wondering if they would still be there where it came in again to drown them.

It was late afternoon in Tinton Falls. Elise Gower stood at the centre of a vast group of townspeople, near the river that led to the feature that had given the town its name. The gentle rushing of the water was a contrast to the fear all around.

They were all staring at the sky now, the prickliness of sunburn catching their faces, and they couldn't do anything to shade themselves. Every now and then, a military helicopter sped overhead, eliciting a vast cheer from the crowd. They were a sign that, at least, not everyone in the country was behaving like this. Elise called to the others that they were obvious here, that soon rescue parties would arrive, or, at least, someone who was wondering what was going on. Some of those around her were saying that this was some kind of government experiment, but Elise tried to argue them down.

She felt she was arguing against the thing in her head, which had things to say that were different to her own views, and was saying them in sounds she couldn't even hear.

So they waited. They didn't know what for, but they could feel that they were waiting to do something. Elise could see, out of the corner of her eye, her daughter, with the slim bump above her hips. She could only pray that they would all be disturbed from whatever horrifying thing it was that they were here to do.

Dawn was approaching on the steppes. The workers of the former collective farm felt something change as they stared at the sky. Something in the sound that came from Anton had altered.

They all felt it at once, a convulsive imperative inside them.

They opened their mouths, and a terrifying sound burst out.

The scream rose into the brightening sky.

Kennet looked up from the laptop. 'I'm sorry, Doctor, but … we have to bomb these people. Or at least eliminate the leaders with the Shalka in their heads.'

The Doctor went to look at the images that were now coming in from all over the world, of screaming people with their faces turned to the sky. 'Could all the governments of the world be persuaded to do that, within the hour?'

'Doubtful. No time. But what else can we do?'

The Doctor seemed to consider something far away. He looked quite romantic for a moment, Alison thought, lost in contemplation of something good. 'Oh, I can think of so many things… But for the moment,' he snapped back to Kennet, 'you can trust me.' And then he looked straight at Alison. 'And her.'

'What?' said Joe.

The Doctor went to Alison and put his hands on her shoulders, looking intently at her. '*Homo sapiens* has minutes to live. I have to engage the Shalka. And I can't do it without you.' He shrugged. 'So no pressure.'

Alison stood up and took his hands in hers. 'Just show me what I have to do.'

Kennet was looking at them, puzzled. 'Doctor, I don't think –'

'No time, Major!'

Joe had got to his feet, was staring desperately at her. 'Alison, please!'

She couldn't help it. She rounded on him. 'Go on, Joe, ask me to stay with you! In the circumstances, are you really going to do that?! Are you?!'

He surprised her. He just dropped his gaze, understood, finally, where all this had been going for so long. 'No,' he said.

'We can talk when I get back.'

He managed a smile. 'Go. Go on. Save the world.'

The Doctor had been glaring between them, visibly twitching. Now he grabbed her hand and pulled her towards the door at a run. 'One hour, Alison! Come on!'

As they raced towards Kennet's office, where the Doctor had left the TARDIS, Alison jumped at the flash of light from a picture window. They stopped and stared out. A moment later, a vast clap of thunder rolled across the valley where the empty town lay. Then more and more lightning, hitting buildings, playing about the hills with the ferocity of a strobe.

Above them, storm clouds were rushing in, the forces of nature convulsed and speeding towards the school.

'It's started already,' whispered the Doctor. 'The ecosphere is reacting to the scream.'

Kennet packed up the laptop and grabbed his files from the table in the classroom.

'I'll go and see to the troops, sir!' yelled Greaves. He grabbed Joe by the arm. 'You come with me!' And they dashed out to find shelter as the rest of the Green Jackets had, in their improvised barracks in houses near the school, or, the poor devils, out on patrol somewhere.

Kennet ran to the RT room and took a moment to check that all flying units were down and safe. Then he returned to his office, just in time to see, as he opened the door, the last shadow of the TARDIS fade away, taking the noise of rending space and time with it.

'Good luck, Doctor,' he called to the air. 'And God speed.'

Chapter Eighteen
The Death Principle

The workers from the former collective farm stared up into the sky, their throats already starting to feel cracked and aching.

They knew the weather was changing around them, that the air was changing, making them lightheaded as they screamed. They could feel the wind speed rising, rippling at their clothes, the dust flying into their faces.

And then, under the scream, they heard another high sound. They saw the dark shapes in the sky, coming at them out of the sun as it rose.

They understood that the aircraft were there to put an end to what they were doing, to kill them. Many of them welcomed that.

But then the scream suddenly differed. Information was pouring from their throats now, was being broadcast.

From the ground around them burst green forms, breaking the soil, their eyes staring in the sunlight. The creatures stared up into the sky beside them.

They started to scream too.

The dark shapes in the sky dashed in, became fighter aircraft. Their missiles and bombs were about to be launched, they were so close.

But the scream hit them.

One of the aircraft fell from the sky in a spin, cartwheeling tail over cockpit, like it had lost the power to fly, or the air around it had been ripped away. The pilot ejected, but his chair rocketed straight into the ground, to be consumed a moment later by the shape of his craft, astonishingly touching the earth. And then reducing pilot, aircraft and all to a sudden fireball that turned metal and flesh into flame.

The noise and heat of the blast seared over them, but they kept screaming.

The other fighters fell at greater distances, either falling from the sky, or being hammered straight into the ground, the creatures leaping from one point of lava to another, flashing their heads up and down, sending their screams interlacing in all directions, emptying the skies with deadly precision.

There would be more. The tears ran down the faces of the friends and colleagues in the scrublands. They were working, they knew now, for these creatures from hell, for the forces of death.

Alison was exploring the control room of the TARDIS, putting her hands on things, finding no dust on any of the furniture, getting close to the console to feel its reassuringly deep technological hum. The last time she'd been in here, she'd been lying down, her head wounded, surrounded by soldiers, on the way back from the warehouse units. She'd hardly had time to understand where she was before the journey was over.

This time she allowed it to amaze her, to engage her senses fully. The central column was rising and falling, which the Doctor had said meant they were in flight. He'd then told her he'd be back in five minutes, and vanished through an inner door. That had been ten minutes ago. Vague electronic noises had come from further back in the depths of the machine, as though the Doctor was operating some complex equipment.

Bigger on the inside than the outside. Such a simple thing to say, but what it meant was ... beautiful. That there really could be magical boxes that contained more than any tiny human imagination could fit in them. It sort of said that the silly stuff from childhood might all be true.

And the monsters. Them along with it.

She glanced over her shoulder, and saw that the man she'd taken to be some sort of butler when she'd glimpsed him earlier had stepped out from between the rows of shelves, where he'd just apparently finished replacing some books, and was now regarding her with what looked very like distaste.

'You remind me of all the others,' he said, unbidden. 'Horrifyingly.'

'What's that supposed to mean?' Alison took a step towards him. 'And who are you, anyway?'

The man came forward to meet her, raising his eyebrows as if he were addressing a particularly ill-tempered pet. His eyes, Alison realised, were really quite lovely. They were amazingly deep. Like pools of something that led down into ... a maze. Alison found herself feeling dreamy, on the verge of sleep.

'I am the Master,' he said, his voice suddenly commanding. 'And you will –'

The Doctor breezed in. 'Evening!' he called.

'– come to like me when you get to know me, my dear Miss Cheney,' the Master finished, moving swiftly to go and stand beside the console.

Alison blinked, feeling that she'd missed something.

But now the Doctor was talking to her once more. 'I've just been in an extreme state of meditation, in readiness for what I must do. Hard to clear your mind of all its baggage in five minutes, but there.'

He sang a single, rather rough, note. Even if Alison, who'd

never studied music, didn't recognise it, she knew it was only halfway towards whatever it was trying to be.

'What do you think?' he asked hopefully.

'A touch flat,' murmured the Master, with a look of extreme displeasure.

The Doctor went to a cupboard and grabbed a spray, which he applied liberally to the interior of his throat. 'I learnt to do that,' he called, 'under Dame Nellie!'

'Don't worry,' the Master purred back. 'One would never guess.'

Alison looked between them. These two had obviously known each other for a very long time, but their double act wasn't really appropriate in the face of the fear that was rising inside her. 'What are you two going on about?' she asked. 'I thought this was serious!'

The Doctor turned back to her, and put the spray down slowly. The look on his face told her exactly what he felt. 'Serious? Alison, this is me being *deadly* serious.'

Prime stood at the sonic controls, screaming into the device, delighting in the way its voice was manipulating events all over this world. It was a fine planet, a luxurious mass of rock that would soon be a perfect place for its people to thrive.

Very few of its warriors were present in the base now. They were scattered around the world, defending the human slaves and managing the scream process. The technicians had joined them, making sure the sonic network remained in place and alive to every subtlety.

A familiar sound disturbed Prime's concentration. It turned to see if what it thought the sound to be could possibly be true. As it watched, the blue box exterior of the Doctor's space-time craft materialised once more on the podium where it had previously been imprisoned.

Prime conveyed to its people that it would leave the

scream to their own initiative for a few moments, and turned with its remaining warriors to face the new arrival.

The foolish lower creature had actually returned!

The Doctor hit the red control that opened the doors and said farewell to the Master, who looked anxiously after them as they left.

'Isn't the Master coming with us?' Alison asked.

'No,' replied the Doctor, stepping out into the cavern. 'He can't leave the TARDIS.'

Coming towards them were three Shalka warriors, poised, ready to scream. Behind them Alison could see Prime. She wanted to ask the Doctor exactly what his plan was, or why the Master couldn't leave the ship, but instead of doing anything sensible, the Doctor pointed upwards, affecting to admire the décor. 'You know, without so many Shalka about, you can really see the architecture. See that spiral on the roof?'

'Oh yeah,' muttered Alison, glancing up. 'Very Gaudi.'

'Now there was a man who knew a thing or two about string. Lucky I was there when he ran out. You're a very informed barmaid.' He was all at once looking at her again, seemingly interested in nothing else, even as the monsters approached.

'I gave up a degree in history to live with Joe.'

He nodded slightly, his eyes glittering in the low light, as if now he understood.

'Doctor!' The creature called Prime had surrounded them with its warriors. It spread its arms, indicating the TARDIS. It sounded mocking. 'See the technology you command! And yet, you distract, you de-emphasise, you *talk*. I think that's all you can do!'

Only now did the Doctor acknowledge its presence, with a friendly grin. 'My, you sound happy!'

'In a few moments, we will add this world to the Shalka Confederacy!'

The Doctor jauntily leant on the shoulder of one of the warriors, who looked to Prime, unsure what to do, and finally stayed put, hissing awkwardly. 'Ah yes, your "empire of a billion worlds". I have a horrible idea that now I know where that is.'

'I think not, Doctor.'

With a hop, he walked through the surrounding spiral of Shalka and wandered into the centre of the cavern. Alison, feeling that also gave her licence not to be surrounded, followed him.

'You're fond of rocks like dolphins are fond of water. So how might you travel between worlds? I used the TARDIS scanner to search for recent meteor debris, plus traces of the radiation that might suggest a miniature wormhole.'

From the lamp on top of the TARDIS there unfolded a projection, a pan across a desolate landscape on what Alison recognised was still Earth. A volcano stood piercing the clouds. On its slopes lay two dead bodies, regurgitated by the earth, painfully twisted into lava. Alison shuddered at the familiar sight. Around them lay the remains of a rock, which the picture zoomed in on, obviously the remains of a meteor. The image fluttered then vanished. Alison could imagine the Master carefully timing his actions at the console to create the most theatrical impact.

The Doctor turned to address Prime again. 'You seek out worlds that are in ecological trouble, and then you pounce on them with one of these things, a targeted meteor containing one of your people, plus the seed of a wormhole.'

Prime let out a long hiss. 'We take the weakest of the herd: Soltox; Duprest, Valtanus...'

'Dead worlds. Lost civilisations. History says they destroyed themselves.'

'They did most of the damage. Then we finished them off. Billions of Shalka live there now. Underground. Not getting into ridiculous wars like lower creatures. We inhabit eighty per cent of the worlds of the universe. Those you regard as "dead"!'

Alison saw the Doctor's nostrils flare. He'd finally got this monster to boast about what it did and how it did it. He stepped forward towards Prime. Alison realised, with a little jolt, that he was actually angry now, that he'd become furious at these cosmic things that meant so little to her.

'So you're it,' he said. 'The great limiting factor of the cosmos. The death principle! If cultures wander down an ecological cul-de-sac, you grab them by the throat and throttle them!'

Prime came to meet him. The two aliens stood glaring at each other, eye to eye. 'And when the Earth's original atmosphere has been stripped away, and raw radiation has cleansed the surface, millions of our kind will arrive through the warp gate and live off pure volcanic energy!'

Kennet was on the telephone in his office, trying to speak into the receiver over the noise of the storm that was raging outside. He'd already talked to his family, told them to get down into the deepest part of the house. Now he was going to stay here and keep the comms web going, try to make a difference.

Dawn was breaking outside, they'd already had a little longer than the Doctor had anticipated. It was as if mother Earth was holding on, trying to fight back. 'Yes, I know!' he was yelling. 'It's chaos out there! It's chaos out *here*!'

He ducked reflexively as the window burst inwards, shards of glass smashing against a far wall under the force of a hurricane. Every piece of paper in the room suddenly came alive and was swept away.

He pulled the telephone into the corner with him, and carried on in the face of it. 'Just get me through to someone in the Cabinet Office ... I don't care! Anyone!'

Dawn came up like thunder that day.

The radiation was already driving the atmosphere into a frenzy. But now, as the first rays of direct solar light flashed across the sea from the Netherlands, Britain began to experience what the rest of Europe had already discovered. Trawler crews grasped their faces, crying out as the dawn burnt directly into their flesh. North Sea oil-rig workers fell to their knees, suddenly sick with radiation.

The sea at the shallows of the coast started to boil and froth. Then the line of fire hissed inland, the direct sight of the sun burning and blazing and setting fire to haystacks, roofs, whole forests. In seconds, columns of smoke flew westwards, mercifully blotting out the path of the erasing, searing sun.

'This is why I was sent here,' the Doctor said solemnly. 'In all my travels as a Time Lord, I never saw it. You're not predators. You're death incarnate!'

Kennet realised that nobody was talking to him any more. The receiver in his hand was dead. The land lines must have gone down in the gales.

He was about to scramble to his feet and head for the RT room when the door smashed open. Greaves tumbled into the room. He managed to fall against the wall, and stared at Kennet.

His hands were red, burnt. His face was a mass of blisters.

Kennet realised, horrified, that he'd run back into the school for him. He backed towards his desk.

'Sir!' Greaves shouted. 'Get away from the window! Sir! The sun! It's hard radiation!'

Kennet felt his hand roasting in the moment it connected with a shaft of sunlight that shone through the broken window onto the desk.

He snatched it away, and found it was sunburnt. 'The ozone layer's being stripped away! We need to organise the men, get some kind of protection!'

Greaves stumbled again, and managed to right himself, lying panting against the wall. 'Protection?' he laughed. 'I think it's a bit late for that, sir! This is the end of the world!'

And then something blasted through the window, and the room became darkness and flying shards, and Kennet fell into the darkness also.

Tidal waves, made from the heat of the sea, burst across the eastern seaboard of the United States and the west coast of Ireland.

The seas off Japan rolled and crushed the cities on the coast.

The reflected radiation from the Australian desert made the electronics on three airliners short out, and they returned in emergency runs to the nearest airports, airports with which they were no longer in radio contact, the whole electromagnetic spectrum roaring with hard radiation. Satellite signals, relayed by craft designed for the hard radiation outside Earth's atmosphere, would have remained uninterrupted, but their broadcast was through the rushing void of the terrestrial electromagnetic atmosphere.

In bunkers deep beneath mountains, on all the continents, those who looked after the leaders of the world had begun, in moments, to assemble emergency staff, to switch on emergency nuclear power sources, to view the catastrophe from whatever surface viewpoints they could contact. It had all happened so fast that in many cases the executive officers who should be running things had been caught in the open, miles from cover. The grey men who had spent all their lives taking orders looked at each other and wondered if they could rule. If there would be anything left to rule. They had been raised expecting war, but this ... this was more like the last trump. The hand of something huge had descended on the planet, and the enemy, small as they were when seen from satellites, seemed to possess a power too big to fight.

A nuclear weapon had been launched from an aircraft carrier, borne on a cruise missile. It had been melted by sound as it approached its destination. Various countries had released sprays of biotoxins into the wind, intending to fell hundreds of their screaming citizens at the merest touch. These sprays had been rebounded by the weather, turned away by the scream, only in a few cases had they folded over the people, and then not enough had fallen.

Lava had broken open the crust, where it could, and had surrounded the screaming thousands with a rough land defence. The Shalka appeared in their hundreds on the surface, knocking down any aircraft that attempted to get close to their slaves, their screaming becoming a wall that allowed the greater scream, the scream that was killing the world, to blast at the atmosphere, like a blowtorch through liquid.

The nightside of Earth glowed, the aurorae blazing from both poles. The death of the planet screeched its way into the consciousness of space, broadcasting itself across the light years.

Like so many before it.

Prime began to laugh. It allowed itself that now. It could hear that the latest triumph of its race was not far away. It could hear the scream reporting all the details of victory. Soon it would be time for the warriors to move out onto the surface, the beautiful, clean, empty surface, finding the last of the lower creatures and killing them in person.

That was always the most satisfying part of the process.

It looked down at the lower creature that stood before it, with all his presumptions, and laughed even louder. It could allow itself one more luxury now.

The luxury of killing this 'Doctor' in its real form.

Cracks appeared all over the surface of Prime's humanoid body. They criss-crossed with a sound like an egg hatching. The green mass underneath burst free, steaming in the air of the cavern.

It thrashed and shook, throwing off the remains of its former shell. The humanoid form had packed the creature inside tightly, folded its structure many times. Now every organ could swell to its proper size. Its lungs collapsed into breathing tubes that sucked in the volcanic gasses from the vents across the cave with the joy of new birth.

A new armour hardened around this true form. New eyes opened above the towering presence of a full Shalka Prime, a War Chief of the Shalka Confederacy. It had the bulk of a fighting animal, the opening hood of a master of sonic combat. It knew not what people the Doctor claimed to represent, but they could not be lords of time while its own people were the lords of all time and space. Its limbs and tail rippled with controlled killing power.

The Doctor took a step back, his gaze sizing up the vast figure of unfolded power that had grown above him.

'Call us death if you wish, "Time Lord"!' Prime bellowed. 'For we bring extinction to the entire human race!'

Chapter Nineteen
The Doctor and the Monster

The few remaining Shalka warriors in the cavern grabbed the Doctor and Alison, and took them to a rock wall, where their screams rapidly fashioned chains out of the rock itself. The chains were secured by locks, which didn't look like they were made for keys, just a hole that would focus a quick scream and spring the manacles. A labour-saving device as befitted a great civilisation. So, the Doctor thought, he wasn't going to have to bother with any of that yogic hand-slipping stuff. Jolly good.

He saw Alison flinch as the manacles were secured around her wrists, but they were only warm. Prime didn't want its captives harmed until it was ready to do so. The Doctor suppressed a smile. He'd angered its pride just enough to get it to that place. Warrior races rarely treated war as a rational exercise. Certain South American tribes had kept captured royalty prisoner for exactly a year before then killing them in ritual combat. Prime wanted its plan to be complete in front of the Doctor, wanted to rub his nose in it, before killing him.

They might be something he'd never seen before, they might control most of the dead worlds of the cosmos, but they were still militarists, and thus predictable.

He let that smile come after all. And he was still the Doctor.

Alison nudged him as best she could from her own chains. She'd been watching Prime, in its new body, as it returned to the controls, screaming with greater variation and oscillation now into the 'microphone' that stood centrally there. 'Why is it keeping that going?'

'The Shalka share the scream like whalesong,' the Doctor whispered. 'A way to transmit a lot of messages between each other at high speed.'

'The sonic internet?'

The Doctor looked sidelong at her. 'And that machine adds automatic co-ordination. It keeps all their slaves doing what they're supposed to be doing, without the Shalka having to think about every little command. It must be able to record, play back, relay and boost the screams.'

'Their sonic service provider!'

'Stop that.'

She managed a smile. 'What are you going to do?'

'Oh, I'm already doing it. Using that same hairpin of yours I used to open the hardware store. *Like* the hair, by the way. There.'

With a flick of the wrist, his chains opened. He drew back a little, pleased at Alison's amazed expression, to hide the fact behind her, and turned his attention to her own shackles. 'Now hold still.'

'Okay,' she whispered, still staring at him.

Death had arrived in the world.

Trees were flying in the hurricanes of the night, as the air mass of the Earth contorted, trying to get away from the transformation that was being wrought on it, and away from the heat that was roaring onto the half of the planet that was seen by the sun.

The seas were boiling, heaving, eating the coastlines.

Lightning torn from the frenzied atmosphere was dancing across cities, adding to the fires, the fires becoming firestorms.

The people hid, in caves and in cellars, reduced to fearing their own sky, burnt and bewildered.

Except the slaves, at the top of it all, who stood, defended, still screaming, destroying their own world against their will.

The Doctor's fingers worked nimbly at Alison's chains.

'A friend of mine,' he began, 'Andy Warhol was his name, said: "They always say that time changes things, but you actually have to change them yourself." Wonderful man. He wanted to paint all nine of me.'

'What are you talking about?' She didn't seem at all impressed.

'Just getting my courage together.'

Her chains fell to the floor and he slid the hairpin back into his sleeve.

'Thank you.'

He glanced across to where Prime and its warriors were still sharing that deadly scream. They had a few seconds. And there was something important he had to try to explain to her, something she was missing. It was him against the machines. Always. A big personality against too many that were too small. He stood for things. And he was just getting that back now, he didn't want to lose it again, he wanted to explain it. 'In time,' he began, 'I hope you'll allow me my eccentricities, Alison. Sometimes they're all I, or the world, have got.'

'Is that why you brought me down here? So you could do this in front of me and save my life?'

He felt himself get angry and defensive, and bit down on it. 'Of course not. That would be sheer vanity! I need you in a very practical way.' He would have liked to have gone on, but there was no time. Whatever she might think of him, and he realised now that he cared rather horrifyingly about that, he didn't do his talking while people were dying.

He took the jar from his pocket, unscrewed the lid with one jerk of his hand, and dropped the tiny Shalka he'd pulled from her head into his palm. The blow between his hands had only stunned it, and the oxygen inside the jar had kept it in stasis. He could feel it coming alive again in his hand.

He looked at Alison again, trying hard not to be a stage magician. But then he thought that blast it, he was what he was. He threw back his head, tossed the Shalka into the air and swallowed it like a dratted performing seal.

He hadn't expected the sudden pain that made his head jerk back. And then the darkness.

The tiny Shalka fell into the Doctor's digestive system. It had a small consciousness. It knew its purpose. It had been hatched to link with lower creatures. It knew the whole grand structure of the Shalka Confederacy was above it, and better than it.

It found itself now inside a lower creature, so it did what it always did. It reached out tendrils of fine silicon to join with and infest the physical structure of the animal. It would establish links that would feed it from the beast's system, where no nutritious gasses could be found, and then use its scream to contact the great scream of the Shalka, and move the creature as its masters saw fit.

Except that this time its fibres were intercepted.

Aggressive neurons sprang from tissue that should not bear them. This was not a lower creature, this just looked like a lower creature! Terror seized its small mind.

Then the neurons were upon it, and energy roared from them into the Shalka.

Alison had seen the Doctor stagger, his eyes rolling. Then he'd fallen back against the rock wall, breathing hard, in some sort of trance. Just as well the Shalka were so engrossed in their screaming. They probably already knew that he was becoming one of them. How could he have been so stupid as to deliberately put one of those creatures inside him?

She steeled herself, and then decided she had to do it. She slapped his cheek as hard as she could. 'Doctor!'

His eyes snapped open. He was staring at something beautiful, in the far distance, beyond human sight. 'Oh,' he gasped. 'What it must be like. To escape the reliance of all life on other life. To take sustenance directly from worlds.' He managed to focus on her, breaking into a spacey grin. 'They take good care of their planets, Alison, after they've transformed them.'

She slapped him again. Harder. 'Don't let it take you over!'

He caught her hand before the third time. 'Stop slapping me! I wasn't!' He sounded hurt. 'My neurons were linked to it. I was learning from it and reprogramming it.'

'Oh.' She pursed her lips. 'Sorry.'

'I can understand the scream now. All that beautiful information. That was the pleasurable part. Now here comes the dangerous bit.' His eyes became serious again. 'Don't move until I tell you.'

He'd suddenly stopped sounding like an amateur.

Alison nodded. She wanted to wish him good luck. But it seemed redundant.

The Doctor stepped from the wall, let his chains fall away from him, and headed across the cavern towards the Shalka.

The Doctor tried, as he approached Prime, to think of what the most obvious thing to do in these circumstances might be. Obviously, one could dive for the controls, perhaps even try to attack Prime in some way. What could he possibly be attempting?

Hang it all, he decided. He didn't need an excuse. They wouldn't look for one. He was going to have fun, blast it.

He took a deep breath and spread his arms wide. 'What

good is sitting alone in your room,' he sang, his voice wavering uneasily around the proper notes, 'come hear the music –'

He stopped as they turned and looked at him, their mouths open to attack. And well they might. Liza would not have been proud. Next time the Doctor saw her, if there was a next time, he really had to tell her of the use her signature song had been in saving the planet. If there was a planet.

Prime left them to it, going back to its work.

The Doctor stepped quickly aside, wanting their full attention. 'I must say, I'm getting tired of all your "oooh". *Nul points* says the Time Lord jury!'

They swung to follow him.

'Tell me honestly, am I irritating you yet?'

They all screamed at him at once, which was what he'd wanted. But he hadn't expected it to hurt quite so much. The scream battered him physically, rippling the skin over his muscles, blasting his face like a wind tunnel. It was like being hit with sledgehammers, over and over. He could feel how this would bully humans, how their minds would bend under the sound as their bodies did.

Just as well he wasn't human.

They stopped just short of killing him. Prime must have given them orders to that effect. Ah, he had, he could read it in what he just heard. Just. So this was working... But it was going to take a while. He lay on the floor, panting, tasting the blood in his mouth. It would be quite easy to stop this right now. Another burst might well kill him. He didn't know if he was going to get to where he wanted to go before it did.

But no. Alison, her friends, even Kennet. A whole world of people. Just him to protect it.

He leapt to his feet and laughed at the monsters. 'You'll have to do better than that!' He walked right up to them and looked them in the eye. 'Look how *strong* the lower creature

169

is! Look how he stands up to you! A billion worlds?!' He swung his arms wide, mocking the bullies, his favourite thing in the whole universe to do, which was good since it might be the last. 'Top predator of the cosmos?! You're just a bunch of one-penny jelly snakes!'

They screamed at him again, harder. The blows concussed his chest and back.

He wouldn't let himself fall this time. He dropped to one knee. His mind was racing through what it was learning, pushing at the tiny Shalka inside, hearing more and more that what was flaying him was language, words of power, not just violence, but information he didn't quite yet understand.

He felt the darkness thumping in his skull, felt the blood falling from his nose as the tiny arteries in his brain gave way.

Knowledge would always conquer force. He knew that. Cleverness beats fists. Those surrounding you who are hitting you are hitting you because they are desperate, because the power of your intelligence scares them.

His mind turned inwards, his eyes closed. He was going to fail. He mustn't let himself think it. He remembered a great man, with whom he'd once sparred, one of the greatest warriors of the world, who'd nevertheless known that his skill as a fighter was the least impressive thing about him. He'd been a master of words as well. In one of his most desperate moments, he'd held on in the face of a terrible beating, knowing that on the other side of it, if he could just keep standing up, there was the victory of intelligence over might.

A sharky smile came to the Doctor's face. 'Hit me again, George!' he snarled, determined.

They pressed in, the pressure of the scream making him sway, the force of it bruising every inch of him.

He kept concentrating. He searched for understanding.

He found it.

He opened his mouth and out burst a single, pure note.

The surrounding Shalka burst into an expanding fog of tiny green particles, a rain that splattered against Prime, the controls, and slapped a circle of green onto the floor around.

Silence hit him. He turned to look at Prime, allowing himself a moment of unadulterated pride. 'Perfect pitch,' he murmured. 'Finally!'

Prime was regarding him with what he hoped passed for new respect in Shalka body language. It had ceased its scream, watching him carefully as he approached the control desk, from which the scream communications continued to issue. It inched round the desk, keeping it between them.

That spiral pattern again. The Doctor kept walking, continuing the circle, making sure he was facing the creature.

'I think,' he told it. 'Therefore, I win.'

'You haven't won.'

'You've kept your human vocal chords.' Of course. It would want to use them to gloat before it killed him.

The huge Shalka inclined its hooded head slightly. 'Which doesn't prevent me from doing … this!'

The Doctor tried at the last second to scream back, but he was too late. The blast of sound Prime had emitted knocked him off his feet and sent him flying backwards to hit the far wall.

He slid down it onto his feet again, keeping the groan inside, dusting himself down.

'Amateur!' hissed Prime. 'You could only destroy an unprepared or inexperienced Shalka! We have a tradition of sonic combat!'

The Doctor feinted, opening his mouth for a moment, and saw Prime react, ready. He resumed his prowl around the control desk, both of them waiting for an opening. This talk of sonic combat was intriguing. The Doctor was an expert fencer, obviously, a member of Salle Paul, pupil to the great Italo Sentilli, tutor to the Chevalier d'Eon and Abraham Lincoln. He had been denied Olympic medals only by his reluctance to adopt a national team and, thus, a nationality. His experience with the blade, together with his new understanding of the principles of the scream, learned by using his inner Shalka to soak up great gouts of the language, made him just about able to duel with Prime on its own terms.

Just about.

'And I,' he returned, keeping their eyeline level as they circled the desk, 'have a tradition of getting in the way.' Out of the corner of his eye he saw Alison watching, wondering what was going on, wondering if he had anything up his sleeve or was just making it up as he went along. A little of both. He smiled at the thought.

'You are not preventing the destruction of this world by delaying me,' said Prime. 'The scream continues to operate without my personal direction.'

'But with the knowledge of your whole system in my head, I'm eventually going to get the hang of this.'

He noted where they'd reached in their circling motion, and took a big breath again.

Prime got there first again, the blast sending the Doctor flying. He'd got an arm in the way and for a moment he thought it had been shattered. The impact of the wall winded him. But he leapt to his feet again.

He was so close! He skipped sideways the last couple of steps, and watched as Prime circled the desk, following him. 'Or perhaps I'll just –'

Prime's scream sent him flying again.

Across the room.

But this time he'd been ready for it, rode it like a tumbler.

Jumped back to his feet straight away.

And was now standing exactly where he wanted to be.

Beside the switches that activated the warp gate. '– get you to fire me in the right direction,' he finished.

He grabbed the switches and heaved.

The pattern inside the warp gate changed once more. It became a black hole again. Suddenly, everything in the cavern leapt into the air.

Prime's powerful arms grabbed for a handhold, but they missed, and the great mass of its body went flying. Towards the warp gate, towards the Doctor. It roared as it fell.

The Doctor was holding onto the controls as the gravitational pull dragged him sideways. His fingers were turning white with the strain. It was like hanging from a ledge that was suddenly pulled sideways, a great fall beneath him.

Prime landed across the warp gate. It was too large to pass straight through. Its hands grabbed one side, its tail thrashed to put the bulk of its body in the way of the other. It screamed at the Doctor. The blast hit his hands.

He couldn't grit his teeth through a moment of such agony. He had to let go.

He fell across the body of Prime, both of them struggling in the rushing maw of the warp gate. He managed to spin, to get his hands to the very edge of the surrounding rock. Prime thrashed beneath him, trying to twist its head so it could blast him into nothingness.

If they fell now, it would be to their deaths. There would be no more escapes from this black hole. Everything that wasn't held down in the cavern flew at them and past them, into the swirling abyss: rocks, pieces of small equipment, a storm of volcanic gasses that buffeted them as they blasted by. At any moment one of the objects would strike one of them, and randomly choose who won and who died.

The Doctor and the monster struggled on the edge of their doom.

* * *

173

Alison had grabbed her chains as soon as the appearance of the warp gate vortex had changed. Now she had been dragged sideways until she was hanging, screaming, pulled horizontally across the room.

A tiny sound came to her under the scream, the roaring of the air and the rushing of the volcanic gasses. The rock that had been extruded from the wall to form these chains was narrowing, warping … about to break.

She slapped out a hand to try and grab for the wall –

But then the rock bonds broke.

She flew across the room.

She hit the floor, rebounded, and stretched out an arm as she skittered to her feet once more.

She had grabbed the warp-gate control console.

She hung on, desperately moving hand over hand to keep a hold of it.

She was just a few feet from where the Doctor was holding on himself. She held her own terror down and found that she was equally frightened for him.

It looked like he was going to lose.

Prime struggled into a position where it could finally look the Doctor in the face. It took in a great inrush of air, ready to blast him from his handhold. 'Die, Doctor! Die!' it bellowed.

'That's just it, Prime!' The Doctor was just about holding on. But he couldn't lose. He couldn't make a noble sacrifice. He had to win this and then do much more before the Earth was safe. 'Life won't!'

And he lashed out with his boot.

The blow caught Prime just at the moment it unleashed its scream. It had been concentrating on that moment of victory. Its hands lost their grip on the warp gate, and its tail couldn't find leverage.

The great beast fell into the black hole, screaming vengeance as it went.

That scream blasted the Doctor's fingers from their slim hold on the gate rim.

He flew into space, arms and legs flailing, looking at the black hole that would in a moment consume him. He had a second to think of things left undone: of the one he'd lost; of all his lost people; of Alison and the people of Earth.

And then Alison's hand grabbed his.

His feet missed the abyss by inches. He swung in an arc.

He saw she was hanging from the controls by one hand, holding onto him by the other.

He managed to swing to the other side of the gate, grabbed a handhold and held on. 'That nodule!' he bellowed at her. 'The big one! Hit it!'

Alison hauled herself back to the controls, found the right button, looked to him for confirmation for an instant and then bunched her free hand in a fist to punch it as hard as she could. As hard as a scream would.

The warp gate became a wall of rock, switching itself off completely.

The Doctor and Alison fell to the floor.

The Doctor jumped to his feet, bounded over to Alison, and swept her up to a standing position. Then he jumped in the air, punching it, letting out all his relief and the pain of his bruises.

'Oh yes!' he yelled at the bare rock. 'Yes!'

Prime fell, screaming, into the void.

It vowed vengeance for the Shalka as it fell. It remembered the joy it had felt in crushing the lives out of the lower creatures with the scream that sundered worlds. It cursed the Doctor with its last screamed and steaming breath.

And then it hit the mathematical nothingness of the singularity that lies at the heart of the black hole.

And it knew no more.

Chapter Twenty
The Final Battle

The Doctor grabbed Alison by the hand and rushed her over from the warp-gate controls to the bigger control column with the 'microphone' set into it. She was amazed at how swiftly he could switch from triumphant to urgent. It was as if the triumph had been a luxury he'd allowed himself, something he'd been missing for so long that he had to indulge himself in it when it came.

'Quickly!' he gasped now. 'Hundreds of Shalka have taken up positions just under the surface to protect the slaves and direct operations!' He listened for a moment to the warbling scream that still came from the control desk. 'They're starting to ask why they haven't had any central commands for the last couple of minutes, but they're more than capable of getting the slaves to finish the job!'

'How long have we got?'

'The atmosphere could react and change any second.' He grabbed her by the shoulders again and looked into her eyes. 'Alison, do you trust me?'

She wanted to slap him again. 'Oh, how needy are you? *Yes!*'

'Then this is why I brought you here.' He turned aside for a moment, decorously shielding her from what he was doing. A moment later he spun back, holding the miniature Shalka in his palm. He was looking seriously at her. 'I want you to take your passenger back on board.'

Alison was horrified by the thought. But only for a moment. The world couldn't afford her horror now. 'Right.' She started to pull the dressings from her forehead.

The Doctor helped her as best he could with one hand. 'I've put it into a deep sleep. Being a Shalka, it can communicate with all the others via the scream. It grew in your head, took sustenance from your biosystems, already connected to a human brain, so it was easy for me to mentally reprogram it. But I can't make full use of it, because my brain isn't human. Only you can do this. It'll plug your brain into the Shalka network.'

The wound was exposed now. The Doctor looked at her for confirmation, and she nodded. He placed the Shalka at the wound, moved it around a little ... and that was a terrible feeling in itself ... and then it slid inside.

Alison was glad that she'd been unconscious the last time that had happened. 'I am going to be okay, aren't I?'

'I wouldn't risk losing you,' he whispered. 'You know I wouldn't.' And he meant every word.

'It just feels so...' She felt something change inside her head. 'Oh. Oh!'

It was different to when she'd been passively carrying this creature around. She hadn't felt connected to it at all then. It had just been telling her what to do, a one-way street. But now ... now she could all at once hear everything the Shalka was hearing. The scream opened up, became a vast, beautiful pattern of racing information.

She realised with shock that she was right at the centre of it. She saw what the Doctor had meant. It was glorious to see, glorious to be part of.

'You're in charge now,' said the Doctor. 'You're the centre of Shalka operations. I've made the tiny Shalka think that it's a Prime. Tell the slaves to shut up. The Shalka will try and stop you. You mustn't let them!'

178

Alison took a deep breath and closed her eyes. Just for a moment, she found she was thinking about Kim.

Lala and Elise and Anton and all the other slave leaders were connected by so many things. The air they breathed circulated and sustained a carbon cycle that unconsciously included every living thing. The chemical reactions in their bodies were sustained by minerals formed in the same cluster of distant supernovae, billions of years before the Earth was formed. Genetically, they had more in common, as did the whole human population of the planet, than any random tribe of chimpanzees.

And now they were all standing with their immediate friends and family around them, staring into the sky and making death with their mouths.

But then, all at once, they became aware of a new voice. It sounded like it was talking into their ear. They heard it as part of the scream, each in their own language, translated by whatever it was that was in their heads. 'Listen to me, everybody,' it began, hesitantly. But it became stronger, more confident. 'I'm one of you. A human being. You're free! Free!'

The crowds around them swayed, distracted from their task. Mouths closed, eyes looked round. The control of the scream had weakened to let this communication in. Indeed, the message of the scream now *was* these words!

'Stop the scream!' she yelled. 'Stop the scream!'

Hoarse cheers and sobs broke out. People fell against each other, helped each other stay standing, just starting to think it was over.

But then, in all the locations where the slaves stood, the creatures that had 'protected' them from soldiers and missiles and aircraft appeared, roaring to the surface, their own screams battering them back to what they'd been doing before. The orders were *not* countermanded! The slaves would continue!

The slave leaders wept and yelled and tried to fight. This was worse than it had been before, to have hope taken away from them!

The Doctor watched with pride as Alison's lips moved, her voice audible only as part of the scream. She was arguing with the whole of the Shalka presence on Earth, trying to change the scream into something that freed, fighting the invaders of her planet on her own.

If she could only succeed, then the Doctor would destroy the scream controls here. The pattern would be broken, the individual Shalka warriors on the surface would not be able to put such a vast network of control back together again once it had gone. They would come here, but the Doctor would assemble enough military here in the TARDIS to make them sue for peace. He would carefully reset the warp gate and send their army home. They would know better than to try here again, and the humans would know to look out for asteroids that sought out planets with failing ecologies.

It would be messy and awkward and dull and full of setbacks and take ages. But peace was like that. He'd leave about halfway, when he was sure it was going to work. Off on his way, alone again, free of these trying humans and their violence.

He looked back to Alison, and something gave him pause. Free of them. Indeed. Alone again. Like he had been for so long...

Alison gasped, putting her hands to her head. 'They're trying to drown me out!' she said out loud. 'Trying to take control back!'

The Doctor grabbed her hands. 'You had the willpower to

fight them on your own. Now you've got all those people on your side. You *can* do it!'

A vast noise cut into the end of his words.

Alison managed to stay focused, her eyes still closed, but he looked up and saw that the rocks at the other end of the cavern were crumbling away from an immense lava flow that had seared open the rock wall.

Through the gap came, as fast as it could slither, the giant colony creature, the worm inside whose mouth the Doctor had once ridden. It bellowed as it came, its huge jaws open, its bulk ready to flatten them. It rushed forward.

The Doctor closed his eyes for a moment. No more time. All hope for peace gone.

All right.

'Change of plan,' he told Alison. He grabbed the microphone. 'Am I speaking to the Shalka now?'

He could hear Alison and the Shalka they'd shared translating his words directly into the scream.

'Yes!' she shouted.

'Are you all on the surface, all trying to control every single one of those humans on your own, spinning all those plates at once?'

'Yes!'

The bulk of the worm was nearly upon them. Its vast mass was growing bigger by the second.

'Well then,' said the Doctor. 'This is how it feels to drop them.'

He let the scream burst from his lungs and throat.

A pitch-perfect note. A thrust in sonic combat. At the moment when the whole scream was listening, open, vulnerable.

The giant worm stopped, reacted, twisted –

And exploded.

One moment it was there, the next moment it was an

expanding blast of green skin and innards.

The green mess flew everywhere, covering them, splashing into every corner of the cave and filling the air with a fine green mist.

All over the world, Shalka on the surface felt the scream inside their bodies become a dagger that twisted –

And burst them.

They had been tense in an environment they loathed, not on their guard inside.

They flew apart at a cellular level. Into a mist that was too dissipated to ever reform.

The guards surrounding the slaves became flying blasts of green.

The technicians in the tunnels became lines of strung out plasma.

The Shalka that remained in the oxygen tent in the Doctor's laboratory suddenly filled it as a dead green gas.

Across the planet, the thousands of Shalka vapourised and died.

And the slaves fell, exhausted, injured, collapsing into each other with grief and relief.

The scream of the Shalka had been silenced.

Lala found his mother had gathered him up in her arms, while his father frantically brushed away the remnants of something from his forehead. Everyone around him was falling into each other, sobbing and praying, as the waves burst around their legs. Some fell into the water, but others helped them up. Nobody could really speak.

Dad led him and Mum and Aj up the beach, to the rocks, where they lay down with many other people who were slowly walking or being dragged out of the water. The moon was setting above it now. Everything looked beautiful.

Lala asked if he was going to wake up now, and Mum said yes he was and kissed him.

Elise Gower went straight to her daughter and asked if she was okay. Ann stopped sobbing long enough to say yes she was, and they held each other for the longest time. Elise's husband found them there after a little while. Fellow council-folk soon found their way to the hugging group, but didn't feel it appropriate to join in. They just sat mopping their brows or shading themselves or crying or, perversely, laughing in the shade. A few people even started to drift home. Prayers were said out loud. Most folk wanted to stay together, but they didn't know why.

A helicopter landed in a clearing in the park, and a group of marines ran towards them, shouting for them all to remain calm.

Elise raised her head from Ann's shoulder and shouted to them that the council was over here, and that they'd missed all the excitement, and that they'd better remain calm themselves if they were going to be waving those guns around.

She saw the astonished look in her husband's eyes and found, to her surprise, that suddenly, for the first time, she was crying.

Anton wiped the thing away from his forehead, and looked around at the stunned faces of his friends. They were sitting down now, coughing and spluttering. The smoke from the crashed aircraft didn't help.

Anton wondered for a moment if they'd really been going to bomb them? Ah well. It was to be expected.

He went to find Val and his boys, and led them back towards the farm. 'Aliens,' he spat. 'You can always beat them somehow.'

* * *

The Doctor wiped the fine green mist from his eyes.

He looked around the cavern, and staggered. He had to hold himself up by the control column.

He'd actually done it.

He leaned back into the microphone and whispered to the now silent cave. 'Come to the cabaret.'

Alison had opened her eyes, and was now looking at him in awe at what they'd done together. 'They're gone,' she said.

'Vapourised. All of them.' He took a moment to blow a fine green dust from the wound in her forehead, and then blew the air from his nose dismissively. '"Amateur" indeed!' He wandered off into the centre of the cavern, his hands jammed into his pockets, looking around at all the devices, all the civilisation that would now become just dead rock, gradually or swiftly folded back into the planet as the Earth recovered.

But Alison didn't come with him. She stood, leaning heavily on the control deck, staring into space. 'We could have used the scream to fix the atmosphere,' she told him, almost accusingly. 'Not just to stop the Shalka, but to get rid of all the pollution. To set up big carbon sinks on the edge of deserts. To make the world green again. All I needed was another couple of seconds.'

The Doctor reached out and wiped a fingerful of green goo from the blue of the TARDIS. He felt awkward with her. But he wasn't going to stop telling her the truth. 'I wouldn't have allowed it,' he said, trying to sound offhand. 'Humans can sort out the problems they make for themselves.'

She came over to him slowly, shaking with delayed shock. Green droplets were starting to fall from the ceiling, in a fine rain. There were great creaks and groans as the structure started to lean in on itself, no longer having the scream to support it. 'Every time I think I understand you…' she said.

The Doctor thought for a moment, and then just said everything that was inside him, letting her look directly into his eyes for what felt like the first time in a long while. 'I feel the same way. I don't like the military, but I have so many friends in it. I say I do not kill. But then I exterminate thousands.'

She seemed to understand. She stopped shaking, after a while, and came to a conclusion. 'Look. You do your best to keep all the plates from smashing. You don't have to be *perfect*. Okay?'

The Doctor found himself smiling like that was the nicest thing anyone had ever said to him. 'Okay.'

He reached forward and kissed her like a daughter on her extremely messy forehead, taking care to avoid the wound. 'So,' he said, 'tea?'

And he planted a gobbet of goo on her nose.

'Oh,' she sighed. 'Lovely!'

The Doctor threw an arm around her shoulder, and led her back to the TARDIS, where they could both get cleaned up.

Chapter Twenty-One
Farewells

The squalling weather outside seemed to have died down.

Kennet was tending to Greaves' wounds in a sheltered corner of the office. He'd upended the desk to offer them some protection from the solar radiation. But in the last few minutes the light reflected off the walls hadn't felt so scalding. The major had taken a medical pack from the sergeant's belt and was applying a tube of gel from it to the burns on Greaves' face. 'It's only antiseptic, Sergeant, hold still.'

Greaves winced. 'Permission to howl, sir?'

'Permission denied.' The major finished applying the gel, then stood up. Distant sounds were coming from the window. Engines. The wind had dropped to a level where he could hear them. And there was something about the taste of what was coming through the window. Burning, of course, but ... something about it felt like spring.

He cautiously reached a hand into the light, and it didn't burn. 'Smell the air, Greaves!' he said, excitedly. 'I think we're going to be all right!'

'Who's "we", sir?'

Kennet sighed heavily once more. 'Greaves...'

A teapot of exquisite Arts and Crafts design stood warming on the TARDIS console, gently reflecting the light that washed over it from the column that rose and fell with flight.

186

Alison stood with a cup of sugarless tea in her hands, only now feeling the full weight of what had happened to her over the last couple of days. She smiled at the thought of the tea. The Doctor had offered her sugar, but had seemed pleased when she'd turned it down. She wanted to go and sit in one of those big old armchairs by the fireplace, where there was now a blazing log fire, but there were only two of them, and with the Doctor out of the control room she didn't think she could. She'd only go to sleep anyway.

As soon as they'd got in, the Doctor had rushed her to an ornate bathroom, which seemed to be connected to some sort of swimming bath, perhaps even an entire health spa, and had waited on the other side of a marble wall while she tossed him her clothes. She'd only just eased herself into a bath that had prepared itself and smelt of all sorts of herbal concoctions (and was at just the right temperature) when a hanger with those same clothes on, all now clean and pressed, had been thrown back over that same wall to land elegantly on the hook.

The Doctor had only stayed in the control room, when she'd returned to it, long enough to offer and produce the tea. That left her with the Master, who had inclined his head in welcome from where he was reading amongst the book cases. But he didn't look particularly welcoming to her. He had an expression on his face that said something was troubling him, and perhaps Alison was it.

Which was why she had said nothing to him, just taken her tea and wandered, checking out the spines of some of the books. She could be wrong, but she thought the shelves were somehow reacting to her, offering up books she'd never heard of on subjects she found interesting. So much history. And so much of it written at the time, or in the far future. She reached for a history of now, a chronicle of the years 2003-2010. But then she withdrew her hand. She wasn't sure she wanted to know what they'd said, what the next few years were going to be like, if she was mentioned.

She realised with a little shock that she'd feel weird to think that she was going to be part of it.

So she'd walked away from the books and ended up in front of the old grandfather clock, its ticking slow and comfortable. She reached a hand up again to play with the hands, wondering what time could mean inside the TARDIS, but then a shadow fell over her, and she let her hand fall once again.

The Master was standing there, regarding her.

'This place is so huge,' she said.

'You have seen but a small part of it, my dear Miss Cheney.' He paused for a moment, and his voice became harder. 'Tell me, do you plan to stay long enough to explore?'

'Stay?' It was like he'd heard her most private thoughts.

'With us.'

She turned away a little. 'I don't think I've been invited.'

He laughed. It sounded gracious, full of bonhomie, but also somehow cold. '*He* would never invite you. And neither would I. Because I am by no means fond of you.'

'So why do you call me "my dear"?'

'I call everyone that.'

'Oh.'

'However, loath as I am to admit it, you offer him a companionship that I do not. One he has not allowed himself for a long time.'

Alison didn't want to keep looking him in the eye. She drank up and went to get herself another cup. To her surprise, the teapot seemed to be just as full as it had been before she'd poured this cup. 'What happened?' she asked, trying to sound casual with her back to him. 'To make him such an … emotional island?'

The Master sighed. 'It is for him to tell you the whole story. But… I think he sees an echo of it in you.'

188

'Have you always travelled with him?'

'By no means.' He came to stand close to her again. 'I was of aid to the Doctor after he had lost…' He paused and thought better of it. 'During the events that so damaged him. In return, he offered me a last chance for salvation.'

He reached up with one hand and, to her amazement, removed his face. She stared at the electronics that flashed away beneath. The eyes still followed her, and the complex muscles around the mouth still formed a half smile. 'An offer I was foolish enough to accept.'

He replaced the face plate, and flexed his features. 'As those who punish us are always sending us into danger. And I doubt we will ever, as the Doctor promised me at the start of this journey, reach the place he calls "Bognor Regis". Of one thing I am sure, however. He wants you to stay and share his exile.' He gently placed a hand on her arm, and she didn't feel scared at his touch. She felt now that he'd shown her something very important of himself also. 'Trust me.'

'Exile? Exile from what?'

That was, of course, the moment the Doctor chose to burst in, carrying an awkward bundle of umbrellas under his arm. He was spotless once more, every inch the gentleman again. Alison took a step quickly away from the Master, and realised with a smile that the Master had done exactly the same thing at the same moment. 'You left the umbrella stand in the Zeppelin hanger!' the Doctor cried accusingly at him. 'Again!'

Alison looked between them and quietly repeated the words to herself. 'Zeppelin hanger?'

The Doctor stepped out of the TARDIS and snapped open the largest of the umbrellas. It was pouring with rain. The sky was full of it, grey and white, across the dark green of a typically English field. Now, thankfully, there was typically English weather to go with it. The ship had landed in mud.

He helped Alison down off the step. She declined the smaller umbrella and accepted his arm under the larger one.

There was a road just ahead, and around the corner, the TARDIS's navigation systems had assured the Doctor, there would be the school where he'd set up his lab and Kennet had made his headquarters.

He had a heavy heart, despite the freshness of the rain. He hoped there wouldn't be a difficult conversation during this walk. He was very bad at those. His conversations with the Master never touched on emotional subjects. He just hoped things would work out without him having to do anything so terrible as to say anything more.

He took out his asthma inhaler and allowed himself a quick puff.

'Couldn't you have landed back at the school?' asked Alison, glancing up at the sky.

'My control over the old girl's a bit erratic. Shame that worm never told me how it works.'

'Couldn't you have got us back *after* it had stopped raining?'

'It won't.' The Doctor hopped over a swiftly forming puddle. 'Not for ages. The Earth needs to sort itself out. The English will love it. Probably conquer the world all over again.' His face fell for a moment. 'Which would be bad.'

'If I stayed with you, could we go back and see the pyramids? Find out who really built them?'

For a moment he thought about knocking that aside with a joke about how he didn't like to boast, but… But that would be cruel. He couldn't decide what was for the best, whether he was being selfish or not. And now he'd been silent too long. 'The TARDIS can travel to any time or place,' he said, finally.

She looked angry, was going to push him for a real answer, but thankfully from up ahead came the sound of an engine.

A jeep was approaching, driven by Greaves, with Kennet sat in the back and Joe beside him. They'd obviously been spotted from the school, or from one of the helicopters that were doubtless now flying again.

'Ah,' he said quickly, 'here comes your boyfriend. So all's well that ends well, eh?'

The jeep stopped beside them, and Kennet leapt out of the back to shake the Doctor's hand and slap him rather too heartily around the shoulder. 'Doctor! The Prime Minister and the US President want to thank you. The UN has already been in touch about a closed session. And I believe there's even talk of a parade!'

The Doctor glanced sidelong to where Alison and Joe were looking at each other. 'Oh, let's not get all mushy, Major. Leave that to the Shalka, eh?' He decided that he had no place here, finished shaking the man's hand, quickly turned to Alison, preparing to leave. 'So,' he said. 'This really is ... goodbye?'

He hadn't managed to keep the question out of his voice. But he did manage to turn and head off back to the TARDIS.

'Doctor, wait!' she called.

He turned back, looking puzzled. 'What on Earth for?'

He was aware that he was looking at her intently. But he wasn't sure what he was willing her to do.

He saw her decide. 'I have to say goodbye to Joe,' she said.

'What?' He smiled. As if this was a complete surprise.

'Alison?' Joe was staring at her, stunned.

Greaves had got out of the jeep. The Doctor strode over to him, intent on distracting the military men from Joe and Alison. 'Greaves, how fabulous, you've got a tan!'

'Permission to thump him, sir?'

'Suits you, Sergeant, good for you to get outside.' Kennet and the Doctor shared a look of mutual understanding as they walked a few paces away from where Alison and her boyfriend were having a very strained conversation.

'So,' said the Doctor. 'Tell me everything. Casualties, damage, the ecology. Don't spare me.'

Kennet smiled. 'Thousands. But not millions. Absolute hell. But hell that lasted a little under two hours. Thanks to you.'

The Doctor patted his arm. 'You may want to invest in boats. Sand bags are up, I hear. And the bottom will have dropped out of the sunbed market.'

He was looking at her like a drowned puppy. It was a look she'd expected, without having really realised it, for quite a few months now.

'The Doctor can drop me off at Mum's place,' she said.

'Why can't you come on the train with me?'

'Because I'm *bored*, Joe! I want to *do* something! This is my chance to travel in a time machine!'

He looked angry with her for a moment. But beneath that, there was something kind. The look that had made her care about him in the first place. He looked across to the Doctor and called out. 'Doctor, how do you know you'll be able to get her back?'

The Doctor looked surprised at Joe, and almost pleased. 'Time machine, Joe. She's probably back there already. Go on, phone up her Mum and see.'

Joe took his mobile from his pocket, and had to look in the memory for the number. 'Hello, Mrs Cheney?' he said when he'd got through. 'Is Alison there?'

He listened for a moment, then cut the call.

'Oh, I see,' he said, looking at her. 'You're not.'

Alison looked between the two men, or rather the man and the alien. The former was hurt, but had assumed the best. The latter was pleased, but had assumed the worst. Or at least, some worry about the future was making him frown.

'Well,' she told them both. 'I guess now we know, don't we?'

Joe closed his eyes, then tenderly put his hands to her face, and kissed her forehead. 'Don't forget your keys.'

She showed them to him. 'I'll see you soon.'

She turned to see that the Doctor and Kennet were walking off again towards the TARDIS. They'd nearly got there. Kennet was consulting a palmtop, reading off items to the Doctor, who was nodding along, looking serious.

She took a last look at Joe, wanted to kiss him, but knew that would feel joyful and inappropriate, and ran off after them.

Joe stayed where he was.

'Doctor!' she called out, catching up with them.

Kennet had raised his hands, having obviously come to the end of a long list of reasons why the Doctor should stay. 'Doctor, you can't just saunter off again! Not on your own!'

The Doctor's eyes met Alison's, and he grinned. 'You're right, Major. Not on my own!'

He took her arm once more, and fished in his pocket for the TARDIS key.

'Erm, Doctor!' Kennet stayed where he was, looking a little uncertain of himself.

'Yes, Major?'

'You don't…' the soldier squared his shoulders and made it sound like an entirely routine request, 'fancy an extra hand?'

The Doctor threw back his head and laughed. And after a moment, Kennet smiled too. 'Not enough room, Major,' he cried, his eyes sparkling with the obvious lie of it. 'She's smaller than she looks!'

To Alison's horror, the sounds of take-off had begun from the ship.

'Ah, the Master wants to go…' The Doctor glanced back to Kennet, his eyes interrogating him, just making sure for a moment that he hadn't overstepped the mark. He looked, for a moment, like he'd been when Alison had first met him, afraid of everything he did. He'd changed so much, she realised, just in that time. She looked forward to seeing what he did next.

The Doctor's confidence wasn't misplaced anymore. Kennet shook his head, sighing in mock resignation. He raised a hand in farewell, and the Doctor grinned back, and guided Alison to the TARDIS door.

'Does it always have to make that awful racket?' she asked as he fumbled with his key.

'I'm afraid you'll have to get used to that.'

'Is there anything else that I'll have to get used to?'

'Ship's rules!' The door swung open, and he ushered her inside. 'No running, no jumping, no pushing ... and no slapping!'

She tutted at him as the doors closed behind them. She was also looking forward to the two of them seeing what there was to see in all of time and space.

Kennet went back to where Greaves was telling Joe that he had a cousin who Joe really ought to meet. A fellow doctor, actually. And Joe had just started to say that he'd had just about enough of doctors.

But then Kennet took them by the shoulders, and turned them to look at what was happening in the field across the way. Something that none of them might see again, and had never thought they would see before.

The TARDIS dematerialised, leaving only the shape of itself in the mud.

The Doctor and his friends were off on another adventure.

The Making of 'Scream of the Shalka'
By Paul Cornell

The first thing I knew about any of this was an e-mail that was forwarded to me by my agent. It came from Jelena Djordjevic, a producer in the field of development at BBCi. It asked me if I'd be interested in writing a new BBCi *Doctor Who* animation project.

I calmly called my agent back and told her that, upon mature reflection, I would indeed be interested in such a project, at least to the point of getting a meeting together. Then I jumped around the room yelling.

It came at a good time for me. I'd just been dropped from two TV series at once (and I'd yet to talk to the various old pros who told me that it happens all the time), probably because I'd been writing for them both at once. My confidence was at an all-time low. And here I was being given something I'd always wanted to do.

I called up Jelena and arranged the meeting, then called up my old friend Rob Francis at BBCi and asked what this woman was like. 'Sitting next to me,' was the first line of his reply, but he assured me that Jelena was 'a force for good'. Rob's going to be famous one day. He's BBCi's bold venturer into LA, the one who gets invited to Amber Benson's parties, the one who has a monster in the *Buffy* X-Box game named after his e-mail handle. He weighs things up carefully and has a very cool head.

I immediately assumed that I'd got this gig because Rob and James Goss (the BBCi producer, who I vaguely knew from conventions) had spoken up for me, because that's how writers get most of their work, through word of mouth, but that turned out not to be the case. I'd worked with a BBCi producer called Martha Hillier before, and she'd been the one given the responsibility of finding a writer for *Who*. She'd consulted several other producers, and my name came up a couple of times. Meanwhile, James Goss and Martin Trickey (the executive producer of *Shalka*, who I'd also worked with before) were apparently reading all sorts of *Who* work, doing their own author search.

Anyhow, however it happened, there I was. I came in to BBC Centre House for an initial meeting with Jelena, Martin and James. Martin explained what was going on. The success of the webcast version of *Shada* had made BBCi more confident than ever that its webcasts were reaching a big audience, an audience that went beyond the bounds of *Doctor Who* fandom. Also, the animation provided by Cosgrove Hall for *The Ghosts of Albion*, a webcast on their *Buffy* site, had convinced them that it was possible to create a truly animated *Doctor Who*, not as *Shada* had been, an audio play with limited animation illustrating it. Thirdly, the existence of Big Finish's *Doctor Who Unbound* plays had made BBCi aware that the BBC in general were no longer worried about the idea of regenerating the Doctor. BBC Films had been pursuing, for many years, a film deal based on the property, and that department had always previously insisted that no new Doctor be cast, thinking it would spoil any future announcement of their own new Doctor. As Martin Trickey discovered when he went to talk to them, and to people like Alan Yentob, who'd expressed an interest in *Doctor Who* in the past, every relevant department of the BBC was now happy to see a new BBC Doctor. As it turned out, of course, they were happy to see two. But nobody knew that then.

This is proof of Martin's formidable negotiating skills. He's the most gentle of men, but he really knows his facts, and anyone arguing with him has to be prepared to face down a barrage of precisely chosen information, all delivered with a slightly bemused smile. James and Martin together are like good cop/bad cop, or rather lovely, sweet cop and nice, well-informed and, you know, really-actually-the-boss cop. James is one of the nicest men I've ever met, someone who just wants everyone to have a nice time and get on. His ability to diffuse tension comes through actually dragging the tension out of a room into himself. He suffered more than any of us over the various stresses of the production, particularly during his first encounters with fandom. He'd been a fan as a kid, and knows what a Drashig is, but had never linked up with organised fandom and is still deciding how close he wants to get to it.

Martin and James had decided that the biggest possible splash could be made by regenerating the Doctor and, by our second meeting, they'd confirmed that they could do that. Together, they and the rest of BBCi's Cult section (Ann Kelly, Daniel Judd and Rob) had come up with a shortlist of possible Doctors. It was split into areas like young and old, male and female, and included all ethnicities. One name kept coming up.

Meanwhile, a start had to be made on the story. Jelena and I went for lunch in the BBC canteen. I was raised as a BBC boy, in love with the corporation, in awe that a building like TV Centre could be a box of mysteries where *Basil Brush*, *The Goodies* and Terry Wogan lived side by side with *Doctor Who*. It still gives me a little thrill that one of the doormen at Centre House has started to recognise me. 'Coming in to talk about something else that'll never get off the ground, sir?' he says, in my fantasies. He's far too polite to do that in real life. So it was lovely that here I was, finally, in the place I'd always wanted to do this, doing it. I was eating an apple and planning new *Doctor Who*. I tried to seem blasé about it.

Jelena was straightforward, funny, and as I swiftly discovered, good with story. She had made a small yelp of surprise and pointed at me accusingly when I had replied to some continuity joke that Rob made, which pleased me: they'd hired me because I was a writer, not because I was a fan. She knew nothing about *Doctor Who*, which, I assured her, was a strength. I had to be able to convince her that what I came out with would work dramatically. I couldn't play the 'it works because it's *Doctor Who*' card. We discussed what story shapes *Doctor Who* had used in the past, and I talked about how, even with the 'infinite budget' of animation, a traditional *Doctor Who* feel depended to some small extent on budget limitations. We still needed to represent a small community of people under threat by a hostile alien force that hasn't, as yet, completely shown its hand. The alternative would be vast cosmic battles, but everyone saw that going there would lose us some of that *Who* feeling. The real trick would be to do 'base under siege' and then pull back the focus to show the widescreen picture that animation could give us.

Step one was the monsters. There should be some, they should be the main threat, and they should be an entire race of them, an attempt to create something new, in other words, in the classic *Who* monster tradition. Martin wanted to make this threat ultra special, to make it universe-shattering, a thought that we kept in our heads throughout the development process, and which I personally thought was a bit of a trap. So many *Who* projects have floundered by attempting to be about 'the greatest adventure of' or 'the biggest danger in the history of' our hero. But three drafts in, I was able to satisfy Martin's note by making the Shalka the 'great limiting factor' of the cosmos, the reason that civilisation doesn't spread everywhere. I'd recently read Stephen Baxter's

Manifold series of SF novels, which ask the same question: mathematical projections indicate that civilised alien life should have passed through Earth's stellar neighbourhood at least twice by now, so why haven't they? What stops great galactic civilisations from arising? In the *Who* universe, the answer to that question is the Shalka. And I think in retrospect that Martin was right to give us that motivation.

The other factor that shaped the Shalka was the matter of design. The shape of the snake is one of two fears that every baby is born imprinted with, an instinct to get away from the danger they represent in the wild. (The other such fear is that of the spider.) Television *Who* had done snakes on a couple of occasions in the past, but the shape was one which live-action effects had a great deal of trouble achieving in a convincing way, and thus natural new ground for us to break using animation. Besides that, it was easier and quicker for animators to make such monsters move convincingly than it would be for them to work on humanoid villains.

Here's the first note I wrote on the monsters, which shows how far our thinking proceeded afterwards:

The SHALAKOR are a race of intelligent parasites that spread from world to world via meteorites. They consume the by-products of industrial technology, so they prefer to feast on inhabited worlds where the carbon cycle is out of control. They seed the crust of a planet with their stone-like eggs, then create two black holes, one at either pole of the planet, which they slam together at the centre of the world to detonate it, sending their eggs flying off into the cosmos at close to the speed of light, ready to infest more worlds. They themselves are all killed in the process, but they see this as a worthy sacrifice, for the ongoing life of their species.

* * *

199

The SHALAKOR are silicon-based creatures, made of brittle rock, made mobile by magnetic force fields and lava-like blood in their bodies. They're like living statues. They can swim through volcanic rock by using their vibrational powers to liquefy it in front of them. They have greater difficulty with other kinds of rock, and prefer to remain below ground, where they feel most secure. SHALAKOR soldiers are normally snakelike in form, but they have a humanoid cast of leaders and planners, and also breed giant snakeforms and other specialities. They have complete control over what forms their eggs produce.

The SHALAKOR evolved as predators of carbon-based life on their own world, where they competed with a humanoid technological species. They won that contest by detonating their own world, becoming a purely space-faring, nomad species. Their culture is entirely based on what genetic memories remain in the race memory of the egg. They regard carbon-based life as not really alive, not really intelligent, entirely expendable. Before destroying a world, they get the industries there to pump out as much waste and carbon as possible, so they can feed well and have their Breeders create as many eggs as possible.

The environmental aspect was something Jelena suggested early on, and I welcomed a chance to give the story an ethical 'oomph', not only because of my own green concerns, but because such ideas had often informed the traditional *Who* we were trying to emulate.

The reasons for the changes made to the above plans are interesting: I felt, in the end, that the Shalka (as they came to be renamed after a scary encounter with that other top predator, the Orca, at Kelly Tarlton's Underwater World in Auckland, New Zealand) would look rather ridiculously 'metaphorical' if they fed directly on industrial products. Our initial thought was that they were simply boosting the carbon emissions of factories and power stations all over the world, which would have been too cheesy for words. Also, their desire for self sacrifice, and their lack of contact with other members of their species somehow limit their ability to be *Who* monsters in the classic style. I'd initially given them a religious aspect – Kennet and the soldiers find the bodies of the meteorologists in an early draft, covered in symbols – and made them fanatics, but I came to feel, along with the whole team, that we just didn't want to go there, even if that would make the aliens a truly modern nightmare. Their plan, plus the magnetic fields that hold their bodies together, in this version, also makes no reference to their central ability, the sonic scream.

They're a bit all over the place, they don't mean and do one big thing, as *Who* monsters should (the Cybermen want us to be like them, the Daleks want to exterminate). Quite late on, we were still toying with the idea that the Shalka would get their slaves to mix and release chemicals to alter the atmosphere, making great metal release spheres in the factories. But, again, this gives them an awkward lack of focus, and also allows the humans an easy means of halting their plans.

It was Jelena who guided me towards logic on all these matters, and insisted that the Shalka should be about their scream, and she was absolutely right.

It also doesn't help that the above plot reminds one somewhat of the Sixth Doctor story 'The Twin Dilemma'. It's very difficult to write a traditional *Doctor Who* story without going over old ground. I was determined that I wouldn't go the route that some very traditional *Who* stories of recent years go: parading a series of the show's 'greatest hits' in terms of plot points and dialogue, and hoping that nostalgia will do the job. But I didn't expect to fall at the first hurdle by completely duplicating an old plot!

Other differences between the original plot and where we finally went included the fact that Alison Cheney was initially to be a cinema usher, because I'd talked to Martin early on about this being a 'base under siege' *Who* story that made use of modern city locations like multiplex cinemas. (This time it was incoming producer Muirinn Lane Kelly who insisted that if I wanted Alison to be an 'everywoman' then she should have the most ordinary possible job.) The Master was originally intended to be a hologram of a previous Doctor. I'd suggested the Fifth because I thought his kind and open personality would provide a nice contrast with our rather more harsh and edgy Doctor. But two thoughts struck me over the weekend of the Gallifrey One convention in Los Angeles: firstly that holograms had been done to death in previous telefantasy; secondly that it would be much more interesting to give our Doctor a virtual companion who he could have a complicated, somewhat dangerous relationship with. The Master, in his new form, could be someone programmed to do the nastier things that our emotionally wounded and defensive Doctor couldn't bring himself to do. I remembered whispering that in Ann Kelly's ear in the bar one night. Ann is a great judge of when something's logical and when it isn't. She's also garrulous and loves a party. And, fortunately, she can keep secrets like a safe.

The last big change was that the geologists in the opening scene (who appeared in the second draft because we all felt there was some upfront threat missing if we just started with the Doctor) were initially doing their work in Iceland.

Perhaps it's at this point that the huge contribution made to this story by New Zealand and New Zealanders should be mentioned. My wife Caroline and myself had delayed our honeymoon by a year because we'd been so busy. Having finally settled that we were flying off to New Zealand in early April of 2003, it came as some surprise to get my dream commission a couple of weeks before I was due to vanish for over a month. (I'd just failed to be considered for an ITV drama series for exactly that reason.) I told BBCi that I'd be in touch via my laptop, and would be able to deliver multiple drafts of the plot from down under. (I e-mailed in the first draft on the day before I left, or so I thought.)

We landed in Auckland in the early hours, and like my meteorologist, were immediately struck by how clean the air was. The environmental themes of Shalka were to be reinforced by five weeks living in a country where the environment is the central issue. We drove down the west coast of the North Island in a camper van, having met up with Paul Scoones, the editor of New Zealand's premier fanzine *TSV*, and his wife Rochelle in Auckland. We'd got to the lovely city of Hamilton before I checked in at a cybercafé, and found, to my mild annoyance, that the *Shalka* plot hadn't reached the BBC. Something in their firewall of anti-virus programs had rejected the enclosure of the plot document itself. Annoyance turned to panic when I found that the floppy disc drive of my laptop had been damaged, so I couldn't simply take the document out on a floppy, put it in a cybercafé computer and send it again. No café was willing or able to physically attach my computer to their system. (One lovely lady in a particular cybercafé tried to move heaven and earth for us when she learnt I'd worked for *Casualty*, her favourite show, but the technology defeated us.) So BBCi had to face the prospect of not getting their plot for another five weeks, when the stern deadline of a November release had been drummed into us all as being only just achievable as it was.

In short, I was facing losing my dream commission.

We'd popped in to see Jon Preddle, a New Zealand fan of long standing, when we arrived in Hamilton. He kindly let us have use of a printer so we at least had a hard copy from that point.

But, of course, as the document headed '*Doctor Who*' came out of the printer, Jon stared. He understood right away what he was looking at. I'd signed some vast secrecy agreements about this project, and now had to get Jon to agree not to mention it as well. I'd been asked on convention panels if I thought the show would ever come back, or if I would ever write for it again, and had fended off such questions as best I could. Or sometimes just lied. Online I'd been asked who I'd cast as a new Doctor, told the questioner it would be Richard E. Grant, and then worried about it for days afterwards. Myself and the rest of the BBCi bods had been guests at the wonderful Gallifrey One convention in Los Angeles that February, and had managed drunken revelry in the bar as always, amongst crowds of fans and friends, without having given away the secret that made us smile to each other. I'm not ashamed about any of that, it's my job to keep the secrets that my bosses want kept. However, it was difficult spending a lovely afternoon in Wellington, in a coffee shop with Gary Russell, later that holiday, without mentioning anything to him. He was such great company, as he always is, and I felt like a complete Judas. (Despite the assurances that BBCi had been giving me all along the line that this project wouldn't affect future webcasts being Big Finish productions.) But orders are orders. When it came to the time for Big Finish to be told about the project, James called them first, and I called immediately afterwards to tell Gary it was me that was doing it. He was the first person outside BBCi to offer me his congratulations, and has been very kind when he could have been horrible, which is why this book is dedicated to him.

To Jon Preddle's eternal credit, he kept the secret completely, and thus I kept my job. I decided to fax the hard copy from his bank to the BBC. We travelled to Waitomo Caves hopefully, and I found a lady at a tourist information office there willing to let me try to fax thirty pages of type-script to the other side of the world. But there were technical problems, and the problem of the bill … it would have cost over five hundred pounds! I decided that a few days wouldn't make much difference either way, put the plot in an envelope, and put it in the mail. As I let go of it into the post box I asked the lady how long it might take to get there. 'Six, seven weeks…' she replied.

I'm sure they could hear my scream in Centre House.

I still don't know if Jelena ever got that package.

Finally, under the impression I was suffering the effects of some kind of curse, I managed to call a friend of Caroline's back home in the UK. I got him to break into our house, acti-vate my computer, and re-send the plot to … well, everyone even vaguely involved, just in case. It worked, and I could continue my honeymoon, with lengthy plotting sessions being conducted between me and Jelena over a mobile phone late at night on campsites in the middle of a very lovely nowhere.

When it came to submitting the next draft of the plot, Jelena took my horrified screams of frustration to Martin, who just placidly said that I should enjoy my honeymoon and get back to the plot when I got home!

So the rest of our holiday was spent enjoying that wondrous country, not giving away the secret to any more people, and walking, astonished, through many volcanic land-scapes. (Most of them having played some part in the *Lord of the Rings* movies.)

By the time I got back to Britain, I had a new draft of the plot ready to send, and was immediately able to get to work on the script for the first episode. Minor changes were made all the time, for instance, in early drafts all the Shalka can talk as well as scream. This became problematic, as one of the things that had become a bit 'of its time' I thought about previous *Doctor Who* was the conversations monsters tended to have among themselves. It's what Gareth Roberts calls 'squabbling rubber', where various ranks of monsters (usually just two of them) discuss their plans, perhaps argue a bit, and declare that everything is 'excellent'. The limited vocabulary of such scenes indicates that their credibility had become suspect: they had already got to a point where they were only playable without inducing laughter by treading very carefully. We decided that the less the Shalka talked, the more dangerous they would seem. It would give them a worrying power in the face of the Doctor's continual monologue.

Another major change, and a very welcome one, was that after the first draft of the first episode I was told that I should write not for audio, with added notes for the animators, with the thought being that the script should make absolute sense to those who couldn't see the pictures, but as a full animation script, meaning that the final version wouldn't be slowed down with characters describing what everyone could see. That confidence in the animation was already there at BBCi.

I wasn't party to the animation process itself, so Cosgrove Hall will have to forgive me. Hopefully the full story of their vast contribution can be told elsewhere, with many illustrations.

Sometime after the first draft of the first episode had been written, I was told that Jelena would be moving onto a script-editing apprenticeship on *Doctors*. I wished her well: she'd always wanted to go into production, and had been working on *Who* while waiting for that opening to come up. Here's Jelena herself on her time on the show:

I got involved with Doctor Who *very late in my life. I had a lot of catching up to do and had a lot of people explaining what it was all about. Cheers guys. I took what I learnt on board and decided with the good people of BBC Cult that we had an opportunity to do something other than what had been created so far. I then realised that was quite easy for me, not so easy for the* Who *aficionados on the team. Sometimes lack of knowledge is a wonderful thing. Not so wonderful for the guys when I upped and left them after the initial script idea was formulated. I'm glad that my departure to daytime TV didn't stand in the way of what is undoubtedly an exciting adventure for a new Doctor. May he have many adventures and let's hope I can be involved till the finish post next time.*

Our new producer would be one Muirinn Lane Kelly.

Muirinn is a sharp, engaging, very social, team player. She has big ideas, she applies them to the matter at hand, and she likes you to argue back. Before coming to us, she'd been on *Grease Monkeys*. She's also earned my eternal respect for having a hand in creating the 'blobs' that spout lines from the BBC archives to hilarious effect between programmes on BBC3. She brought with her her own gang of contacts, largely drawn from the theatre, but also from a social life that I can only stare at, blinking in astonishment. For instance, for a long time she was talking to one of the biggest British pop stars about appearing in *Shalka*, and another rock star (and secret *Who* fan) under Muirinn's encouragement nearly persuaded his Hollywood actress girlfriend to take part!

Muirinn, once more, knew nothing about *Who*. She had to be persuaded to stop referring to him as a super hero.

She learnt swiftly, and by the end of the production was declaring confidently that 'the Doctor doesn't swear' when Richard added a (very mild) oath to one of his lines. She seems in control of everything at all times, the ideal quality for a producer.

Muirinn took me for a meeting in her office, and immediately asked me all the most basic questions about the project. For example, why did I want to write *Doctor Who*? I replied that it was because I'd been bullied in the playground, and suddenly found myself coming out with a little essay I seemed to have had in my head all my life, which touched on all the things that *Who* actually means to me. I think she does that a lot, finds out what makes people tick like that, where the passion is. If I'd said 'because it's a television institution' or 'it's a laugh, innit?' I think things would have proceeded a lot less smoothly.

She was responsible for casting the show, choosing the director, and asking the most central question, until it became, rightly, the most important thing we were thinking about: what was the Doctor going to be like?

From the start, I'd decided that we shouldn't do a regeneration scene. They're only really sustainable in a show which is going to run for many more weeks and will be around long enough to give you a solid grounding in the character of the lead. What you don't want, for new viewers, especially new viewers who are going to get a fifteen minute dose, is a lead who is confused, isn't himself, and is recovering from a process that in itself points out that there's a huge backstory here that they don't understand.

I wanted the Doctor mobile, himself and whole from moment one, and that was one of those decisions that everyone just ran with, because there isn't really an alternative. The other good thing about this strategy was that it got out of the way of BBC Books and Big Finish, not providing them with a solid, limiting end to their Eighth Doctor stories, not stepping on their toes. I was determined that this production took care not to erase or alter anyone's continuity, in the hope that those who had been cared for might thus accept and adopt us.

That implies that the ninth incarnation has been the Doctor for some time. But how long? The change having been made only recently would say to the audience that they missed something. So it's going to have happened a while back. And that while gives us time to give the new Doctor a little bit of backstory, a few character hints that suggest that he's different to what we've seen before, that he's moved on, and that, again for the sake of the other storytellers in this universe, exciting and big things are going to happen in their continuities, stories that they're free to tell. It will hopefully intrigue the viewer in the way a hero with a secret often does. And not only that, it gently says that this isn't just a rehashing of old material, something so in awe of the past that it's constrained by it. The message should be: this is the same old Doctor, but his life has continued.

I like *Doctor Who* to be gothic. I like the hints of gothic romanticism that inform the character of the Doctor in the Jon Pertwee and Tom Baker eras. When I was a kid, I almost found the character of the Doctor as scary as the monsters, and the TARDIS, and everything about the show. Here was, after all, a man who specialised in monsters, and a vast magical box that might contain more of them. He came from that world of threat and terror, even if he was a good force within it. The unpredictability and anger of a man who wasn't reassuring or comfortable was something I wanted to bring to the Ninth Doctor. And it would be good if he had a reason for being like that, a gothic secret, something that drove him … it all came together.

It's also nice to be able to give the lead character an emotional journey in his initial presentation to the audience, somewhere for him to go. He needs to change at the start of this story, and Alison gives him the chance to do it. But not so much, hopefully, that we think he's going to be vastly different again the next time we meet. In effect, we did the things regeneration is for, rather than doing a regeneration.

Here are my initial notes on the character of the Ninth Doctor:

The DOCTOR is a hero. An alien. Unpredictable, witty, the absolute master of sudden and resolute action. He improvises brilliantly, using his vast experience of the universe and a pocket full of useful bits and pieces. Not part of any organisation or system, resenting having to work within such. He's an intellectual, he'll always go for the peaceful solution when he can see it. He prefers the little to the big, the domestic to the grand. He's asexual, unattracted to humans. Or perhaps to anyone. Or perhaps his great degree of civilisation and kindness just mean he's above that sort of thing. He's incredibly brave and angry at cruelty.

BUT: not long ago he lost someone he cared about. Maybe he couldn't do anything to stop it. Maybe it wasn't his fault. But from now on he's not going to have anyone close to him that could possibly get harmed, so he can rely on his own instincts and skills without having to look out for someone else all the time. It's made him harder and colder inside, and completely unwilling to trust anything but his own judgement.

Perhaps he's lost the little stuff a bit and, to save himself from pain, now only deals with the big stuff. He's more at home battling monsters than having scones for tea.

Which is wrong for him. Not what he's really like. So this story is about him regaining the little things in life by meeting ALISON and letting her into his life.

I'm amazed I got through that without saying 'never cruel or cowardly'. I'd still stand by all of that.

How the Doctor looks is at least as important as what he does, and I had some solid ideas there too. Here's my original description:

He wears a sombre Edwardian suit, in black or dark brown, with boots and waistcoat. He could walk down an Edwardian street without anyone looking twice. No eccentric additions, no question marks. Perhaps a college scarf (Keble), when it's cold. Pocket watch, gloves when cold, a big floppy handkerchief.

Some of which has been altered (for the better) by Cosgrove Hall, who decided on the cape. But the general thrust of it, that these should be clothes rather than a costume, is something everybody ran with.

The matter of choosing a new companion isn't something which one can approach lightly either. Here are my original notes about Alison:

ALISON is taking a year out before starting her degree in history. She's working at a cinema to pay her way and to see lots of movies. She lives at home with her MUM, DAD, and little brother, KEV. She doesn't have a boyfriend right now. She's waiting for someone amazing to come along at university: she's set her sights on the unobtainable.

When the monsters came, she got just as scared as everyone else. She'd love to do something brave, but is waiting for something that would work. She's seen too many people killed to do anything stupid.

She seizes on the DOCTOR as the one unafraid person, the hero who's going to save them all. And she swiftly gets completely bowled over by him, amazed by who he is and what he represents.

Until it becomes clear that he's only looking at the big picture, and doesn't care so much about the small stuff. That he doesn't do the warmer human feelings anymore. That, she doesn't like. She tries to get him to talk about it, but he won't. ALISON wants the DOCTOR to be a very human hero, producing a tension that he can't quite resolve between his origins and how he appears.

In the end, of course, he decides that he likes her, that he wants someone around, that he still likes the parts of his character that she wants to encourage.

ALISON has always wanted to see the past: her heroes include Napoleon and Churchill, and she really wants to meet them. She's open to all sorts of adventure, and regards the idea of visiting other worlds in the TARDIS as a gleeful emotional rollercoaster. She does the frivolous stuff he's still wary of: looking down the wrong alley on an alien planet. She's too inexperienced to know what's dangerous, and is sure the DOCTOR will get her out of it. She wakes him up like having a kid wakes up a staid parent. But in many ways she's his intellectual equal: he can't see the point in studying history, it's just stuff to hop past, but to her it's a weave of cause and effect.

Soon, the DOCTOR and ALISON are going to be best friends. But one always suspects that, given the slightest hint, she'd want it to be more than that.

James Goss had made two big suggestions at the start of this whole process. Firstly, he wanted there to be a sweet and rather mad old lady in the story, because he liked characters like that, so I found Mathilda for him. Secondly, he thought that a good place for a companion to begin, in a story which touched on a real world setting in what was hopefully a very modern BBC way, would be as half of a relationship that had come to a natural end. In a very early draft of the plot, Prime (or Control as the character was called then), took over the body of Alison's boyfriend by covering him in boiling lava, and that was why he had a humanoid shape.

James Goss takes up the story:

We at BBCi originally had the idea that the Doctor's companions should be a couple who'd just split up. After all, what could be worse than being lost in time with the last person in the universe you wanted to see? Not being writers, we all thought this was very funny. Especially leading to lots of fun if one or other companion developed a crush on the Doctor, with hilarious consequences. Paul naturally nodded and smiled when we explained this to him. He's a professional. He knows not to let on when he's being sold a lemon. He then delivered a treatment in which Alison and her boyfriend argued, split up ... and then he got boiled alive by lava. Thus neatly cutting out any potential love triangle japes.

Paul sweetly explained that there's a difference between setting up a healthy tension between two of your main characters, and having them behaving unsympathetically all the time. You can't just introduce them as unhappy, miserable people, constantly bickering and then expect your audience to care for them deeply. So, out went the boyfriend, and in came the family. By the time Joe came back, he'd changed completely. And was rather adorable in his own, puzzled way.

I remember seeing Craig Kelly flicking through the script.

'I'm not coming back, am I?' he sighed.

Of course, there are a lot of other daft, and not so daft, ideas that were batted around. There was a point when (hahaha) we were toying with keeping the identity of the Doctor secret. Paul suggested having the TARDIS materialise, and a strangely dressed stranger emerge, sniff the air, and then walk off in an eccentric way. Richard E. Grant then emerges from the TARDIS, waves at the shuffling eccentric and says 'Bye then!'

Another idea that could, frankly, have been rubbish, was the Doctor's mobile phone. This was one of Jelena's suggestions. She was quite cross that, for some reason, the Doctor didn't have one. 'I can understand that he doesn't have sex. That's fine. But what's wrong with him having a phone?'

And it's true. We were a bit nervous about the idea. But there was no reason we should be. After all, the Doctor used phones and radios all the time in the TV series. I think the thing we were most scared of was the phone turning into a magical gimmick: not just a phone, but also a sonic screwdriver, gun, force-field-scrambler and portable food machine. As it was, Paul was very careful. It's just a phone. A part of the TARDIS, yes, but just a phone.

Well, most of the time. It's only more than a phone once. And this caused a fair amount of contention. We were all nervous about the Doctor's phone suddenly having the power to transport him back to the TARDIS. But Paul did have the Doctor falling down into a wormhole with no other way out. And he argued (very persuasively) that, if we showed the phone doing this just once, and explained that this was the only time it could ever do this, we'd then established that the Doctor had a phone, but that it no longer had any exciting McGuffin powers.

* * *

In the end, as James says, we wrote the boyfriend out altogether, and gave Alison a family instead. In the first drafts, the family all had small speaking parts.

It took Muirinn to say that the family, including a small child who had two lines, were a waste of resources, and that Alison could just as easily talk to a single character, which took us back to the boyfriend.

By this time, the scripts were almost ready to roll. It was time to turn what had only existed on the printed page into something real.

I first met Wilson Milam at a meeting at Centre House. He had a vastly annotated copy of the script, and some serious questions. Wilson's about eight feet tall, with a careful Seattle drawl, and a laconic calm that sometimes erupts into great, enthusiastic energy. You immediately know when you meet him that you're in the presence of a safe pair of hands. He'd only worked in the theatre previously, and he brought from that experience a heavy emphasis on logic and character. He'd again had no previous experience of *Who*, and watching him apply his powers to this new field was an exciting experience.

His first question to me was: 'So how come Prime doesn't need to scream when it descends into the earth?' And I realised that Prime should indeed do that. There were lots of similar points, where Wilson had interrogated the logic of what I'd been doing and found it wanting. His advice, and at several points his dialogue, rounded and supported what I'd written in a wonderful way.

The first thing he did was to work on the scream, booking the recording studio before time so that he and the sound engineers could play on the same afternoon that Muirinn locked me in her office for a final burst of rewrites based on Wilson's notes. Those are the moments a writer loves, working against the clock with a team who are all committed and all pulling in the same direction.

Wilson's lack of knowledge of *Who* went from the point where he was calling the lead character 'Mister Who' to the point where he took me aside during recording and said: 'There are separate mini-genres within this genre, aren't there? Would this story be what you call "base under siege"?' He'd eaten up a pile of reference books that James had lent him (including James' own beloved and felt-tip pen benoted copy of Peter Haining's *A Celebration*) and had gone from neophyte to informed cultural critic in two weeks. Some of my favourite times during the production process were when Wilson called me up, usually long after everyone else's working day had finished, and would knock lines and character readings back and forth, always looking for something more, something better. His ability to coax added depths out of actors and his energy and desire were all revelations to me. He's going to be huge.

I'll let Wilson take up the story in his own words:

I had the time of my life working on Scream of the Shalka. *I'd watched* Doctor Who *wren growing up in Seattle and loved it, not least because it was a doubly foreign world for me, involving as it did not only alternate galaxies and time travel, but also a foreign country with radically different accents, clothing, and hairstyles, which I was completely unfamiliar with.*

So working on Scream *was a chance to reacquaint myself with the Doctor knowing much more than I did then, as well as the added bonus of – having become a director in the interim between those early TV days and actually coming to London – being able to work with actors I'd long admired, all of whom threw themselves into this alternate world we were creating.*

It was a gorgeously collaborative effort from the start, from early meetings with the producers and the writer working out the intricacies of just what a Shalka invasion involves, to the sound engineers pioneering the way forward on what a Shalka scream actually sounds like, to all the actors riffing off each other trying to get that extra added moment out of a scene … even if the scene at hand happened to involve the reaction of a dozen smallish Shalka hissing at your best efforts at singing show tunes.

Things I will always remember: the sound studio coming to a halt one afternoon over the question of whether the TARDIS could start up before the Doctor was actually inside (yes); working out the sound of Prime splitting out of its humanoid form into a proper Shalka shape; figuring out just what would be the sound of Shalkas exploding all round the world. But always, always, always, I will remember days and days of listening to various and sundry options of Shalka attack screams, Shalka communication screams, Shalka hissing screams … screams and screams and screams.

I hope we've honoured the brilliant Doctor Who *tradition, and I hope this new addition will keep the* Doctor Who *spirit alive for both old and new audiences.*

Muirinn and Wilson vanished at this point, whispered some magic words at various celebrity nightspots, and returned with a cast. (There are some things that writers just don't get to see.)

Top of the list was Richard E. Grant. He'd been the name staring out at us from the possible cast lists for months. I took care, while I was writing the scripts, to watch some of his *Scarlet Pimpernel* episodes, and wrote the character especially for him. Sir Percy's double life said things about the Doctor: his outward confidence, his inner vulnerability as displayed by his cutting and sometimes caustic wit, and his sheer joy at defeating an enemy he's passionately opposed to. I didn't re-watch his appearance in Steven Moffat's comedy *Who* episodes *The Curse of Fatal Death*, enjoyable as it was (I'm a huge fan of it, and besides, Steven was my best man), chiefly because I remembered the most vital thing about it: that Richard E. Grant had successfully defined a Doctor's character in thirty seconds of screen time, having never heard of or seen the series before that date.

I was also very pleased by the casting of Sophie Okonedo as Alison. Sophie had recently appeared in *Spooks* and the movie *Dirty Pretty Things* and has some real depth as an actor. I thought she and Richard would strike sparks off each other.

The read-through is something a writer dreads. You've put a lot of time and energy into your dialogue, and then you're locked in a room with a bunch of actors who, quite normally and professionally, will read it through as if they're reading from the phone book, or worse, adopt funny voices or horribly overplay it. That's just how it always goes. Acting at a read-through is actually regarded as being a bit of a no-no, as it can be seen as an attempt by the actors to overrule the director, whose plans for the piece are at that point not known.

This is also the point where the script ceases to be the writer and script editor's baby, and is given completely over to the director and actors. From here on, the writer is only present in the production as a courtesy: one's work here is done.

Knowing all this, I was determined to show up at TV Centre on Friday 13 June (there's an auspicious date!) with not a care in the world, determined to smile along at everything and not worry if Richard E. Grant decided to play the Doctor as a sperm whale.

I was to be pleasantly surprised. We all trooped in to find Richard, the thinnest man I've ever met, sitting rather nervously watching daytime TV in the plush meeting room set aside for the read-through. He was polite, a little distant, uncertain. He seems from his own writing to be someone who has great difficulties with being famous, who likes people not to react as if he's familiar, to get to know him as a person. At that time, however, I was suddenly convinced that he'd read the script and hated it.

I smiled along, not a care in the world.

Mal Young, the BBC's Head of Drama Series, popped in, affable and cheerful as ever. True, he was down in the depths of TV Centre for a meeting next door, true he wanted to see Richard again and have a chat. But his presence made us all pull our socks up.

The whole cast assembled except Sir Derek Jacobi (the Master) and Craig Kelly (Joe). (Rob Shearman and I like to joke that Sir Derek ran back and forth between *Shalka* and doing *Deadline* as an Unbound Doctor for Big Finish, and the dates do get rather close to each other!) Connor Moloney (Greaves) and Sophie (Alison) were funny, bouncy, telling lots of jokes. Jim (Major Lawson) was very dry. Anna Calder Marshall (Mathilda) was full of actor stories. Diana Quick (Prime) announced that she'd said yes as soon as she heard she was playing a *Doctor Who* villain because she'd been saving up some *Doctor Who* villain acting all her life. And her performance really says that: not hammy, just blissfully powerful and committed and old-fashioned in the way of someone who really knows the show.

The surprise came from Richard. He played the part, established the character, right then and there, growing visibly more relaxed all the time. And everyone else acted along beside him. At the end of Part One, where the Doctor introduces himself, he got to the end of the scene, then

DOCTOR WHO

bounced to his feet, pointed at his chest, and cried out: 'I *am* the Doctor!'

And by that time we all knew that he really was.

I've never enjoyed a read-through so much. It gave us notes on some things that didn't work, it let us see we could establish some new relationships that weren't there yet (Connor and Jim established a comic partnership as major and sergeant that we mined more and more). But more than anything else, it told me that thanks to Wilson and Richard and these actors, it was all going to be okay.

At the end of the read-through, Martin brought in photographers who took pictures of all the cast front and sideways in 'mug shot' style in front of a white screen. These would be used as references by the animators, so that all the leads (with the exception of Diana Quick's Prime, obviously) would be drawn to look like the actors that played them.

Then there came another big moment. Martin had got the ancient TARDIS prop out of the BBC scenery dock, and had had it assembled in the middle of TV Centre, by the fountain. The whole cast gathered in front of it, with some traditional images of Richard peering out from inside the door being taken by BBCi photographers.

We were sure that that was the end of our secrecy, there and then, although the feeling of something big happening more than made up for that. It was lunchtime on a sunny Friday, with dozens of BBC employees hanging around eating lunch in the sun, or just passing on their way to it. I'll let Ann Kelly take up the story from here:

Mostly my involvement with Scream of the Shalka *consisted of keeping my mouth shut. I must admit, I was amazed that no-one cottoned on more quickly. Especially as we held a photoshoot with all the main cast and the TARDIS in the 'doughnut' of Television Centre, nicely placed for hundreds of prying media eyes to see us. Somehow, no-one managed to put two and two together, although we had a couple of nasty moments. A surprised looking Mr Geoffrey Bayldon, flushed with acclaim at his performance as the Doctor in the Big Finish audio* Auld Mortality, *walked past with a suspicious glare at the TARDIS. Shortly afterwards, we were joined by Nev Fountain, of* Dead Ringers *fame. 'That's torn it,' I thought, but turning adversity to our advantage, we simply stuck the long-haired, waistcoated comedy scribe in front of the TARDIS and took a photo of him. Nev looked quite the part, so made a very effective decoy indeed. When everything was finally revealed, it was a great relief to me. Especially as I somehow ended up at a party in a flat lined with* Doctor Who *videos that evening.*

We were sure that day that we'd all get home to find the internet ablaze with rumour. But like on so many occasions during this production, the supposed fan intelligence network inside the BBC failed to work.

The next time I saw the cast and crew was on the day I was invited to come and watch a bit of the recording. The audio was to be recorded first, with a representative from Cosgrove Hall in attendance throughout, making notes so that the finished visuals perfectly matched the audio tracks. The studio was just down the road from TV Centre, but Caroline and I were pleased to run into our old friends from *SFX Magazine*, Stephen O'Brien and Nick Setchfield, at Paddington station, and we blagged our way into their expenses-provided taxi! They, and the lovely Ben Cook from *Doctor Who Magazine*, were there to meet the stars and talk to the production team, with Mark Wyman arriving the next day to do the same for *TV Zone*.

A few tables and chairs had been placed outside the studio on this sunny day, but the coolest place to be was inside the air-conditioned building. Wilson was nowhere to be seen, absolutely concentrating on every moment of production, and Muirinn was a blur, run off her feet. Richard and Craig Kelly, who sweetly introduced himself as if I wouldn't recognise him from *Queer as Folk*, were hanging out in the lobby chatting, Richard with one eye on Royal Ascot and the other on entertaining the reception staff with continual banter about royalty and racing.

Wilson arrived to lead me into the studio, the scene being recorded being the explosion of Alison's house. I was impressed with how relaxed the control area of the studio was, with Wilson sitting at a desk covered in papers at the back, and an experienced team of cheerful audio engineers in front. The special effects had been prepared in advance, and the 'boom' of the explosion was so dramatic and loud it made everyone laugh in shock. Some TARDIS effects were taken straight from an ancient BBC Sound Effects LP, for the greatest possible veracity to the subject matter.

The brightest surprise was, again, the acting. Encouraged by Wilson to improvise and add their own moments, the cast had found whole new levels of meaning, Richard and Sophie particularly giving the Doctor and Alison an edge of care for each other from almost the point when they first meet. Richard's ideas verged from the magnificent (I still have no idea what 'rumpity' means!) to various asides that have been left on the cutting room floor, with him joining the grand tradition of *Who* leads who've brought lots of themselves to the role. The vast majority of it was absolutely spot on, showing he'd put a lot of thought into the character. Sophie came up with the wonderfully precise description of the Doctor as 'an emotional island'. Wilson would listen to a take, then run into the recording area, making swift adjustments. He'd pushed the actors so hard, used to a theatre tradition of rehearsal after rehearsal, that he was running to make up for lost time. He proudly played back the Doctor's answerphone message to me: and I laughed my head off. I knew that I could just relax and enjoy this.

James Goss was present throughout the recording:

The studio recordings were interesting, and occasionally fascinating. What was surprising was the sheer energy Richard E. Grant brought to the part. We've done enough interviews with actors to be deeply suspicious when they start talking about 'energy', but with REG it's rather true.

He bounded round the studio, whirling props over his head, hooting, roaring, running and pounding tables with what my mum would call vim. No take was ever quite the same. Take One may have been angry excitement, Take Two would be casual boredom, Take Three would end with him leaning over and licking Sophie.

This was most obvious when he was doing his 'it's the end of the world' acting. Sophie would ask: 'How long have we got, Doctor?'

TAKE ONE:
REG: (Deadly serious) 'I'd say humanity has an hour.'

TAKE TWO:
REG: (Frantic hurry) 'Humanityhasanhour!'

TAKE THREE:
REG: (Deadpan) 'I'd say humanity has ... (yawn) ... an hour.'

TAKE FOUR:
REG: (Icy calm) 'Humanity? I'd say it's got ...' (lurches forward, opens his jaws around the microphone and roars) AN HOUR!'

Of course, Wilson and Richard both worked really hard on getting the Doctor to sing. Richard E Grant is, perhaps, not famous for his singing. Paul's dénouement called for the Doctor to sing. Quite a bit. Something that both Richard and Wilson found … interesting.

It was fun sitting in the booth while Richard revved himself up to try and hit a note one more time. The sound engineers would look on encouragingly, but gently turn down the volume on the speakers. Richard would breathe in. Slowly. Sophie would wince, and clap her hands over her ears…

… And then some noise would come out.

The singing bits are still my favourites in the play. It's somehow really endearing having a hero who sings his enemies to death.

Rob Francis also insists that he played his part:

At last it can be revealed: I played Doctor Who for the BBC! Okay, that's probably a bit if an exaggeration. My debut probably won't go down as one of the most memorable in the series' forty-year history. No post-regenerative trauma followed by questionable fashion decisions for me. When Who *archivist extraordinaire, Andrew Pixley, writes the definitive list of actors who tackled the Time Lord, I probably won't even merit a mention below the guy who played William Hartnell's robot double or stuntman Terry Walsh in a curly wig.*

Nevertheless, for one glorious minute back in July 2003, I was the Doctor, or at least his hand. Sitting in on the post-production for Scream of the Shalka, *we reached a point in the script where we needed the sound of the Doctor sketching a diagram on a blackboard.*

Since Richard E. Grant had long since left the building,

I was asked the sixty-four-thousand-dollar question: 'Do you want to be in Doctor Who*?' I'll say I did! Armed with some real chalk and some not-so-real blackboard (it wasn't even black) I dutifully gave my best impression of a Time Lord illustrating volcanic rock formations in the North of England for the microphones.*

I toyed with the idea of tapping out a chalky secret message in Morse code: ROB WAS HERE or suchlike. Sadly my knowledge of Morse is confined to the letters S, O and, er, S again, so it was not to be.

Late alarms included a web search that revealed that Shalka was also the name of an Irish folk rock band (I've yet to hear them, but I like the sound of what they do). After much consternation, we finally decided that that wasn't too worrying. What was strange, though, was what else the search revealed: that a large meteorite that landed in India many years ago had been given the name 'Shalka'. I don't remember having known that before, but I suppose it's possible that I did, then it sank down into my unconscious and resurfaced when I thought about meteorites. It still feels like spooky synchronicity, though. Or perhaps that should be serendipity.

There was also a bit of a hoo-hah when Martin, having sworn us all to secrecy, left his copy of the script on a tube train, and unknowingly went to ask about it at a lost-property office run by the boyfriend of a *Doctor Who* fan!

We gathered in a playback theatre in Centre House a month later, to listen to the whole edit of the soundtrack. We'd all gone on to other things: Muirinn to the new season of *Grease Monkeys*; myself to new TV pitches; James, Martin and the gang back to the usual stress of the BBCi Cult section.

I'm usually incredibly critical of my own work when I first see the final version. I hear every little flaw at ten times the volume. But this didn't feel like my work, this felt like an episode of *Doctor Who*.

That was quite a surprise, having completed my childhood ambition only to find that it felt like *I* hadn't done it. But in many ways it was the nicest possible feeling. It felt like I hadn't imposed myself on something, but just quietly continued it. At the time of writing, I've seen a couple of images from the animation (the Doctor looking steely and perfect, Alison, a really good capture of Sophie's look), and look forward eagerly to seeing the whole. I also look forward to where this goes next.

I remain immensely proud of *Scream of the Shalka*. I hope you enjoyed it too.

SERVANTS OF THE SHALAKOR

Reproduced here is the original outline for what became Scream of the Shalka, *as submitted by Paul Cornell to BBCi. While the central core of the story remains the same, details - including the title and the realisation of the Doctor's character - are very different from the final script.*

Part One

THE DOCTOR, a dark, Byronesque figure, lands his TARDIS in the deserted car park of a multiplex cinema complex in a British new town in 2003.

It's not where he expected to be at all. He curtly tells the powers he assumes are watching him (the Time Lords, though we won't say that out loud), that he's not happy with them sending him into situations where something terrible's going to happen. He plucks a blue mobile phone from the alcove on the front of the TARDIS and heads off.

He finds the place almost deserted. It's nine o'clock on a Saturday night, but already the staff are packing up, heading home. Nobody will tell him what's wrong. Everyone's afraid.

A weird, alien, point of view, based on vibration, follows the DOCTOR from a low angle as he walks the empty streets of the suburbs, finding everyone quietly at home, the sounds of television on the night air, but nobody driving, nobody walking. Nobody out in the open. No animals either. There are weird stone statues every now and then, human figures contorted into grotesque shapes.

He finds a BAG LADY in a shop doorway. She's not quite sane. She tells him she left her house because the floor wasn't solid enough. She used to have twenty-eight cats. But they all ran away. All the pets have fled this town. But nobody human can bring themselves to leave. And visitors never think of coming here. The DOCTOR feels a vibration beneath his feet: it terrifies her. The DOCTOR calms her and moves on.

We see the cinema car park becoming molten beneath the TARDIS, opening up. The TARDIS is drawn into the ground.

A young couple, ALISON and DEAN, are yelling in a car outside ALISON'S house. It's a blazing, relationship-falling-apart row. Enraged, he leaps out of the car and yells that he's had enough. Of her, of this place! *They* can take him now! She pleads with him to get back into the car, but, driven beyond endurance, he starts yelling at the ground, daring *them* to come for him.

The DOCTOR knocks on the door of a house, and finally gets someone to let him in. It's a family, the RAZZAQS, who are trying to act perfectly normally despite being terrified of something. The DOCTOR realises: they feel they're being watched, told to act naturally. Amazed that he doesn't know what's going on in this town, they ask him who he is, where he's from, why he's dressed like that? The DOCTOR tells them he's a traveller who doesn't want to go home. He's dressed like this because this is what they wore where (or when) he last was, and he can't be bothered to change every time he goes out of his front door.

* * *

ALISON is pleading with DEAN to get back in the car, screaming as the ground starts to vibrate. DEAN thinks better of his madness at the last moment, and tries to run. But from beneath him erupts a geyser of hot gasses and lava, burning away his flesh with an agonised scream.

There's a noise from the cellar. The family tense. Something's moving down there, coming up the stairs. The little boy, ABDUR, can't help but say it out loud. It's the monsters. The DOCTOR tells them that's why he's been sent here. He's an expert in monsters. He gets the family to stand behind him and faces the door to the living room expectantly as the sounds draw closer. The door creaks open. They're coming!

ALISON stumbles to what's left of DEAN, a skeletal stone shape, rock formed around his skeleton. She reaches out but can't touch him, the stone is still too hot.

Suddenly, 'DEAN' opens his eyes. And starts to laugh.

Part Two

The door to the RAZZAQS' living room bursts open. It's just the wind. Everyone relaxes. And then the monsters burst in.

They're snakelike human-sized beings that look like they're made of stone. They slide up out of the floor, the floorboards breaking open around them. They have arms that can be folded back into their bodies, and faces like statues, with glowing eyes. They bellow that they are the SHALAKOR, and the human parasites are their slaves. They want to know which of the parasites is not of this world?

* * *

229

The DOCTOR grabs a heavy bookcase and heaves it onto the floor between the SHALAKOR. The impact seems to confuse them for a moment. He hustles the RAZZAQ family at speed out of the house, and onto the top of the car, from where they leap to run along a nearby wall. They have to keep off the ground! The creatures' eyes aren't much use, they seem to sense movement through ground vibrations. A rumbling follows the fleeing family, and suddenly a geyser of lava bursts up nearby.

ALISON is running from the skeletal statue that used to be her old boyfriend. Whatever it is, it seems to have retained all DEAN'S memories, and goads her with them as it pursues her. ALISON runs straight into the DOCTOR'S party.

The DOCTOR grabs a crowbar and knocks DEAN'S head from his shoulders without breaking his run. ALISON is horrified, but the DOCTOR grabs her by the hand, leading his party towards a garden centre. That wasn't a human being, that was a vehicle made from the remains of one, by silicon-based beings who want to be able to use human senses. And beheading it very probably only delayed it. He's worked that out in the last few seconds. When ALISON continues to protest, and wants to go back, the DOCTOR coldly forces her on: he knows what he's doing!

Behind them, 'DEAN' replaces his head on his shoulders, and, using molten lava from the ground, re-attaches it. He reports to the rest of the SHALAKOR that he has accessed this human parasite's senses and memory once more. He will pursue the alien parasite. Meanwhile, the SHALAKOR are to order their human slaves not to enter the garden centre. He heads off after the DOCTOR and his party.

* * *

The DOCTOR finds his human companions unable to move, scared to enter the garden centre. They're like rabbits in headlights, made catatonic with fear by a vibration from the ground. The DOCTOR uses rhythmic singing to snap ALISON out of it, and drags her with him. He needs the help of a local. He doubts the aliens will hurt the RAZZAQS, it's him they're after, and if he can find what he's after he can give them a big surprise. He gets ALISON to lead him to the fertiliser section.

The SHALAKOR, with 'DEAN' at their head, close in on the garden centre, sliding through the ground. They go straight past the RAZZAQS and enter the building.

The DOCTOR is getting ALISON to frantically help him in constructing a large fertiliser bomb at a spot he ascertains by means of resting a spirit level on his palm. She asks him how come he didn't get scared like she did? He tells her he's not human. She gets to see the contents of his pockets as they complete the bomb (and he finds a little powdered some-thing to add to it): a ball of string, a multi-bladed weird knife, bits of electronics, all very practical, if eccentric, stuff. So DEAN is dead? Yes, he tells her. There's not much he can do to help her get over it. He doesn't do that sort of human feeling. ALISON says she's sure he did once. That's why he's driven like this, isn't it? Because monsters killed someone he loved? He looks awkwardly at her – And then the monsters burst in, led by 'DEAN'. The DOCTOR lights the fuse on the bomb, and leads ALISON by the hand through the aisles, dodging to and fro, leading the SHALAKOR in circles, throwing silly insults at them, and at the last moment pulling ALISON through an emergency exit, and into a ditch. The garden centre explodes in a fireball that produces a seismic pulse that bounces the gravel off the ground.

* * *

In front of the building the RAZZAQS recover and run. Lights come on all over, people start to sob and collapse in relief, freed from the controlling vibrations as the SHALAKOR, stunned, swim away into the ground. 'DEAN' goes with them. The fireball brings outsiders: the emergency services at first, and then the armed forces, helicopters heading in. The DOCTOR leads ALISON back to where he left the TARDIS, saying they can get cleaned up. But the TARDIS has gone. The DOCTOR runs onto the patch of tarmac where it was, and it collapses beneath him with a blast of sizzling air. He falls into the chasm below.

Part Three

The DOCTOR falls, hits the wall, kicks himself away from it, and grabs a handhold. He climbs back to the surface, and ALISON pulls him out. They look down into the hole. It descends seemingly forever. But a roaring is coming from far down there. The DOCTOR calls for ALISON to run, as behind them a geyser of lava seals the hole. The SHALAKOR are in total command of tectonic processes. And they've got the TARDIS, which is how they realised the DOCTOR was an alien. ALISON asks if the DOCTOR'S ship is going to be safe. The DOCTOR says that the TARDIS has some very tough defences…

Deep beneath the Earth, the TARDIS is secured by lava to a pillar of rock, and SHALAKOR are setting up rocklike equipment to examine it. The doors are hauled open by two giant pincers of rock, and 'DEAN' marches in to inspect the aliens' prize.

He's met by the smiling holographic form of the FIFTH

DOCTOR, who introduces himself as the ship's security system. The TARDIS remembers its crews, and he's someone the current DOCTOR, the NINTH, by the way, loves to chat to. If they want to get any further, they'll have to get past him. The SHALAKOR try. The holographic FIFTH DOCTOR warps the interior of the TARDIS to hold them at bay and finally throw them out.

The DOCTOR walks to the football stadium, and welcomes a helicopter containing a Royal Engineers bomb squad. He explains that he put certain trace chemicals into the explosion that he knew the authorities would detect and come running after. This town has to be evacuated, right now. Meanwhile, he needs subsurface maps, access to geology experts and a cup of hot, sweet tea. The ENGINEERS laugh until he throws a wallet at them containing every security pass in their command structure, and spiels off codewords. One radio call and they're calling him 'sir'. The DOCTOR chooses a local school and asks for all the assistance to be brought there.

ALISON, feeling left out and grieving, follows the DOCTOR at a distance, watching him. Until he calls her to come and help him set up the schoolroom. Okay, she can stay for a while: he feels responsible for her. But she's not to put herself in danger. Around them, the evacuation of the town proceeds.

A military man, MAJOR THOMAS LAWSON, who's been authorised to deal with the DOCTOR, arrives. He has great difficulty with the DOCTOR'S way of doing things, a difficulty which the DOCTOR seems to encourage. The DOCTOR points out, with the aid of his group of GEOLOGISTS, that the town stands on top of a plug of volcanic rock, which goes diagonally downwards, intersecting with some nearby caves. The easiest descent into the aliens' own tunnels would be via the caves. He wants to go down on his own, but LAWSON insists on accompanying him, with a special-forces team. The DOCTOR arranges for ALISON to delay being evacuated until she's got her belongings together, but nobody, herself included, wants her to come along.

'DEAN' and the SHALAKOR watch the above conversation through their vibration sensors, seeking to understand what the alien parasite values. They'll be waiting for him.

The DOCTOR'S team head down into the caves, with helmet lights and weapons. The DOCTOR says he can sense the direction of the TARDIS, so he should be able to track it. He wonders aloud what the SHALAKOR wanted with the town and its inhabitants. He's quite bitter towards the soldiers, needling them in a Michael Moore way. They come upon the first signs of SHALAKOR presence in the caves: a long abandoned chamber with some desiccated human corpses, covered in symbols. The bodies are Maoris, brought here all the way from New Zealand, through the Earth's crust. They've been sacrificed in some sort of ceremony. The DOCTOR is noting the symbols when a roaring is heard from the depths. There's something much bigger waiting for them down there.

ALISON, having gotten her stuff, is evacuated in the back of an army truck. But as it leaves town the truck finds its wheels running in lava, and the soldiers onboard are ambushed by SHALAKOR rising up all around them. ALISON is grabbed and dragged off underground.

Part Four

The DOCTOR and his army escort encounter a huge worm-like beast made of stone, with the face of one of the SHALAKOR set small on its hide. They can come in any size. LAWSON attempts to use high explosives on the monster, and the DOCTOR can't persuade him to stop. So he tells the major to use his grenades at a particular point, with the apparent aim of starting an avalanche. Instead, it creates a rockfall, cutting the running DOCTOR off from the military, leaving him alone inside with the beast.

The DOCTOR waits until the beast roars, and then jumps into its mouth. He finds a hiding place amongst the teeth, and uses his mobile to call the TARDIS.

The FIFTH DOCTOR is being held at a distance from the console by a force field the SHALAKOR are using to try and get in. He can't answer the phone. Instead we get to hear the DOCTOR'S answerphone message.

The DOCTOR, frustrated, allows himself to be taken down into the depths. He steps out of the mouth of the monster when it arrives at the SHALAKOR'S headquarters, miles below the surface, and asks to meet their leader. He's brought to 'DEAN'. He says he's here to make peace between the humans and this race of arrivals. 'DEAN' tells him that's impossible. The SHALAKOR arrived here a century ago: a clutch of their eggs inside a crashing asteroid. They did what they always do when they find a new host. They bury deep inside it, multiply, and begin to worship their deity. Through human sacrifice, the DOCTOR notes: that will have to stop. 'DEAN' laughs at him. What he calls humans are parasites, stripping the nourishment out of their hosts over millennia.

They're not really people, any more than the DOCTOR is. They are interested in his TARDIS, though. It's a religious object to them. If he will allow them access, help them to understand the ship, they'll offer him transport to any-where he likes. The DOCTOR turns them down: he should make his offer clear. He's here to broker peace between the SHALAKOR and the humans … or destroy the SHALAKOR.

'DEAN' has had enough. He has ALISON brought forward. She's already been in captivity down here for a couple of hours. The soldiers with her have been killed. They've seen him worry about her. If the DOCTOR won't do as they say, they'll throw her into the lava. ALISON tells the DOCTOR not to do anything terrible because of her, but he can't face this. He gives in, utterly and completely. He enters the TARDIS and deactivates the security systems, switching the FIFTH DOCTOR off when he protests. He shows the SHALAKOR the basics of how to operate the TARDIS systems. All the while, he can't look at ALISON, who starts to feel horribly guilty.

Once 'DEAN' has learnt all he's after, he tells the DOCTOR that he lied. There's no point in making bargains with para-sites who will all be dying soon anyway. The DOCTOR'S is a particular honour, not granted to all: he's to be sacrificed direct to the deity. He's led off in chains as the SHALAKOR start moving religious items into the TARDIS and decorating it with their rock art. ALISON is to be exposed to the beauty of the deity. This can happen at the same time as she watches the DOCTOR being sacrificed to it.

The DOCTOR and ALISON are thrown down smooth vertical tunnels, and plummet, plucked here and there by force fields, deep down into the centre of the planet.

* * *

And then suddenly they're in a huge chamber, where giant SHALAKOR craft have created a gigantic space, taking up all of the Earth's core. Before the heat and pressure kills them, they're picked up by a SHALAKOR ship, with 'DEAN' upon it. He's switched minds with a new host SHALAKOR body. The DOCTOR doesn't understand how this can be here: without a rotating mass of iron, how is Earth's magnetic field still present? 'DEAN' tells him the SHALAKOR have duplicated it with their incredible force-field technology. The parasites will only die when they wish them to, not from solar radiation beforehand.

The craft moves closer to something shining at the very centre of the vast cavern. Streams of matter connect it to the walls, as a disc of superheated matter flashes around at intervals. It's a small black hole, getting bigger over years as it slowly sucks matter from the Earth's interior. This is a manifestation of the SHALAKOR'S god. They brought it here with them when they landed. It's been feeding ever since. Getting bigger, faster and faster, it will eventually consume the world. And now, the DOCTOR is to be its latest victim. He tries to struggle, but 'DEAN' throws him out of the craft. He falls into the black hole's event horizon and vanishes as ALISON screams his name.

Part Five

THE DOCTOR has gone. ALISON, stunned, is taken back to her cell. She's been 'exposed to the deity', and her head aches as a result.

MAJOR LAWSON and his squad have finally made their way to the SHALAKOR'S headquarters. In hiding, moving slowly to escape the SHALAKOR'S senses, they watch as ALISON is imprisoned, and decide to rescue her to learn more of the SHALAKOR'S plans.

They manage to break into the cell, but are detected, and a savage battle ensues. LAWSON'S men get the worst of it, being killed in numbers.

We join the DOCTOR, falling on his psychedelic journey to the centre of a black hole. He's decided to stop breathing. Threatened by gravitational currents that could rip him apart, he grabs a piece of debris and surfs them down. He feels the presence of a mind within the darkness, and starts to communicate with it. It's the universe-wide group mind of the SHALAKOR, the deity the species worship, as the DOCTOR bitterly notes. They're so in love with themselves! The mind is pleased by the DOCTOR'S sacrifice, looks forward to him being crushed by the singularity at the heart of the black hole instead of, as it grants to its children, being transported to another black hole elsewhere. THE DOCTOR tells the mind that he's done enough sightseeing. He takes his mobile phone from his pocket, and unfolds it into a TARDIS door, which he steps through and closes behind him. (It is a part of the TARDIS, after all!) A moment later, as the group mind roars, the door vanishes.

THE DOCTOR finds himself in immediate danger inside the TARDIS, as it's filled with SHALAKOR. He takes a tuning fork from his pocket, hits it against the console, hits a control to make the ship vibrate and uses the changeable interior to slide the stunned SHALAKOR out.

He follows them, and sees ALISON running towards the TARDIS, the last few soldiers being cut down as they protect her. He calls to her and LAWSON, who looks like he's about to sacrifice himself to save her, and bundles them both into the TARDIS as the last soldier is killed. The TARDIS takes off, fights against the force fields of the SHALAKOR for a moment, and gets away.

ALISON is relieved and guilty at once to see the DOCTOR, LAWSON angry at him for the death of his men. The DOCTOR tells him he expected him to head back to the surface. LAWSON says that makes him a fool as well as foolhardy. The DOCTOR shrugs that off, lands the ship, and virtually pushes ALISON out. She looks round to see that she's in her hometown of Sheffield, as she mentioned to the DOCTOR when they discussed her evacuation. She looks back to see the TARDIS taking off without her.

The DOCTOR takes LAWSON back in time to 1908. They witness the SHALAKOR meteorite crashing into Siberia. The TARDIS's sensors pick up a gravitational anomaly on board the lump of rock: a tiny black hole, brought along with the eggs. The black hole burrows straight for the centre of the earth, causing a vast, planet-rocking impact, the Tunguska explosion. The DOCTOR lands the TARDIS in the molten crater, grabs a liquid-nitrogen spray, and dashes out, leaping between the rocks, until he reaches the eggs, now swirling along in the magma. He tries to spray them, to crack and kill them, but he can't make his limbs do it. He yells at the sky, and heads back to the TARDIS, defeated.

He explains to LAWSON that he can't change what he knows to have happened. He can't end this here. It's a legal law that the powers that force him to work for them turn into a physical one. At least maybe LAWSON now sees how much responsibility he takes on. Exactly, LAWSON replies, the same responsibility as he takes on concerning the safety of his men. A contrite DOCTOR comes to a better understanding with the major, and heads the TARDIS back to contemporary times.

Meanwhile, ALISON is seeing headlines about a 'terrorist gas attack' down south, a state of emergency, a town cleared. Angry with the DOCTOR for dumping her, she goes to her parents' house, changes, gets a bag together, leaves a note and heads off to the railway station. Travelling to London on the train, she feels a pressure in her skull. Something actually seems to be forcing its way out. She looks in the mirror. There's a bulge. It's actually pulling her to the west. The pain is too much. She has to follow the pull. But they're between stations. She pulls down the window, squeezes herself out of the gap and throws herself from the train screaming.

Part Six

ALISON is terribly injured by the impact. But she manages to get to her feet, pulled along by the force in her head. She has to move in a certain direction. And something's helping her, force fields that spring up from the ground and keep her limbs braced.

The DOCTOR shows LAWSON, the PRIME MINISTER and the Cabinet, a liquid hydrogen spray that could halt or destroy an individual SHALAKOR. He demonstrates it on one of the creatures the military have captured and kept stunned with the DOCTOR'S repetitive beats. They have a group mind, so he feels no qualms about killing one. But this is a sideshow. He needs to find out what the aliens are doing.

* * *

'DEAN' watches the demonstration from below. It doesn't matter. They knew the alien parasite would find such a weapon. The plan can continue.

The DOCTOR and LAWSON, meanwhile, have gone to Jodrell Bank, and are consulting with a worldwide radio astronomy network. The DOCTOR summarises what they know: the SHALAKOR aren't just waiting for their black hole to gradually eat the planet. They took over that town for a reason. They're planning something: but what? He bets they take black holes like that with them wherever they go. A black hole inside a planet should give off a particular infra-red signature. He programs the network, and gets an image back from an infra-red astronomical satellite: a sky full of such sources. So the SHALAKOR are sucking matter from the interior of planets across the galaxy. But where does it go? He reverses the program, and finds just one source, a white hole, orbiting the galactic plane. That's their grand cause, what they think planetary populations, or parasites, get in the way of. It's a slingshot ship, designed to escape the Milky Way, and send the SHALAKOR off to conquer the next galaxy, the Andromeda Spiral. LAWSON asks why he should be concerned about such huge things? Because, the DOCTOR tells him, to launch it, the SHALAKOR would need a sudden vast injection of energy … like Earth being sucked into the black hole in a single moment.

ALISON finds herself making her way across country to a wooded area. In the wood, she meets the RAZZAQS. They say they were evacuated, but then felt the need to move. To come here? No. To find her. The old BAG LADY is here too. Indeed, lots of people ALISON knows from the town. Everyone is still themselves, angry and frightened: they felt the same need to find her that they felt to stay in the town.

They're still slaves to the vibrations from underground. But ALISON realises something horrible: she's the only one with something inside her head.

The DOCTOR, brooding, overhears one of the soldiers who worked on the evacuation talking about the behaviour of the evacuees. He took some to a nearby town where their relatives lived. They didn't unpack, but asked their relatives if they could borrow food and money so they could move on. The DOCTOR asks LAWSON if they've followed where the evacuees went. LAWSON starts making phone calls.

ALISON finds more and more people from her town entering the wood. Including her GP, JENNY BROMLEY. ALISON gets JENNY to give her a local anaesthetic, and to start exploring her skull to find the thing in her head. Around her are clustering more and more locals, as if waiting for orders from her.

The DOCTOR and LAWSON have discovered that none of the evacuees stayed where they were sent. They all left again within a day. But where have they gone? The DOCTOR puts together a bank of TV sets and watches every news source at once, running back and forth to a map. He's looking for odd crowds, hitch-hikers, people walking away from traffic jams. LAWSON beats him to the location by seconds with a satellite photo: thousands of people moving into a wood in Suffolk. What's there? It's what's nearby: a USAF base, storing nuclear missiles. The DOCTOR flings open the doors of his TARDIS: they have to get there right now.

JENNY finds a stone lump inside ALISON'S head, but when she touches it is ripped apart by a blast of gravitational force from the stone. ALISON finds her limbs moving. She's heading for the lights of the USAF base. The people all around her move to follow. They get through the fences by piling their bodies and climbing over them. They head for the hangers containing the nuclear weapons. The GUARDS try and stop them, but find it difficult to open fire upon conscious 'zombies' who call out that they can't stop themselves, who plead with them not to shoot. But finally the BASE COMMANDER has no alternative but to give the order to open fire, cutting down the rows of people in front of ALISON, who's now right in the way of the next burst.

Part Seven

The TARDIS materialises between the slaves of the SHALAKOR and the soldiers, bullets bouncing off it. The slaves keep marching, but the DOCTOR gets out and yells at the soldiers to stop firing. LAWSON follows him out and backs him up with his own men.

The DOCTOR finds ALISON, and holds her still, examining the bulge that appears at the front of her skull. He can see, from the incision JENNY made, that there's a stone in there, a broadcast unit for the vibrations the SHALAKOR are using to control the slaves. The SHALAKOR deity grew it inside ALISON'S brain by directed pulses of radiation. The DOCTOR asks ALISON if she trusts him. She says yes. The DOCTOR says she's wrong to, grabs the stone out of her head, screams at the burst of gravitational energy it blasts through him, but nevertheless plucks it out and falls, apparently dead.

The slaves turn to follow him, but he's not moving. They stop and wait. LAWSON, remembering the DOCTOR'S methods, sets up rhythmic chanting which gradually eases the slaves out of SHALAKOR control.

All the while, ALISON is pleading with the DOCTOR to still be alive. He grins at her, opens his eyes, bounces the stone pellet in his hand, says he has an idea, throws the stone into his mouth and swallows it. Inside the DOCTOR'S brain, we see the pellet linking to his neurons and taking them over.

His eyes glaze over. He says now he can see it all, can understand it from the SHALAKOR'S point of view. He asks ALISON and LAWSON to consider what it must be like, feeling that one is made of the same primary stuff as planets, feeling that that stuff should serve its own purpose, that carbon-based life forms with their tiny minds are parasites who don't really think, not like silicon-based life. Not over huge scales. Not over millennia! LAWSON gets out his gun and warns the DOCTOR, and he looks sighingly at him. He's accessed the SHALAKOR group mind, not been taken over by it. He just likes to give humans a bit of perspective.

LAWSON gets a radio message, saying that armies of 'conscious zombies' are closing in on nuclear sites in India, China and Israel. The DOCTOR says it would be foolish to assume that the SHALAKOR only exposed one person to their god, or only hypnotised one town. LAWSON must try to organise world defences to keep the nukes away from the slaves. The Doctor is off to the heart of the problem, to the edge of the Milky Way. He opens the door of the TARDIS and asks ALISON if she'd like to come with him. Not knowing quite why, but feeling properly wanted by the DOCTOR for the first time, ALISON agrees.

We see the armies of slaves break through defences in

various parts of the world, at great loss of life, and lay their hands on nuclear warheads. SHALAKOR appear out of the ground and, where they're not fought off with freezing weapons, take the nuclear devices down into the depths with them. They use lava bursts to keep back human soldiers.

'DEAN' exults, deep under the Earth. He's following the trains of humans, working on the weapons, taking them all to one point deep under the crust. The explosion they're going to set off will connect a molten spar of the Earth's crust direct to the black hole, which will then consume the entire Earth in a millisecond.

The DOCTOR is quiet as the TARDIS lands on a vast, rocky world. Outside is the glory of the whole Milky Way galaxy, seen from side-on. He extends the atmospheric envelope beyond the ship, and he and ALISON step out to take a look. This is the SHALAKOR'S galaxy-spanning ship, packed with eggs, waiting for the burst of energy from Earth's moment of extinction.

ALISON asks the DOCTOR how they're going to stop it? The DOCTOR laughs. Stop it? Either she and LAWSON are extremely gullible, or he hasn't lost his skill at lying! They're not here to stop the grand plan, they're here to take part!

He turns to her and his eyes are those of a SHALAKOR.

Part Eight

ALISON says she should have realised. She can still walk. The force fields are still supporting her injuries. The 'DOCTOR' laughs in an evil way once more.

* * *

245

The 'DOCTOR' takes her for a tour of the ship, explaining the desire of the SHALAKOR to rid the universe of all that fake, pretend sentient, carbon-based life. The real stuff of the universe is the rock, not the flesh. The rock is mutable, it can be taken away from the parasites, saved, reconstructed into things like this intergalactic vessel. He shows her the controls. Originally it was to be launched by a hatchling, with instructions transmitted from the black hole down below. But now he'll do it.

ALISON asks him why he brought her along, and realises the 'DOCTOR' doesn't know. Perhaps that was something the real DOCTOR wanted. Why? Suddenly, she realises. She starts talking to the 'DOCTOR' like he's DEAN, reminding him of things they did together. Of the good times.

We see inside a visualisation of the SHALAKOR group mind, as the DOCTOR, chained and gagged, struggles, concentrating, helping her.

DEAN'S mind surfaces and manages to say a few words to ALISON through the 'DOCTOR'. He says he's sorry, he wishes he could do something to make up for everything. ALISON says he can. He has to go back into the group mind and find the DOCTOR'S consciousness.

In the dreamscape, DEAN enters the DOCTOR'S cell, and, fighting the SHALAKOR that are appearing all around him, and removes the DOCTOR'S gag. The DOCTOR makes a tremendous effort, declares who he is, and breaks free.

With a scream, the DOCTOR is himself again. He hugs ALISON, then throws her aside and grabs the controls. With his last moment of willpower he made the SHALAKOR bring her along. They've only got seconds. SHALAKOR are hatching all around them, rushing out of the black hole inside the ship from all over the universe and sliding up through the ground to intercept the DOCTOR and ALISON.

ALISON grabs the freezing weapons from inside the TARDIS and fights the aliens off as the DOCTOR frantically works the ship's controls.

Inside Earth, the slaves have brought the nuclear weapons to the correct place, in SHALAKOR tunnels at the base of a particular cave system. An enslaved SCIENTIST is hitting makeshift controls on one weapon, yelling at those around him to stop him. 'DEAN' anticipates glory. The destruction of Earth is only seconds away.

The DOCTOR hits his final button just as the SCIENTIST'S unwilling finger is reaching for his. He's reversed the direction of the black-hole system. Suddenly, mass is sucked from the interior of the ship they're standing on, and chucked out of all the black holes to refill the centres of all the planets. The planetary quake on Earth causes the SCIENTIST'S finger to miss the button. The shock of having the system reversed sends the SHALAKOR group mind into catatonia. SHALAKOR everywhere become statues and crumble into dust. The ship beneath the DOCTOR and the now once more horribly injured ALISON starts to disintegrate. The DOCTOR grabs her and hauls her into the TARDIS as everything falls apart. A moment later, the ship explodes.

The DOCTOR lands the TARDIS back at the USAF base, and gingerly leads ALISON out onto terra firma again. He's used his craft's advanced medical technology to heal her limbs. He tells LAWSON that the SHALAKOR have been stopped, perhaps for millennia. The Earth has its iron core back, he arranged an exact reversal. LAWSON asks him to stay, in case they try again, but the DOCTOR says he has to be on his way. Hesitantly, he tells ALISON that perhaps he has lost sight of some of the things that save the world: the little domestic things. Would she like to teach him about those? And see the universe with him? ALISON accepts.

The DOCTOR leads her into the TARDIS, closes the door and the ship dematerialises. The DOCTOR and his companion are off on their way to another adventure.

Acknowledgements

This is my chance to thank the people who helped make *Scream of the Shalka* what it is:

Martin Trickey and James Goss – whose idea it was to do this, and who had to deal with the most stress.

Jelena Djordjevic – our first producer, who shaped the idea so much and gave me loads of support during the writing.

Muirinn Lane Kelly – our next producer, who got it over the line, cast it so well, and brought her Flying Circus along.

Wilson Milam – the best director I've ever worked with.

Rob Francis, Daniel Judd and Ann Kelly – who kept the secret, provided all sorts of back-up, and were our first fan critics.

Sarah Keeley – who provided meteorological advice.

Karen Baldwin – who provided research help.

Jon Preddle – who made numerous attempts to help me send the scripts off my failing laptop from New Zealand to the BBC.

Alastair Smith – who finally broke into my house for me and e-mailed the scripts to the BBC while I was in New Zealand.

About the Author

PAUL CORNELL has written scripts for *Casualty*, *Children's Ward*, *Coronation Street* and *Holby City*, as well as his own CITV series, *Wavelength*.

His SF novels *Something More* and *British Summer Time* are out now from Victor Gollancz.

His comic series, *Xtnct*, runs in the *2000AD* magazine.

His Who career covers books, audios and comic strips. He's the creator of companion Bernice Summerfield, now the star of her own series.

He lives with his wife in Oxfordshire.

Recently published:

Emotional Chemistry
by Simon Forward
ISBN 0 563 48608 2
Featuring the Eighth Doctor

"Love! Surely one of the most destructive forces in the universe. There's nothing a man – or woman – won't do for true love."

1812 The Vishenkov household, along with the rest of Moscow, faces the advance of Napoleon Bonaparte. At their heart is the radiant Dusha, a source of inspiration – and more besides – for them all. But family friend, Captain Padorin, is acting like a man possessed – by the Devil.

2024 Fitz is under interrogation regarding a burglary and fire at the Kremlin. The Doctor has disappeared in the flames. Colonel Bugayev is investigating a spate of antique thefts on top of which he now has a time-travel mystery to unravel.

5000 Lord General Razum Kinzhal is ready to set in motion the final stages of a world war. More than the enemy, his fellow generals of the Icelandic Alliance fear what such a man might do in peacetime.

What can bridge these disparate events in time? Love will find a way. But the Doctor must find a better alternative. Before love sets the world on fire.

Recently published:

Deadly Reunion
by Terrance Dicks and Barry Letts
ISBN 0 563 48610 4
Featuring the Third Doctor, Jo and UNIT

'With one glance he will destroy your body and wither your soul.'

Second-lieutenant Lethbridge-Stewart gets more than he
bargained for when he is assigned to map out Greek islands at
the end of the Second World War. Even if he lives to tell the tale,
will he remember it?

Years later, Brigadier Lethbridge-Stewart and his colleagues at
UNIT investigate a spate of unexplained deaths and murders.
Meanwhile, the Third Doctor and Jo are caught up in strange
events in the small English village of Hob's Haven.

As preparations get underway for a massive pop concert, a
sinister cult prepares for a day of reckoning – business as usual
for UNIT. But can the Brigadier help prevent the end of the
world? His friends and colleagues are not so sure, because this
time, the Brigadier has fallen in love…

Sometime Never...
by Justin Richards
ISBN 0 563 48610 4
Featuring the Eighth Doctor and Fitz

This Week:
A hideous misshapen creature releases a butterfly?

Next Week:
The consequences of this simple action ensure that history
follows its predicted path...

Sometime:
In the swirling maelstrom of the Time Vortex, The Council of
Eight maps out every moment in history and take drastic measures
to ensure it follows their predictions. But there is one elemental
force that defies prediction, that fails to adhere to the laws of
time and space... A rogue element that could destroy their plans
merely by existing.

Already events are mapped out and defined. Already the pieces
of the trap are in place. The Council of Eight already knows
when Sabbath will betray them. It knows when Fitz will survive
the horrors in the Museum of Anthropology. It knows when
Trix will come to his help. It knows when the Doctor will
finally realise the truth.

It knows that this will be:
Never

Coming soon from
BBC *Doctor Who* books:

Empire of Death
by David Bishop

Published 1 March 2004
ISBN 0 563 48615 5

Featuring the Fifth Doctor and Nyssa.

In 1856, a boy discovers he can speak with the voices of the dead. He grows up to become one of England's most celebrated spiritualists.

In 1863 the British Empire is effectively without a leader. Queen Victoria is inconsolable with grief following the death of her beloved husband, Prince Albert. The monarch's last hope is a secret séance.

The Doctor and Nyssa are also coming to terms with loss, following the death of Adric and Tegan's sudden departure. Trying to visit the Great Exhibition of 1851, the time travellers are shocked when a ghost appears in the TARDIS, beckoning them to the Other Side.

What is hidden in a drowned valley guarded by the British Army? Is there life after death and can it be reached by those still alive? And why is the Doctor so terrified of facing his own ghosts?